TELLY PEOPLE

TELLY PEOPLE

SAM ROSPE

PALINDROME

Published by Palindrome Publishing Ltd in 2022

First published in Great Britain in 2022 by
Palindrome Publishing Ltd
Abbey House, 25 Clarendon Road, Redhill RH1 1QZ

A CIP catalogue record for for this book
is available from the British Library

ISBN 978-1-8380291-8-0

Pre-titles

Sebastian woke up with a sick feeling in the pit of his stomach, the knowledge that something bad was going to happen. Then he remembered *Rough Diamonds*, and realised it already had.

He shifted his bulk from his left side to the right, then back again. It was difficult to get comfortable. The bunk was narrow and hard, the mattress thin. The whole structure groaned and creaked rhythmically, something to do with the occupant above him.

From the window – dim and grey, like the screen of an ancient television – light was edging into the cell. This was Sebastian's second day in prison. Nothing in his life, not even a six-month traineeship at the BBC, could have prepared him for this.

Somewhere down the corridor an early riser began to beat a tattoo on the floor with a blunt instrument. Sebastian's mind returned to the question repeating itself over and over in his head like the catchphrase of a particularly irritating commercial. How did he ever get into this mess?

And – more importantly – how was he ever going to get out, in time for the BAFTA awards?

1 Creative Differences

The Cavalier died somewhere in the middle of Talgarth Road. Blinking in disbelief, Sebastian kicked the pedals as the car rolled gently to a halt across two lanes and a white van neatly removed his mirror. Frantic twists of the ignition key produced nothing more than a sick churning sound that might have been his own stomach.

The tide of rush-hour traffic parted around the stranded vehicle as Sebastian squeezed through the door and dodged towards the relative safety of the central reservation. What looked like a commonplace road junction had become a frenzied killing zone. Urban tanks tailgated HGVs, taxis U-turned without warning, kamikaze couriers and suicide-scooters filled any crack that appeared momentarily between the gridlocked vehicles. The AA promised to join him within three hours and gave instructions to remain with the vehicle. Eight-forty by his watch meant Sebastian had all of twenty minutes to reach his destination. He knew what it was like getting these slots.

He'd been queuing in the garden centre when Albie had called and asked Sebastian to go in his place.

'I'm going to be stuck out here longer than I thought, and I can't cancel Mel Gioconda.'

'Where are you, anyway?'

'Tajikistan.'

'Why?'

'Never mind. Just look like you know what you're doing and don't let her stall the project.'

'But I don't know what I'm doing.'

'You know how to make a gardening programme, don't you? Principle's the same, there's just more of it.'

'Gardening programmes don't have stories and actors and all that other stuff.'

'Sebastian –'

'Anyway, it's only a month until the Giggleswick Floral Extravaganza, I should be working on that.'

'Leave the story to Pete. The rest you don't have to worry about. I'll deal with it when I'm back. Keep it all ticking over until then. Just make sure Mel commissions the next episode.'

'I don't know, Albie. Is this a good idea?'

'Put it this way, Sebastian. There's no one else. If you can't do a simple thing like this for me … why should I entrust you with *Britain in Bud*?'

That was what Sebastian hated about working for Jemma's brother. In the end it always came down to blackmail.

'Where's the meeting?'

'At The Channel. And for God's sake don't be late, she really hates that.'

With Albie's parting words still fresh in his memory Sebastian loosened his tie, which on top of everything else was trying to choke him to death, and started to run.

Thirty-five minutes later Sebastian rounded the last corner and saw the dreary Channel building squatting in front of him. After a brief skirmish with the sliding glass door he fought his way into a mob of sharply dressed, anxious-faced people. Couriers criss-crossed the foyer, shouldering their way through with packages. Above them huge monitors silently pumped out random images.

At the long curlicue of the reception desk the stone-faced receptionist inclined her head by a few degrees.

'Mm?'

'Sebastian Boyle to see Mel Gioconda.'

She consulted her razor-thin screen.

'Your colleague's already here.'

Nodding dismissively at a small figure in the distance, the receptionist pushed a name-tag towards Sebastian and turned her attention to a sleek, black-suited man beside him who seemed faintly familiar. For a second their eyes met. Then Sebastian's mobile slipped through his sweaty figures and he had to bend down and scrabble on the contract carpeting to rescue it.

Making his way past a giggling knot of girl guides, Sebastian hurried towards the lonely figure hunched on the faux-leather sofa. He hadn't met any writers before, but this one was exactly what he'd expected. Besides, his name-tag clearly identified him as P. Clapp.

'Pete?'

The man looked up.

'I suppose you're Sebastian.'

They shook hands.

'You're late.'

'Any idea who that is?' He pointed at the mystery figure, now sparring with the receptionist.

'Probably some soap actor. They're always hanging around in here.'

'Why?'

'Hoping someone will cast them in something decent. Or at least ask them for an autograph.'

'Have you been waiting long?'

The writer laughed sourly.

'Don't worry. You get used to it. Look, she's waving.'

The receptionist was signalling with an imperious flick of the wrist that Sebastian and Pete should move towards the lift.

'Right, then. Have you been here before?'

'Oh yes. I've been here before.'

In the big, battered lift the occupants studiously avoided eye contact. It smelt sultry and they may have connected this with the dark stains spreading out from Sebastian's armpits. Oblivious, he smiled encouragingly at Pete but the writer's gaze was fixed on his feet. The lift stopped at every floor and people got in, instantly falling silent. No one got out. The lift ordered everyone to stand clear of its doors in a synthetic female voice that brooked no argument.

Disgorged on the top floor, Pete eyed Sebastian suspiciously.

'So where's Albie?'

'He couldn't make it.'

The writer shook himself like an old sheepdog, and trotted ahead of Sebastian down the long, dark corridor. Sebastian nudged him.

'This is like being in a drain.'

'In more ways than one.'

Finally the pair reached Mel Gioconda's door. Sebastian yanked his tie straight, took a deep breath, and stepped smartly over the threshold.

Half an hour – or was it ten years? – later, Sebastian and Pete faced Mel and her number two, Jeanie, across an expanse of dung-coloured carpet. For a few seconds no one spoke, adding to the air of tension. The meeting had reached an impasse.

'Or … the guy could be a woman.'

Everyone turned to look at Pete, who rubbed his chin nervously. Was he being sarcastic? No, apparently he meant it. Their main character, the heart and soul of *Rough Diamonds*, could flip gender so far as the writer was concerned.

Sebastian turned from Pete to Mel, then to Jeanie. Then back to Pete again. Was this how it worked? His recent experience, producing a daytime gardening segment for the visually impaired, hadn't prepared him for the creative cut and thrust of TV drama. However, the main difference so far as he could see was the size of the budget. No wonder his brother-in-law was so keen. The thing was not to display his ignorance.

Mel was leaning forward. Pete's comment seemed to have struck a chord. Jeanie, the script editor, teetered on the edge of her seat, not daring to commit until Mel had set the tone. The fate of the series hung in the balance.

'Well …' Mel smiled. 'I feel that's a very … *positive* … step forward.' She shifted slightly in her big comfy chair, feet tucked girlishly beneath her, though Mel was far from being a girl. Her bracelets clanked. Above the sweet smile her eyes were icy.

'Oh yes, it just makes so much more sense with a woman at the centre of the story,' gushed Jeanie. The writer gave her a wintry smile. Sebastian felt out of his depth. His mind was spinning like a hard drive on the verge of meltdown. He glanced across to the corner where Pete sat, shivering. What did he mean, Dan could be a woman? What would that involve? They'd have to sort it out later. Now it was time to close.

'So … is everyone happy, then?'

Mel laughed. Pete's eyes were on Sebastian, then flicked back to Mel. Jeanie leaned forward.

'Shouldn't we just get this script *completely* right first?'

The writer flinched and wearily closed his eyes. Jeanie was young, of course, and keen.

'No.'

'No?' Mel was looking at Sebastian questioningly: how could you, how could anyone, not want to get something completely right? Wouldn't that be lazy and, well, just a little bit *dishonest*? Sebastian had never met anyone with the power of such articulate looks.

'No. We should get this script completely right and *at the same time* … um … explore our new knowledge of the character in the next episode, so Pete can *feed back* what he's learning about him – sorry, her – into the first one.' Now Pete was staring at him too. Well? So Sebastian had done a bit of homework, skimming a couple of books he'd found in the media section at Ottokar's. He hadn't wanted to look a complete idiot, after all.

'Hmm.'

She was on the brink. What had Albie said? Think of it as poker. Liars' poker. It was time for double or quits.

'In fact, I have to say that Pete and I can't agree to reworking Dan as a woman –'

Hold up mate, Pete's eyes were saying, I can't afford to lose this one. Or maybe they were saying something else, it was hard to be sure. His looks weren't in the same class as Mel's. Sebastian, though, understood this bit. They'd reached the moment when the executive was about to dump the whole thing. You could smell it. Sometimes you just had to swallow your principles and do what you knew was right for the project. For getting the project made, that is. Albie had always been very clear on this point. Sebastian watched the writer pick nervously at the frayed cuff of his denim shirt.

'– Unless … you commission another episode.'

The Channel was in deep shit, everyone knew that, even Sebastian. The nineties had brought a production boom but was also threatening to sweep away the old order. Traditional broadcasters were struggling to hang on to what was left of their audience. They desperately wanted successful, popular TV drama. Mel's job was to make sure they got it. And *Rough Diamonds* was just the kind of series their viewers liked. After all, they'd broadcast something almost identical twice already, so it had to be. The question was, did Mel have the vision to see it? Or, crucially, the money to pay for it? The Channel ran on a tight budget. Sebastian gazed at the scuffed lilac paint on the walls of Mel's office, the tired carpet. Even the sofa looked on its last legs, overwhelmed by a succession of thwarted writers, stillborn ideas, dead and dying projects. No wonder the actors and actresses, writers, producers, directors, publicists, and the rest of the circus downstairs had looked so anxious.

'Okay.' Mel smiled. 'First draft in, shall we say, three weeks?'

Sebastian glanced at Pete. 'We can do that.'

Pete looked less sure.

'Thanks, Mel.' They got up.

'Good to meet you, Sebastian. How come our paths haven't crossed before?'

'I've been more involved with, um, the groundwork.'

'Groundwork?'

'You know. The stage before the decking goes down.'

Mel looked puzzled. Sebastian grasped the door handle.

'Bye.'

They made it out of Mel's office and down the grungy corridor, through the makeover glitz of the foyer, and escaped.

'That went okay. Didn't it?'

'How the hell am I going to make Dan a woman?'

'Don't you know?' Pete shook his head. 'Never mind, you'll think of something.' Sebastian peeled off his jacket and wiped his glistening face with a tissue. 'What do you usually do?'

'I suppose she can have lots of intimate chats with her mates, help get the plot out. Maybe a gay best friend.'

'Man-Dan does sound a bit boring.'

'Thanks a lot. What do you know about it, anyway?'

It was a fair question. Sebastian decided to take the script home and read it.

* * *

Albie's office, Sebastian's until he returned, was a converted rabbit hutch in Soho sandwiched between a Thai takeaway on the ground floor and a walk-in massage parlour on the second. As he fumbled with his key Sebastian could hear the phone ringing inside. It was Mel. The commission was going through – but on one condition.

'Can't you give him another chance?'

'He's had five already.'

'But what about making Dan a woman? It was his idea, after all.'

'We'd just be more … *comfortable* with another writer.'

'But –'

'I'm sorry, Sebastian. I can't work with you on this if I'm not comfortable.' Mel somehow managed to convey a sad smile, not an easy thing in a phone conversation, but there was no mistaking the adamant beneath it. Her comfort was non-negotiable.

Unhappily Sebastian replaced the handset and reached into the drawer of Albie's desk for a bar of chocolate. He tried Albie's number again. It seemed to be permanently engaged.

He decided to call Pete's agent. Agnes and his brother-in-law had been friends for years, apparently. Not the kind of friends who went out for meals together, but they talked a lot on the phone and sometimes saw a play, if a client of hers had written it.

Agnes would know what to do.

Sebastian explained the situation and asked if he should phone Pete, but Agnes said he could trust her to handle everything. She'd make sure he was looked after. Agnes had a good heart, Sebastian reflected, although of course as an agent she sometimes had to make herself seem tougher than she really was. He'd met her once and could understand why some people might find her scary. That odd, stretched quality her face had could be off-putting, but she certainly knew her job.

At the brutalist headquarters of ABD, all bright colours and jagged edges, Agnes clipped down the corridor to the glass-walled conference room. She felt sorry for Pete Clapp, of course. It was always sad when something like this happened. But he had to accept that he was at the end of his career. He'd been fairly successful at the start, writing on several of the soaps, and of course *Portia Dale, Private Eye* was quite a hit in its day. But all that was years ago. He was too old school, the young script editors and development executives thought he was out of touch. Living in Chipping Sodbury and dressing entirely in stonewashed denim didn't help. He'd acquired a reputation for being difficult. All he wanted to do was write. He didn't seem to understand that a writer simply couldn't behave like that.

Agnes pushed open the door and nodded to her colleagues, stationed around the horizontal monolith of the table for their weekly agents' meeting. Her violet-lacquered nails drummed impatiently as she summarised the letter she'd received from Pete that morning. It was a typical writer-client whinge: why not sent up for jobs, why no movie rights deal on ten-year-old novel, why no take-up of suggestion to write for *Inspector Pettigrew*, why no invitation to agency summer party? (Answers (1) no ideas or personal interview skills, (2) novel crap, (3) new producer of *Inspector Pettigrew* hated Clapp, and (4) summer party postponed indefinitely.) Agnes went on to remind the meeting that Clapp was currently writing a pilot for a new TV series commissioned by Mel Gioconda at The Channel through small-time independent producer Brunt Productions. Now it seemed The Channel wanted someone new.

Agnes put it to the meeting: given Clapp's letter and obvious dissatisfaction with his career, should they risk losing him as a client by supplying his replacement? Asked what he'd brought to the agency in commission in the past twelve months, Agnes had the figure at her fingertips: £28.90 in residuals from Luxembourg. Her colleagues wondered how Clapp's future looked. Agnes thought, pretty bleak. They agreed and advised Agnes to fire him right away, before he had the chance to leave.

Parrying attempts by the others to get their clients onto the project, Agnes pointed out that this was a formula cops-with-a-twist show for the middle of the mainstream and perfect for her newest signing, Pat Quine, who could use the experience and was quite good enough for Brunt Productions.

Honour satisfied, Agnes left to make the obligatory phone call to her client.

'Hello?'

'Yeah?'

'Pat?'

'Yeah?'

'Pat, this is Agnes Peel at ABD.'

'Oh. Hi, Agnes, how are you? I thought it was the VAT people again.' The slacker voice at the other end of the line didn't sound too bothered either way.

'No dear. Listen, I may have something for you. A producer's making a very exciting new series for Mel Gioconda at The Channel, and he'd like to meet you.'

'Is it greenlit?'

'Not as yet, dear, but it's any day now, it's a sure thing.'

'Cops or docs?'

'Cops. But –'

'With a twist?'

'Exactly.'

'What about the low-budget film?'

'What low-budget film?'

'I sent you the script a month ago. Have you read it?'

'Not yet, dear. You've got time to fit this in first.'

'What's the money like?'

'Not great, frankly, but it won't take up much of your time.'

'Is there a treatment?'

'There's a whole script.'

'They've already commissioned it? From someone else?'

'Yes, dear.'

'What, I'm coming in to clean up the mess?'

'They went to the wrong writer. Now they've come to the right writer.'

'Who did the last draft?'

'Pete Clapp.'

'Clapp? That old hack!'

'Careful, dear, he's a client. Or rather, he was.'

'Oh. Well. Okay, if I can start over. From the beginning.'

'I'll give the producer your number. Sebastian Boyle at Brunt Productions.'

'Who?'

'Up and coming production company, very sharp, good background in ground-breaking drama.'

'Such as?'

'He was associate co-producer on *Inspector Pettigrew*, seventh series. Or was that his brother-in-law? Bye for now, dear, call and tell me how it goes.'

Agnes hung up, typed *Pete Clapp* in the box and clicked. The printer spat out her standard letter of termination.

* * *

Halfway up the Tottenham Court Road a small figure bent over her palmtop computer and laboriously made notes via the pinhead-sized keys.

Pete's new draft. Problems. No story arc!!

Daisy leaned back and looked out of the window at the street outside. It was almost static. Unless, just possibly, the bus was travelling backwards at a very low speed. Daisy sighed and pushed the fringe out of her eyes.

The World of the Series. Is this somewhere we want to spend 49½ minutes? If not why not? Could RD go out pre-watershed? ? (Cut sex in strip-search scene?? And fuck on p. 47).

Daisy worked for Albie at Brunt Productions. She was on her way to a meeting and her head was full of Pete Clapp's script.

Suggestion: make Det. Sgt. Pikestaff a single mum??

Suggestion: make Det. Sgt. Pikestaff a serial killer??!

Sensing that the whole script was starting to unravel, Daisy laid down her stylus and forced herself to look out of the window again. Focus, focus, focus. She intoned the mantra softly. It was only a week since her first self-help seminar and already Daisy felt she was reaping the benefits. It was vital to focus. On what was really important to this project.

Handle Sebastian until Albie gets back. Make a good impression.

Fine, so far as it went. But the kernel. What was the kernel? *Make friends with new writer (v. important).*

Daisy smiled to herself. Now she was making progress. But something still nagged away at the back of her mind. Something she had to do. Focus, focus. Then she remembered. This new writer. Young, Sebastian had said. Daisy picked up the stylus once more and picked out the letters.

Hair.

2   Holding the Fort

Sebastian had arranged to meet Pat Quine in Coffee Republic. It wouldn't have been easy getting him and Daisy and a writer into the office all at the same time, never mind sufficient room to lay out scripts, notes, step outlines, scene cards, three cappuccinos, and all the other essentials of a script meeting. Sometimes, too, the smell of cooking from downstairs could be overpowering. To say nothing of the smell from upstairs.

He'd been a drama producer for two days now and it was proving to be a steep learning curve. Sebastian still wasn't entirely sure how Pete Clapp had left the project and Pat Quine had joined it, but Agnes assured him this was common practice and no one else seemed to feel uncomfortable about it, so he let it go. Giggleswick already felt a world away.

When he arrived, slightly late, Daisy and the new writer were installed in a corner of the coffee bar. Pat looked up and nodded and went on talking to Daisy. She was wearing a figure-hugging T-shirt and her hair seemed different, and Pat seemed very interested in what she had to say. He looked like he might have been a model or a barman before turning his hand to writing. Moody, too, but then writers seemed to be. They'd got themselves cappuccinos but Sebastian couldn't see one for him, so he went and queued up.

As Sebastian sat down Daisy was explaining the story so far and smiling at Pat, but in a serious way.

'So we feel what we really need at this point is a real influx of energy, a new direction, for you to pick up this story and really run with it.'

It struck Sebastian how much like Mel's assistant, Jeanie, she was.

'Pat, hi. I'm Sebastian.'

'Oh? So what do you do?'

'Producer.'

'I thought Daisy here was the producer.'

'Whatever gave you that idea?' Daisy examined the chocolate froth on her cup. 'Daisy's the script editor.'

Daisy gave Pat a conspiratorial smile. 'Pat and I were discussing The World of the Series and we wondered if we shouldn't make it more …'

'Gothic.'

'Exactly!'

'Gothic?' Sebastian was puzzled. The show was set in Carshalton. 'How do you mean?'

Sebastian pulled absent-mindedly at a chocolate croissant. It was weird, he thought, the difference between Pat and Pete, considering they were supposed to be doing the same job. Somehow he couldn't look at Pete without seeing a very old word processor, one of those ancient Amstrads or something, on the desk in front of him. Maybe even a typewriter. He'd looked out of place on Mel's leather sofa, didn't know what to do with his hands. Whereas Pat … Sebastian couldn't imagine him ever sitting down at a desk to write. Probably he lay on his own leather sofa at home and dictated to his computer via speech-recognition software. Or maybe someone else did the writing and he did the meetings. Whatever the system was it seemed to work, because according to Agnes he was up to his eyes in commissions.

He looked up to see Pat and Daisy watching at him curiously. 'What?'

'Pat was wondering how much creative freedom he has here.'

'Well, Daisy, there's Mel and Jeanie at The Channel, and their head of programmes. And something called Compliance, whatever that is. I expect you and Albie need your own input too, of course. Beyond that, Pat, the world's your creative oyster.'

He watched Pat stir his cappuccino aggressively and, Sebastian thought, unnecessarily, since he hadn't put any sugar in it. His own croissant was finished. *Get in, get out. Keep it short.* That was the advice he'd read in *How to Be a Producer*. Sebastian made an executive decision.

'Daisy, you brief Pat on the project and I'll see you back at the office at … twelve. Good to meet you, Pat. See if you can develop this Gothic idea without changing the fundamentals. After all, it is a detective series. Look forward to getting your script.' Daisy could talk creativity with Pat Quine while Sebastian tried to locate his missing brother-in-law.

* * *

Albie had always been the kind of person who liked to keep ahead of the game. Producing corporate videos for companies with more money than taste had given way to a low-rent cookery programme, flower-show reports, a factual entertainment show about extreme scootering. Then, by a progression that appeared entirely logical to Albie but baffling to Sebastian, to making television drama. Most recently he'd picked up on the growing demand for western-style programmes in central and eastern Europe.

These days it seemed everyone wanted their own serial set in their own backyard. As well as universal stories they demanded familiar faces with handlebar moustaches or skullcaps, women with hair like horses' manes and plunging cleavages, face-offs in bars and mosques and market-places. Scenting money, adventurous producers set off to Uzbekistan and Bulgaria, Romania, and Belarus. They helped with equipping studios, casting, scripting, budgeting, shooting. They advised. They invested in the local market and local talent. And, once they'd imparted the priceless gift of soap, they returned home to spend the profits.

Albie had made it sound so simple: put *Britain in Bud* on hold for a month and mind the shop while Albie was off in Tajikistan. Take the meetings and the calls, keep pushing it all forward so *Rough Diamonds* didn't disappear into a black hole while Albie was away. Any questions or problems, just get him on the mobile.

It hadn't worked out quite like that. When Sebastian had called to ask whether it mattered that their hero had undergone gender reassignment, all he could get was a message to say Albie's phone wasn't responding. Sebastian knew that already. What kind of mobile coverage did they have in Tajikistan, anyway? He tried the international operator.

* * *

Pat was back at home reading *FHM* on his sofa when Agnes called.

'How did it go, dear?'

'Okay, I think. Producer's a waste of space but the script editor seems good, a girl called Daisy, and she's going to be running the show once the project gets going, so that's cool.'

'Oh. Sebastian didn't mention that. Anyway, they're going ahead with the commission?'

'Daisy said she'd call you today.'

'Well done, dear. We'll try and sting them for a new treatment too, shall we?'

'Yeah, go on, I've already written it.'

'Good boy. Ciao for now.'

* * *

With a heavy heart Sebastian made his way across London to Waterloo and took the train home to East Sheen.

'Jemma?'

But Jemma was out. Probably, thought Sebastian, struggling after-hours with a tenacious overbite. He ate half a pork pie from the fridge, then looked at the date on the wrapper, dropped what was left into the bin and settled for a glass of wine.

Sebastian sat blankly watching a TV gameshow in which two families competed to demolish each other's home in the shortest space of time, for a large cash prize. He felt sick. Behind his chubby face, disquiet was giving way to anxiety. Where the hell was Albie? Bluffing his way through a meeting was one thing, in a way he'd quite enjoyed it. Now, though, he was sitting behind Albie's desk and running Albie's business.

He worried about the approaching Giggleswick Floral Extravaganza, he worried about *Rough Diamonds*, and he worried that Brunt Productions itself might not be in the pink of financial health. Sebastian had skimmed the most recent bank statement and it wasn't a reassuring sight. Most of all he worried that this charade was shaping up to be worse than any of his brother-in-law's previous ventures – the build-your-own-pizza restaurant, the DVD delivery service, even the garden design business that ended in the small claims court.

If Albie hadn't been Jemma's brother, Sebastian might have thought he was a bit of a shyster. Sebastian had never been completely happy about having his name on the letterhead, being a director of Brunt Productions, but Albie had explained his little difficulty with the law relating to companies and how he needed someone in the family, someone he could trust, to sign cheques now and then. And Sebastian liked making his gardening programmes. He enjoyed travelling all over Britain in his battered Cavalier, and didn't mind being his own one-man crew and sleeping on the back seat when the budget was tight. And the budget was always tight.

But this was something different. With *Britain in Bud* there were no moody writers and inscrutable executives to contend with, just the weather and the M1. Plants had no agents. And there was none of this talk about grabbing the audience and holding them, against their will if necessary. People watched gardening programmes because they liked gardening programmes. Put on ten and they'd probably watch them all. Drama, it seemed, was another world.

Sebastian started at the sound of a key in the lock. 'Bugger, bugger, bugger.'

'I'm in here.'

A pale face appeared at the door, framed in red hair, quivering with anger.

'Bloody buggering lock's buggered again, I thought you were going to fix it.'

'I'll get you a glass of wine.' Sebastian used the coffee table to lever himself out of the armchair, welcoming the distraction from his own dark thoughts.

* * *

Later that night Sebastian and Jemma were in bed.

'Heard from Albie lately?' Sebastian tried to sound casual.

'The less I hear from him the happier I'll be.' She turned to face him. 'Why?'

'Oh, nothing.'

'You haven't let him rope you into one of his schemes?'

'Of course not. I just said I'd help keep an eye on things while he's away.'

'Good. You've got to watch Albie. If you're not careful you'll end up paying *him*. And I'm going to need more than I thought to buy into the practice.'

Since it had gone private, the dental empire Jemma served seemed to expand daily. Local NHS dentistry, meanwhile, receded like a gum riddled with gingivitis.

'Do you have to be a partner?'

'That's where the creative work is. It's that or spend my time scraping caries. How would you like it?'

'Well, I wouldn't. It's just that this a sticky patch.'

'Hmm. Sounds like we might need a filling.'

'Do you think so?'

'Perhaps I'd better take a closer look.' She turned off the light.

3 Input

A few days later in her lilac office Mel was skimming Jeanie's report on the new *Rough Diamonds* script while she worked her Chinese energy balls.

Synopsis: Det. Sgt. Dan Brilleaux (!) is a tough career police officer with a troubled home life who uncovers a web of corruption in the course of investigating an apparently motiveless murder. She solves the murder but fails to nail the biggest baddies while her personal life goes from bad to worse. Plot is bog standard but with flourishes, such as the exorcism in a deconsecrated church. Bit heavy on the Gothic? Also, lots of night exteriors = extra sparks, cherry pickers etc. Suggest stick Dan's frustrating relationship with bisexual recovering alcoholic dancer boyfriend on back burner for early part of series. Also drop incident room blah, seen it all before a million times. Casting for Dan is crucial. Does this make sense as a vehicle for Helen Quigley? If not, then who? Upbeat it's not, and I thought we were looking for sweetness and light on The Channel …

Mel tossed the report onto the pile and buzzed her assistant.

'I'm not going to have time for my weekly with Jeanie. Has she got anything important to go through?'

'Just the new script for *Rough Diamonds*, she said.'

'Okay, cancel and tell Jeanie she can decide what to do with it.'

'Yes, Mel.'

'Oh. And book the car for six-twenty. I need to change and Belinda Barge isn't worth more than ten minutes anyway.'

'Right, Mel.'

'And get us a skinny latte, would you?'

* * *

Sebastian was pleased with the work Pat had done, once Daisy had explained it to him. Pat had taken a routine police show with a twist and given it an extra twist. Then he'd taken out the original twist. So what they had now was a copshow-with-a-twist, but a new twist. Clever. He felt he was starting to get the hang of this drama game, which was just as well since Albie remained resolutely incommunicado.

Pete Clapp didn't see it that way, in fact he sounded quite upset. His agent must have been mistaken when she'd said how happy he'd be with the new arrangement. Sebastian asked him to sort it out with Agnes and hinted there might be an episode for him later in the series once they got the commission, and eventually Pete calmed down enough for Sebastian to get him off the phone.

What Sebastian needed now was the right actress. That was what everyone talked about at the Old Compton Street café when he went in to get his bacon sandwich for breakfast, and again in the Italian deli at lunchtime. Stars. Who have you got?

But how did you get stars? Sebastian didn't dare ask Daisy. He didn't want to look a complete idiot, after all.

Agents. That was it. Stars had agents, just like writers did. You called them up and offered them jobs.

Simple.

Sebastian took a bite of his cinnamon twist and was picking up the phone when Daisy arrived, smiling in that way she had when drama was in the air.

'Guess who I just spoke to.'

'Pat Quine?' They seemed to call each other about twenty times a day. Still, Sebastian supposed, someone had to, and it could hardly be him.

'Jeanie. From Mel's office.'

'Should I call her back?'

'No need. She's read the script. She's got a few notes.'

'Oh?'

'I've called Pat and he's working on them. We should have the new draft in a day or two.'

'Er … didn't you think I might want to have some … input?'

'Do you disagree with the notes?'

Sebastian scanned the sheet helplessly. It seemed to be written in double Dutch. 'No, it all seems quite reasonable. Oh. This. 'Too Gothic'?'

'We've covered that. Did you want to go into battle on any of these?'

'Well. No. I –'

'And I was thinking, what about Helen Quigley? She's perfect for Dan and The Channel love her.'

'Well, I was thinking of the woman in that thing, you know, what's her name … Deanne Davis.'

'But she can't act.'

'The Channel love her.' Where had he overhead that? Caffè Nero?

'That's not what Jeanie said. Why do you think they cancelled *Dead Bodies*?'

Daisy was sounding rather like an up-and-coming producer. Sebastian eyed her nervously.

'What happens next?'

'You set up another meeting with Mel Gioconda. Get her to say yes.'

* * *

'No.'

Mel sat back in her chair. Jeanie smiled earnestly. Sebastian went very pale.

'What? I don't understand. I thought –'

'I admire what Pat Quine's done with it.' Mel looked down at the script on the coffee table. *Rough Diamonds by Pat Quine. First Draft.* Which it was, if you didn't count the seven by Pete Clapp. 'He's really brought something to the project. Only it's something we don't want. This Gothic thing –'

'We've covered that in the latest draft.'

'Have you?' Mel shot Jeanie a questioning look. Jeanie gave a tiny nod. 'Well, it's not just that.'

'What, then?'

'Well, everything.' Mel swung round to Jeanie again. 'Will you take over here, Jeanie, I've got to leave now or I'll never get to the Ivy in time for Sir Ian.' She turned back to the producer with a ravishing smile. 'It's been *lovely* working with you, Sebastian, and I do wish you the very best of luck with it elsewhere.'

As Mel swept out of her office Jeanie at least had the grace to look embarrassed. Sebastian pressed home this tiny advantage. 'What's the problem here, Jeanie? I thought everyone was pleased with the new draft.'

Jeanie smiled unhappily and tugged at her earring. 'It's not one specific thing …'

'Has Mel actually read this?'

'It's more a case of changed priorities.'

'What do you mean?'

'We're really focusing on the pre-watershed Saturday slot now, something for the whole family, maybe with animals. Have you got anything like that?'

* * *

'How did the meeting go?' Daisy leapt up as Sebastian slumped into the office. 'Shall I get the champagne?'

He shook his head.

'What happened?'

'I'm really not sure.'

'Let me guess. They're not looking for a copshow any more.'

Sebastian studied her. How did she know?

'So what's changed?'

'I suppose today there's something she likes more.'

You knew where you were with gardening programmes. Or Sebastian thought he did. Drama just seemed to have so many more … bits.

'Maybe the script had a nicer cover. Maybe it was written by her boyfriend.'

'Maybe it has Helen Quigley in the lead. Did you ask?'

'No, I –'

But Daisy wasn't listening, she was already on the phone, working her ever-growing network of contacts. Sebastian watched, impressed, as she charmed the vital information, piece by piece, from a succession of agents, secretaries, assistants, and providers of miscellaneous personal services.

'Okay. Helen Quigley's attached to a series called *Dark Thoughts*, something Monopolimedia have with The Channel.' Monopolimedia was a big, brash production company that rampaged through Soho's one-man bands like an orc scattering hobbits. 'Mel's just okayed it and the show's waiting for the controller's rubber stamp.'

'What's it like?'

'It's a copshow. But dark. The word that kept coming up was *Gothic*.'

'Uh huh.'

'But listen to this. They have concerns about the script, according to Jeanie.'

'You spoke to Jeanie again?'

'And the writer they'd really like on it is … Pat Quine.'

'Oh. Isn't he working for us?'

'Exactly. So if we can just hijack Helen Quigley, reinstall the Gothic bits, book up Pat Quine so he's unavailable for the next year, and maybe rename our show *Dark Diamonds* … then no one'll be able to tell the difference.'

'Brilliant, Daisy! Let's do it.'

But she was already on the phone, doing it. Maybe there was hope for them, after all.

Pete Clapp dialled Brunt Productions again. And again. The number was constantly engaged. The cowards must have taken their phone off the hook.

* * *

Monopolimedia's purpose-built headquarters, sculpted out of the shell of several old townhouses, had been chosen for its proximity to the stars' favourite restaurants. The executive offices and meeting rooms upstairs owed their inspiration more to exclusive clubs than to other businesses: limed oak panelling, windows that opened, antiques, deep carpets. Beneath them the hand-picked, head-hunted wage slaves worked in a stainless steel sweatshop, assembling television series, entertainment shows and now films with the homogenised efficiency of an upmarket sandwich-shop chain.

'But why should you care about a little piss-pot production like *Rough Diamonds*?'

Bernie Gassman, Chief Executive Officer, adjusted by a few millimetres the position of his Palm Pilot on the otherwise bare surface of his steel desk, then moved it back to its original position. He was dressed in a black suit and open-necked white shirt, at once expensive and anonymous, the uniform of the media business. Jeremy Cavendish, his chairman and partner, who inclined more towards tweeds and bespoke brogues, leant against the door-frame and waited patiently for an answer.

'You know why.'

'Because you don't like anyone else making anything?'

'Because Pat Quine is ours. We've got his film, we've got his next film, we should have his television writing as well. That's the whole point of our operation. Vertical integration. Synergy. That's what Monopolimedia is about.'

Bernie very often spoke like this, in formatted paragraphs, even in public. His small talk usually came in the form of mission statements. 'And Helen Quigley. They stole her from us. Between her and Pat Quine we could package up *Rough Diamonds* into something special.'

'For us.'

'And our associates.'

'But we don't need *Rough Diamonds*.' Jeremy sipped his latte, long legs elegantly crossed, effortlessly blocking the path of the understrapper hovering ignored behind him and waiting for a chance to dart through Bernie's door. 'Let Brunt Productions make it. They'll cock it up, of course.' Jeremy smiled. 'Helen Quigley and Pat Quine will have a terrible time. Then we move in. With sympathy, understanding … and a deal.'

Jeremy's cool was based on many years' experience fluffing celebrity clients. From his early days as a talent scout – after a false start in current affairs – he'd expanded successfully into production, foreseeing the time when TV production would be ruled not by what it was, but by who was in it. If the box was going to be run by the talent, who now liked to get behind the camera as well as in front of it, then Jeremy was ready to oblige.

'Who's the producer?'

'Someone called Sebastian Boyle, apparently.'

Involuntarily, Bernie's hand moved to realign the Palm. It was a tiny gesture and perhaps only someone in Bernie's poker circle would have spotted it. Jeremy preferred bridge.

'Never heard of him.'

'Exactly.'

If Jeremy was old media, all the way back to radio, God help him, Bernie was new media through and through. He'd never worked for a broadcaster, and never would, until Monopolimedia became a broadcaster itself, of course. He'd got into telly through the back door – the fire exit, in fact – via an out-of-hours video piracy scam at a duplicating plant. Bernie had never served time in production, nor spent more than fifteen minutes of his life on set. He hadn't the slightest interest in the difference between a blonde and a redhead, didn't care what a diopter was or where a gobo went or what a best boy did. But he could read – balance sheets, progress reports, business plans, ratings analyses. Sometimes he even read scripts.

'We've got seven other productions to worry about. And all of the development slate. And what about the Golden Globe nominations? We can afford to wait.' And Jeremy sauntered away up the corridor to greet another, recently ennobled colleague.

Bernie waited until he had his office to himself before allowing a small, rarely seen smile to crawl across his face. Then he extinguished it and returned to his survey of production costs in Albania.

4 Your Biggest Fan

In a hacienda outside Chingford the phone was trilling. A tough-looking blonde in a pink tracksuit leant across the treadmill in her mini-gym and flipped on the hands-free. Shrill mid-Atlantic vowels filled the room.

'Helen? How are you, sweetie?'

'I'm fine, Lavinia.' Lavinia Hurdle was her agent, five feet nothing in her kitten heels, but her voice could empty the Albert Hall. 'What's the story with *Dark Thoughts*?'

'Well, interesting situation. Monopoli's offer still stands and they're very close to getting The Channel to sign off on the deal, they say. But another one's just come in.'

'What for?'

'New show written by Pat Quine. You know, he's a hot young writer, doing films mostly but he's got this one TV project, very unusual.'

'Can I do them both?'

'No, sweetie, total conflict, it's either/or. But ... the money's much better on this new show.'

'Much?'

'Mmmph.'

'Mmmph?'

'Sorry, sweetie, I'm eating a bagel. Much.'

'What do you think?'

'Meet them, at least. The producer's called Daisy something, sounds like she knows what she's doing. She wants to have lunch. I've stonewalled Monopoli, so there's time.'

'Okay. Set it up.'

'Will do, sweetie. Bye for now.'

Helen Quigley turned off her phone and concentrated on shifting a rogue half-kilo that had somehow found its way from her birthday dinner to the problem area at the back of her thighs.

* * *

Daisy's focus was beginning to pay off. Things were moving. Now she had to make sure they moved in the right direction. She licked the end of her stylus.

Charm socks off La Quigley.

She looked out of the window at the pedestrians scurrying along Oxford Street. It was funny how she always worked best on the bus. Vaguely Daisy wondered what would happen to her focus if she commuted by tube instead.

Make her feel understood and appreciated.

It was fine as far as it went, but these warm, fuzzy ideas might not be enough to convince Helen Quigley. She had something of a rep as a toughie, after all. What would she want?

Mention Monopoli operate strict no-Winnebago policy. Whereas we believe stars can only give of their best when fully appreciated and properly looked after.

Reassurance. That was a good line to follow.

Tell HQ no nude scenes (NB see she has doctored version of script).

That should help.

Keywords for mtg: integrity … commitment … hit.

* * *

Sebastian had mixed feelings as he stepped beneath the Palladian architrave of Snipe & Abercrombie and into the panelled waiting room with its elaborate plaster swags and waxed floorboards. Copies of *Country Life* and *Horse and Hound* jostled incongruously on the coffee table with *Screen Finance*, *Variety*, and *Intellectual Property Digest*. Everything in the room smelled of money, except him. What did Sebastian smell of? Surreptitiously he sniffed an armpit. Right Guard and fear, not necessarily in that order. People only visited Giles Savernake to chat at the rate of £400 per hour when there was the hope of serious money to be made, or the fear of losing it. Legal advice was, after all, a distress purchase. Sebastian sat down, flipped the pages of *Country Life* and sighed.

It had all happened very quickly. As soon as Mel had heard the magic words 'Helen Quigley' she'd dragged Sebastian straight to her boss's office. Red lights had changed in an instant to green. Without warning *Rough Diamonds* was in pre-production. And Albie was still maintaining radio silence.

'Mr Boyle? Mr Savernake will see you now.'

Giles was old school, or old school with a twist. Inside his office the swags and panelling continued, but the furniture was more *Batman Returns* than *Horse and Hound*. A man in an expensively but conservatively tailored suit rose an inch from a venerable leather chair and held out a hand to his visitor.

'So, Albie got off his arse and got something greenlit, good for him.' Giles was ageless, with the buffed veneer that only regular applications of money can produce. He shook hands. 'Where is he, by the way?'

Sebastian shrugged.

'And you're his – what? Partner?'

'Brother-in-law. And colleague.'

'Right. Trouble is, this Channel deal's shit. Absolute shit. Who negotiated it?'

'I did.'

'You're too nice, Sebastian.' He meant, bloody hopeless. 'What about Brit TV?'

'But it's The Channel who commissioned it.'

'That's the time to get a better offer. I was talking to Brit's head of business affairs and they're obsessed with two things: shafting The Channel and stealing Helen Quigley.' Brit TV was another broadcaster determined to keep its popular audience, tied to their armchairs if necessary. They also had a lot more money than The Channel with which to do the job.

'Well, you've got Helen Quigley, haven't you?'

'Probably. Not committed yet. We're having lunch tomorrow.'

'Sign her up today. Now. I'll niggle away at The Channel's contract and keep them busy in the meantime. Don't worry, nothing too expensively time-consuming. Get a meeting with Steve Bung at Brit TV tomorrow. Bosh.' And he picked up the phone to start on his next client. To do Giles justice, even at £400 per hour that wasn't more than about forty quid. Or did it work like an engineer's call-out charge, charged to the nearest thirty minutes? Sebastian shook the proffered hand again but Giles was already ratcheting up some option deal, and he slipped quietly out.

* * *

Half a mile away Helen Quigley floated gently in a heaving pool of warm water. She'd checked herself into The Lagoon and was now spending the day in the women-only, state of the art health club. This, she reflected, was the best bit – the offers had come in, they were all good, but she hadn't committed and didn't have to if she didn't want to, it was all there for the taking. And she deserved it.

Following Lavinia's advice, Helen had disappeared. While Brunt Productions were pursuing her, along with her ex-husband (some chance! He still had two years to serve), the producer of *Dalston Square*, and another actress rumoured to be a close friend, Helen was safely tucked away in The Lagoon. She'd already had a massage and a sauna. After lunch she'd get her hair done, and her nails.

Lavinia had said it was much better to leave it all to her, and she was right. By now The Channel's director of programmes – Mel's boss – would be calling up, over-friendly, sweating a little, or perhaps even giving in to a bit of bluster. Helen had worked for him, indirectly of course, for seven years now, starting out on *Dalston Square* fresh from drama school and slowly building Rikki up into everyone's favourite minicab controller, but had she ever had so much as a thank you from The Channel? Had she buggery. At their summer party he'd walked right past her to buttonhole some old goat in leather trousers. So now it was time to flex her muscles a little, maybe flex her wings too.

Of course, in the end she'd go back to them, that was obvious. They'd have to match Brit's money, naturally, better it in fact, but she wasn't ready to see a stunt-double Rikki disappear under a mystery car's wheels just yet. And the things they did to you if just upped and left! Well, to Rikki really, but it felt just the same. They'd bring up all that stuff about her fling with Dale's dad and make out she was a slag and had it coming. And they'd say she couldn't handle the schedule any more, the extra episode every week had been too much for her, she'd become unreliable. There'd be hints about drinking, crack, Mars bars, anorexia and bulimia, maybe go so far as clinical depression and black-market Viagra. Those press office bastards, they were capable of anything once they were off the leash.

And their way was best, really, keep Rikki doing her stuff in *Dalston Square* but run *Dark Thoughts* alongside it, build up her rep as a serious actress, decent scripts for a change and classy guest stars, get herself established before cutting loose and heading for the wide blue yonder. Still, it was nice to be asked. She'd just keep her head down for the day, while the suits went postal, let Lavinia handle everything, then turn up at The Channel wide-eyed for her usual call tomorrow and say how nice it was of them to double her fee. Lunch with the other lot sounded fun, but she couldn't have promised anything so it was better to say no. At least no one could get to her here and make her feel bad about it, try to take advantage of her kind heart.

'Helen? Or should I say, Rikki? It's so exciting to meet you in the flesh! I'm your biggest fan. Fancy meeting you here, of all places. In a Jacuzzi!' Helen smiled professionally. The pleasure of being recognised still hadn't worn off completely. 'Yes, it's me. Us. What's your name?'

'Daisy.'

5 Credit Control

It was a very long day. Once Daisy had tracked down Helen Quigley she still had to charm her socks off, or on as it turned out, then call Helen's agent with the actress at her side, embroidering the truth a little but all in a noble cause, then get round to the meeting with Steve Bung at Brit TV and tie it all up. She briefed Sebastian in the taxi, fiddling with his tie and even trying to comb his hair, and persuaded him to let her do the talking.

The headquarters of Brit TV contrasted sharply with the dowdily respectable Channel. An architect-designed carbuncle barely a year old, the building turned its back on the West End to face the City. The high velocity lift shot them to Steve Bung's office somewhere near its apex. Once inside, Sebastian and Daisy seemed to dangle precariously above the streets while they waited anxiously for the man himself.

'Right. You've got Helen Quigley. Is that correct?'

It sounded more like a hostage negotiation than a programme commission. 'Well, we think Helen would be perfect for this part –'

Steve Bung waved away the interruption. He was a big man, a brick shit-house in a Savile Row suit, and seemed to fill the large office, leaving no room for Sebastian and Daisy. He continued in his brusque, Aussie twang.

'And you've got her in – what? A copshow?'

Daisy nodded.

'Right. Give your details to business affairs on the way out, they'll sort it.'

Strange, Sebastian thought, as they plummeted earthwards in the lift. No mention of characters, writers, motivation. No questions about artistic vision or The World of the Series.

'Did you notice, Daisy? He never mentioned the script once.'

* * *

Daisy called Lavinia at Leading Artists with the good news that not only would Helen double her usual fee on *Rough Diamonds*, she would also get a deal with Brit TV for two more shows. No way could the cautious, careful Channel match that and Lavinia knew it. Monopolimedia would take it badly too but that, after all, was the game they were in. If her client was happy, Lavinia was happy. And vice versa.

Brunt Productions had just increased their production fee. Daisy had every reason to feel pleased with herself, which she did.

* * *

At Brunt Productions, meanwhile, a new era had begun. The smells of Thai takeaways and hardcore customers were a distant memory. The new office was only a street away but several rungs up the media ladder. Daisy stood in the conference room, enjoying the optimistic odours of fresh paint and virgin alpaca rugs. She turned to Pat Quine.

'Well, I thought you'd be pleased.'

'I am pleased, it was great when you told me. It's just that now I'm the one who's got to write the bloody thing.' Pat swung his other leg up onto the new leather sofa and groaned. 'Can I have another coffee?'

'Sure.' Daisy put her head around the door, newly coated in lime sherbet green, and summoned their latest acquisition. Sophie was the new runner, which meant she did whatever she was asked, at a run if necessary. At this particular moment she was a waitress. Pat checked out Sophie's piercings with interest as she took the order for refreshments.

'Nice offices. Why didn't we meet here before?'

'We had the decorators in.' This wasn't a complete lie. The unit was one of the first to become available, and workmen were still snagging other parts of the building. It was quite reasonable at only four times the rent of the old office. But, as Daisy had pointed out, there was a lot of work to be done now and it couldn't all happen at a corner table in Coffee Republic.

Sebastian continued to feel uneasy about taking such a big decision without Albie. But Daisy was right, they had to work some- where, and reluctantly he'd taken the shortest possible lease. He'd balked at the rates and again at the furniture, the computers and office equipment, even at Sophie and the cappuccino machine, but in the end Daisy had made him see it all for what it was: an investment. Credibility was key. With this commission they were players now, and they needed to raise their profile. Certainly Pat seemed to agree, his eyes sliding appreciatively over Sophie as she bent to pick up an empty cup.

In his own office Sebastian was just thinking to himself how Pete Clapp would never have been comfortable here when he looked through the glass wall behind Daisy and encountered an unlooked-for opportunity to test this theory. Pete Clapp was standing barely five yards away, arguing with their new receptionist.

Sophie returned from her coffee-making duties to Daisy's office, tapped at the door and went in. Pat was now stretched out full length on the sofa with his arms behind his head, while Daisy sat on the floor. They were both laughing. 'Thank you, Sophie, you're an angel, we're just *dying* for another cappuccino here, aren't we, Pat?' Pat leered at Sophie but continued talking.

'So then the old biddy picks herself up off the floor. She's not dead. And she's not old either. Under all that crap she's got on it's *Mendel*. He never died in the fire. And the thing she's holding is – the *knife*. The one he used. The one they couldn't find at the scene. And he just *stands* there, *staring*. Going mental.' Pat levered himself up just far enough to reach his latest cappuccino. 'And she just says – get this – 'Oh, Tom. ' Kind of sad. That's it.' Pat closed his eyes.

'That's it?' Daisy looked entranced.

'That's it.'

'Just like in that Kevin Bacon movie!' Sophie shouldn't have said it, that was clear right away. Pat shot her another look, her face this time, and it wasn't a nice one. Daisy got the message.

'Thanks for the coffees, Sophie,' she said, with a tiny nod towards the door.

'No worries, that's what I'm paid for.'

'How true.' Sophie heard that, and he meant her to. That was why she gave him the finger. Secretly of course. It was just bad luck that Sophie happened to catch Pete Clapp's eye as he was staring out of the office opposite, ranting at Sebastian. He stopped, mouth open, and slowly went purple. Sophie took her Ericsson out of her pocket and pretended to be reading a text while she hurried back into the kitchen.

Next door Pete Clapp had been wearing Sebastian out.

'Well, maybe we should see what the Writers' Guild has to say it about it.'

'The what?'

Pete rolled his eyes. 'It's the only thing that stops producers like you riding roughshod over writers.'

'Oh. Are you a member?'

'I can always rejoin.'

Sebastian had been trying to talk him down and it seemed to be working, but then out of nowhere Pete Clapp had gone ballistic.

'So you've even got your staff doing it now!'

'Eh? Doing what?'

'That girl who brings the coffee?'

'What's wrong with the coffee?'

'Nothing. She just gave me the finger.'

'Who? Sophie? I don't believe it.'

'That's it, I've had it with this company. My agent said you were crap and she was right.'

'Agnes did? I thought you weren't with her any more.'

'And I'm rejoining the Writers' Guild. Then we'll see who's laughing.'

'No one's laughing, Pete.'

'And I checked the ratings on *Inspector Pettigrew*. Do you know they dropped fifteen per cent when your brother-in-law took over? And what have you done, anyway, that makes you a producer? I looked on the Internet. I couldn't find a single credit.' And with that Pete Clapp was gone. For the time being. Sebastian sat down, then stood up again. He picked up the cappuccino on the table and drank it, then remembered it was Pete's. Personally he liked Pete, but he had to admit their relationship was going through a rocky patch. Sebastian wondered what exactly Agnes had told him. He felt hurt that Pete's Internet search had failed to locate *Britain in Bud*.

From his office he could see Daisy in her meeting. Sebastian could just see Pat Quine, too, horizontal on Daisy's sofa. Fortunately the model-barman-writer had been below Pete Clapp's eyeline. He wasn't a big man, Pete. Pat was lying back, very relaxed, while Daisy scribbled feverishly at a notepad. It looked like it was all going terribly well. Sebastian decided to join them.

'Hi, Pat. Everything okay?'

'Yeah, great. I was just saying to Daisy, I don't think we should meet here again.'

'Why ever not, Pat?'

'The atmosphere's … uncreative. I can't work properly. All this –'

He gestured expansively with his arm: the sofa, the meeting room, the offices … Sophie … '– it's stifling me. My creativity. And it's stifling *Rough Diamonds*.' He gave Daisy a sincere look. 'I think we'd work better at my place. Or at yours.'

Daisy shuffled her papers together. 'Or somewhere neutral. I'll give it some thought.'

'Can I have a word, Daisy?' As Pat loped off through reception, Daisy followed Sebastian back to his office and closed the door. 'Where are we up to with the scripts?'

'Pat wants to write all six.'

'Won't that take him rather a long time?'

'He's working pretty fast.'

'I think we might need more writers. Who is there?'

'How should I know?'

'Hang on. Aren't you the script editor?'

'Yes, but –'

'Why don't you make a list? Let's meet again in … an hour, and go through it together.' Sebastian spun round on his brand new, sculpted aluminium chair and picked up the phone. Daisy remained at the door. 'Yes?'

'I may have, um, given Pat to believe …' Daisy's voice trailed off as she looked at her shoes.

'What, Daisy?'

'Well, promised him, in fact …'

'Yes?'

'Sole writer's credit.'

Sebastian regarded her levelly. 'Oh dear. Well, I'm sure you'll sort it out.' And he picked up the phone again and speed-dialled Bank Frød. The cashflow was proving to be a minefield. Sebastian reached into his drawer for a creme egg. The scripts had become just another part of the jigsaw puzzle that Sebastian was piecing together on his pristine glass and chrome desk. Checking that no one was looking, he opened *How to Be a Producer* on his knees under the desk. He was up to Chapter Seven. At this moment, frankly, he was more concerned with cash flow than with creativity. Someone or something had to pay for all this office furniture.

6 Lists

Slowly but surely Sebastian was adjusting to his new job. The tone on Albie's phone had gone from permanently engaged to permanently unobtainable. Sebastian suspected his brother-in-law was probably steeping himself in the local culture with some friendly guide, possibly female, perhaps in a yak-hide yurt deep in the steppes. Or was that Mongolia? In his absence Sebastian would just have to soldier on alone.

His life now seemed to revolve around lists – lists of things to do, people to see, calls to make. Lists of actors, writers, directors, heads of department, lighting companies. Lists of lists still to be written.

Sebastian pored over *Producing for Beginners*, which he'd found under one leg of the coffee table in Albie's old office, and a paperback called *Do the Deal!* which had caught his eye in Waterstones. The trouble was, all these how-to books favoured different approaches and reminded Sebastian of the many fashionable diets he'd taken up and dropped. Now he was embarking on what one of his guides – he forgot which – called 'the most important decision of them all'. It was time to choose a director.

On his longlist Sebastian had thirty-three names. On his shortlist these had been reduced down to ten. Ten phone calls to ten agents. Simple enough.

An hour later Sebastian had whittled down his director shortlist from ten to zero. Six were busy, two were waiting for a call from Hollywood, one had fallen off the wagon and one just didn't fancy it. Back to the longlist.

Daisy returned with a proposal. Now her areas of responsibility were expanding (an expression that part of Sebastian's consciousness registered with a certain alarm and filed away for processing later), wouldn't it make sense for Daisy to have a junior script editor to help her? After all, lots of this was just donkey-work, pestering agents and wading through episodes of *Deptford Emergency* and *Do Not Resuscitate*. Sophie had read a few scripts for Daisy and now she was ready for promotion.

As he opened his mouth to veto the plan Daisy read Sebastian's mind and got in first.

'It'll be much cheaper. You won't have to pay Sophie much as a trainee – she'll bite your hand off – and I can use my time more cost-efficiently. So, really, it's a saving.'

'And who'll do Sophie's job?'

Silly question. All Daisy had to do was stick her arm out of the window to grab as many media studies graduates as she fancied from the streets of Soho. Apparently some companies asked the runners to pay for the privilege of making coffee. Not Brunt Productions, though. Not yet, anyway.

'Just leave it all to me.'

The scripts, Sebastian reasoned, were a priority, and Daisy seemed to know what she was doing.

'Go on then. By the way, who directed *Parasites*?'

'Damian Spent. He should be on our list.'

Sebastian typed in the name. 'He is.'

* * *

Sebastian had arranged to meet a stream of directors, interspersed with another stream of writers, alternating so that there shouldn't be any awkward crossover in the reception area. So who, he wondered, looking through the internal window with a commanding view over the Brunt Productions empire, was the man immaculate in a cashmere suit sitting next to Bill Block (bomber jacket and baseball cap)? He put down his muffin, picked up the phone, and called Lucy, the receptionist.

'Who's that next to Bill Block?'

'A director called Damien Spent.'

'Bloody hell, Lucy, they were supposed to be kept apart.' All the manuals had flagged up the touchiness of creative types.

'He asked to swap times, he's got another meeting. Shall I send him in?'

The man in the cashmere suit cast a languid eye over the office as he strolled in. 'Hi. I'm Damien. It's Stephen, isn't it?'

'Sebastian. Nice to meet you. Have a seat. Did Lucy offer you a coffee?'

'Never touch it. So, my agent said I should come by.'

'What did you think of the script?'

'Haven't seen one.'

'Oh. We sent one, I think.'

'Did you? I've been in Warsaw. Why don't you just tell me about it.'

'Right. Okay. Well, *Rough Diamonds* is about –'

'Hang on. Did you say *Rough Diamonds*?'

'Yes. It's a very interesting –'

'I thought I was meeting to talk about *Black Oblivion*.'

'What's *Black Oblivion*?'

'A film starring Sherryann DeWitt. No? This *is* Monopoli-media?'

'This is Brunt Productions.'

'Shit! That stupid girl at my agent's. Look, I'm sorry about this.' He didn't sound sorry, just annoyed. 'Wrong everything, I'm afraid.'

'But I did want to meet you. To talk about *Rough Diamonds*.'

'Christ. Not that telly series about the woman who sleeps in a coffin?'

'We've taken that out. In the new script, you'll see –'

'Look, sorry, but I've got to get to Monmouth Street. Could you call my agent, get them to tell Monopoli I'll be a few minutes late?'

'Shall we fix another time?'

'Got to run.'

The phone bleeped. 'Shall I send in Mr Block now?'

Bill Block was not under the impression he was about to be offered a feature film starring Sherryann DeWitt. Sebastian doubted such a mistake would be possible. Bill was a fixture in the self-enclosed world of long-running series. His bleary eyes, shaded from the light by the stained baseball cap, had gazed over sets and locations from *Deptford Emergency* and *Red Alert* to *Do Not Resuscitate* and *Danger Vets*. He had swung from harnesses below helicopters and wobbled on the top of camera cranes. He never flapped and always completed the schedule. He went from job to job, continually in work. He never lost his shooting script, or if he did, it made no difference. Bill Block was very reliable. And very, very dull.

'How do. Read the script.'

'Hi, I'm Sebastian. What did you think?'

'What's the budget?'

'Not finalised yet.'

Bill grunted. 'Lot of night shooting.'

'Quite a lot, yes.'

'Five day weeks, six day weeks or eleven day fortnights?'

'Well, once I've got my production manager –'

'Where are you shooting? London or overnights?'

'Probably London, hard to say yet …'

'You are the producer, right?'

'Er, yes.'

Another grunt. 'Who was that bloke in reception? Looked like Damien Spent.'

'He was here about another project.'

'Yeah? Used to be my runner. Well –' Bill heaved himself off the sofa. 'Why don't you give my agent a ring once you've got a budget and a schedule. If you're interested, that is.'

Sebastian was left with a view of Bill's departing back as he made for reception and the door. The rear of his bomber jacket read *Danger Vets – Series V*. Sebastian looked at the list.

'Who's next?'

Next was Jonathan Krankie. Small, dark, intense, he conjured up the world of *Rough Diamonds* as it was forming inside his head. It sounded an uncomfortable place.

'It's dark. All you can see is this one, tiny, pale gleam. Probably use luminous paint, maybe UV, dunno yet. It comes closer. It's a hand. But – that's all it is. Just a hand. *It's not connected to anything.* It floats … closer. She looks at it, she can't move, she's frozen with fear. Her eye – that's all you can see of her, the curve of one eyeball – stretches wider and wider. Then –'

'Yes?' Sebastian was almost on the edge of his seat.

'Cut.'

'Oh.'

'To one of those huge meat saws, the kind they have hanging from the ceiling in an abattoir. Swinging lazily around. The sound – and that's important, because –'

'It's too dark to see much?'

'Exactly. Just the reflections on the spinning chain of the blade –'

'I think Brit TV will want to see Helen Quigley. More than just one side of her eyeball.'

'Don't they want atmosphere?'

'That too.'

'But there's no atmosphere if you drown everything in light. You can see everything … or you can use your imagination.'

'Given the choice, I think they'd prefer to see everything. Every inch of Helen Quigley, anyway.'

'Then they're philistines.'

'Possibly. But they're also the ones paying for the show, so it may be difficult to ignore them completely.'

'But we have to.' Jonathan's showreel, part of the heap of tapes on Sebastian's floor, supported this view. He'd done his damnedest to ignore the wishes of commissioners and exclude light from everything he'd done. Which, to be fair, wasn't much.

After Jonathan there were two new writers to meet, but Sebastian let Daisy and the newly promoted Sophie deal with them. He could see Daisy was torn, smiling at the nervous pen-pushers but casting anxious, even longing looks at Sebastian's office window behind which a succession of directors appeared, said their piece, and left. There was something about Daisy's famished gaze that made him uncomfortable. He yanked down the blinds on the internal window.

'So, Martin, how have you been finding …' – glance down at top CV on knee, check that name at top corresponds to person sitting opposite, smile, continue – '*Dalston Square*.'

'Shite.'

'I see. Why's that?'

Martin stared at Sebastian as though he was mad. 'Everyone knows it's shite.'

Possibly, Sebastian thought. But they don't usually say so in interviews when it's their only credit.

'So why did you take the job if you think the programme's so bad?'

Another scornful look. 'You've got to, haven't you? Then you move on to something better.'

Not necessarily, thought Sebastian. 'So what's next, Martin? Got anything lined up?'

'Yeah, actually, I'm developing a movie idea.'

'I meant, production-wise.'

'I haven't got time to waste on some crappy series or soap, if that's what you mean.'

'Tell me something, Martin. Why did you come to this meeting?'

'Because my agent told me to.'

'Would you do something for me, Mart?'

'What?'

'Drop this in the bin in reception on your way out.'

'What is it?'
'Your CV. And your agent's client list.'

7 Gut Feelings

Spotting Sebastian alone at last, Daisy put her head around his door.

'Any luck?'

'Back to the longlist.' He glanced at it again. It bore little resemblance to the bold, optimistic document of last week.

'Let me see.'

The best and brightest of the directing elite – the old masters, the young guns, the originals – were all gone. In their place were the foot-soldiers, the malingerers, and several basket cases.

'Oh dear. Listen, there's someone you might try if you're desperate.'

'I'm not desperate. Yet.'

'Just a name to add to the longlist. I've been hearing good things about him. Trevor William.'

'Well, why not. Who's his agent?'

'I'll find out.' Daisy ducked out of the office.

Trevor William was shooting a documentary in Sarawak and wouldn't be back for another week, but his agent sounded very keen so Sebastian put his name down and kept on meeting other directors in the meantime.

To complement the list Sebastian had begun with an elaborately designed chart, with columns for all the qualities he hoped to find in his director. Few of the individuals who'd agreed to turn up in his office had rated more than one tick in any box, and most of them none. Now he was ready to settle for basic competence plus a willingness to undertake the job. Lack of obnoxious personal habits would be a bonus.

Even so, no matter how far he lowered the bar it seemed always to be a little bit too high. Sebastian tried to overlook the blithe overconfidence, the tang of vodka breath beneath the peppermints, the bleary uninterest in Brunt's unique project. But a persistent little voice kept telling him that if he made this choice – any of these choices – he'd live to regret it.

In the meantime it was proving almost as difficult to find an associate producer, the key person who was going to make the whole thing work. There just weren't any available. Sebastian desperately needed someone good, someone who understood the process, someone Sebastian could rely on. Someone who knew what he was doing.

What he got was Dougal.

Dougal was certainly experienced – so experienced, in fact, that he'd begun his career on an early David Lean film in some junior capacity. Apparently he was friendly with Roger Moore and had worked on a couple of the less successful Bond movies. After a faltering career in the film industry Dougal had ended up in telly, which he hated. His blazer and cravat seemed weirdly out of place in nineties Soho, while the quiff of grey hair above Dougal's permatanned face contrasted oddly with Daisy's stylish bob and Sophie's piercings. Still, he had an eagle eye for detail and could budget and schedule in his sleep, which Sebastian suspected he frequently did. The fledgling producer dutifully made the usual calls to check him out – his CV seemed almost too good to be true – and the response was always the same. Dougal's very capable, his former colleagues all said, wearily. It'll all work out fine, if you don't kill him first.

Dougal was already installed at one end of Sebastian's office when Trevor William finally appeared, unannounced and unexpected, at Brunt Productions. He was short and round-shouldered, pale even after Sarawak (had he taken the veil for secret filming?), and exuded quiet confidence. His credits so far comprised his graduation piece from film school (a comedy so black it could have satisfied Jonathan Krankie), a 'hard-hitting' documentary, a kids' show, and a music video for a band which had disappeared without trace. According to his agent he had 'promise'. Sebastian wondered what that might mean. His travels in Sarawak seemed to have left him blissfully unaware that he was the last director in Britain to be considered for *Rough Diamonds*. Neither his agent nor Sebastian was in a hurry to disabuse him.

Accepting the proffered cappuccino, the director took a seat in Sebastian's office and listened attentively to his thumbnail sketch of *Rough Diamonds,* honed by now over many performances and delivered at high speed. There was a silence. Sebastian waited. Trevor William drained his coffee, put the cup on the table and stood up.

'Okay,' he said.

Sebastian looked at him enquiringly.

'You can sort out the details with my agent, can't you?'

'Yes, but – you haven't read the script yet.'

'Don't need to.'

'Well, at least take it with you. Then we'll talk.'

The director put the script into his bag, a serious piece of work that looked as though it probably transformed itself at the tug of a cord into a one-man tent. Then he nodded, and – before Sebastian could say anything else – he was gone.

Dougal said, 'Watch him.' His beady blue eyes gazed over the half-moon spectacles at the closing door. Fascinated, Sebastian watched as Dougal's fingers continued their faery dance across the keyword and budget columns grew and shrank on the screen, seemingly independent of Dougal's conscious mind.

'Why?'

'Just a ... gut feeling.'

Sebastian had already noticed that people in the industry seemed very sensitive to their guts and their feelings.

'I liked him.'

'Well, it's your funeral.'

'It's not as though we've got a huge choice.'

'There's always a choice.'

'Who would you go for? Of the ones who're available and want to do it?'

'Someone who'll shoot the script, on budget, on schedule.'

'Well, yes. But what about someone who'll create this exciting new world, The World of the Series? Cast it with fascinating actors who'll help create characters the audience will really care about? Someone who'll make it an event, must-see television, a signature piece?' Sebastian had been boning up on his latest acquisition, *Producing the TV Masterpiece*.

'I thought you wanted a director.'

'Isn't that what a director does?'

'A director directs. It's like production management, only more so. The rest is just luck and bullshit.'

'Well, I think he's our man.'

Dougal raised one eyebrow. The other was having a day off. 'Have you talked to your executive producer?'

'About this?'

'He may have an opinion. Doesn't Brit TV have approval of the director?'

'Yes, but I understood it was pretty much a formality.'

'They may not see it that way.'

* * *

Daisy had been very disappointed not to join the Trevor William meeting. Sebastian saw her peeking wistfully from the meeting room where she and Phoebe Grolt were up to their knees in step outlines, serial elements, and character arcs. Phoebe's cropped head bobbed violently up and down as she spoke, jangling the jewellery hanging from her crowded and extravagantly pierced ears.

Phoebe was the latest recruit to the writing team and she was talking so hard she failed to notice how Daisy's attention was wandering. After a well-received first play in a small pub theatre Phoebe's career had sunk without trace, resurfacing only when a script editor with a keen memory recruited her to write for the famous so-bad-it's-(almost)-good show, *Tarts and Slags*. Their storylining meetings were famous. Half the writers were soap drudges, the other half bright young things whose gilding had started to rub off, with a few ex-cons and street-walkers thrown in to leaven the mixture. As often as not the meetings ended in a fistfight.

To make up for Daisy's exclusion from director-picking, Sebastian decided to take her along to Brit TV to meet their executive producer, Rick Todge. Also, if he was going to be scrupulously honest – which he wasn't – Sebastian would have admitted that he felt sure she'd handle Rick better than he could. After checking his self-help manuals Sebastian was more confused than ever about this particular role.

Dougal had briefed Sebastian on what to expect. Rick, apparently, was one of those old-time operators from the 'Budget, what budget?' days, when producers swaggered down the corridors of the broadcasters flaunting the size of their overspends. When Rick had been making stuff himself – actually producing it – things had been very different from the way they were now, in the nineties. A guy like Rick would roll into his office around ten, ten-thirty, have a coffee and read the trade mags. Then he'd sort out lunch and get his secretary (they still had secretaries, back then) to book a table. He might flick through a script, or more likely a script report, before the taxi arrived. Back after lunch, about three-ish, there'd be time to make a couple of calls before setting off home early to avoid the rush hour.

According to Dougal the pattern had been similar during production. Send for production car and driver. Drop in on cutting room for coffee and chat with editor. On to location, arriving just in time for lunch. Go to head of queue. Chat to heads of department over second helping of pudding. Visit make-up trailer for free haircut. Earmark rather nice coat seen in wardrobe department, and have it placed in boot of waiting production car. Clap director on back, glad-hand stars, tell everyone how well they're doing, say 'Must get back to the office', and take production car home.

At Brit TV it was all different, of course. Rick's huge salary meant he could afford to pay for his clothes, in fact his employers insisted that he did, and his grey hair was already sleek and groomed. He pointed to a couple of chairs and parked his loafers on his desk.

'So, Sebastian and … Daisy, is it? What are you going to make for us?'

'*Rough Diamonds.*'

'Yeah, that's the one. Steve Bung asked me to keep an eye on it.'

'What exactly does an executive producer do?'

Rick and Daisy both looked at Sebastian. There are some questions that just aren't asked. Fortunately, Rick was in a good mood. The extension to his already substantial home had fallen behind schedule and the builders had that morning incurred a hefty penalty payment. He smiled, showing a lot of teeth, not all of them his own. If the producer wanted to joke he could play along.

'As little as possible, some would say. It's a watching brief. Make sure the producer knows what he's doing, stays on track. Check he's got his ducks in a line.' He turned to Sebastian. 'Have you?'

'Have I what?'

'Got your ducks in a line?'

'Which, er, ducks did you have in mind?

'Helen Quigley I know about. Got yourself a director yet?'

'We're still considering candidates.'

'Well, don't consider for too long.' Rick bent open a paper clip and started cleaning his nails. 'Pick up the ball and run with it. If you want my advice …'

'Yes?' Sebastian said politely.

'You can usually get me at the office on Wednesdays. Only I'm in the middle of something and I've got a problem with the drains to sort out, so it had better be important.'

'Oh. Right.'

'Over to you, then, Sebastian.'

* * *

Phoebe Grolt picked up her phone.

'Hi. Could I speak to Sophie, please? Hi, Soph, how are you?'

In her small office at Brunt Productions, until last week designated the tape store (but as yet there were no tapes to store), Sophie put the call on speakerphone while she rooted around the floor on all fours.

'Hello, Phoeb. Everything okay?'

'Brilliant. Really good. Thanks for the *Saw* screenplay, and those Korean DVDs.'

'No worries.'

''I'll try and work in something, like you said, but I'm not sure quite where yet. It's tricky to get those elements to really gel with English policemen.'

'They were just a suggestion. To inspire you. Shit!'

'What?'

'Hit my head on the desk.'

'Oh. And the note about *Buffy* …'

'Yeah, I just thought we could really do something with that. You know, the young innocent with the power, the old mentor in the background with the experience. Bruno says –'

'Who's Bruno?'

'My boyfriend. He's a director.'

'Oh.'

'Or he's going to be, anyway. He says that's why *Buffy*'s so popular. It's archetypal.'

'Does Bruno have any suggestions for *Rough Diamonds*?'

'He's in commercials.'

'Oh.'

'But it's a way of keeping the Gothic thing going, you see?'

'I thought we had to drop all that.'

'It's what makes the show special. Go Gothic!'

'Right.'

'Call me if you need any more help.'

'Thanks, Sophie. I will.'

Sophie, finally, found what she was looking for among the mounting piles of script drafts that surrounded her desk. She reached across to the original outline document, pushed it aside and picked up the old Nirvana CD. Dropping it into her Walkman – it would be another five years before Sophie could get her hands on a first-generation iPod – she settled down to some serious script editing.

Phoebe stared out of her window across the leafy inclines of Crouch End. It was hopeless. She didn't know what they expected of her, and even if she had known, she probably couldn't provide it. She tugged at the strap of her dungarees and took another bite of the Mars bar. So far she hadn't been offered anything on the new series of *Tarts and Slags*. And they had twenty-six episodes to fill. Phoebe finished the Mars bar without even noticing, a king-size one as it happened. Upstairs at the Bush Theatre seemed long ago and very far away.

Daisy looked through the window in Sophie's door – the only window Sophie had – and watched her sitting cross-legged on the floor, script on lap, lips moving slightly along with Kurt Cobain's. Daisy made a mental note and moved on.

* * *

Whatever Sebastian might be doing, he was painfully conscious of five other things he was neglecting at the same time. He seemed to be in several ruts at once, if that was possible. Everything depended on the scripts, most of which had yet to be written. He had no director. And still he'd heard not a single word from Albie.

It was one thing keeping his brother-in-law's seat warm, quite another to take over his job. Uncomfortably Sebastian wondered how Albie might react to the news that Brunt Productions was now making *Rough Diamonds* for a different broadcaster, based on different scripts, and all being run out of brand new offices in the heart of Soho. What if he didn't like it?

Sebastian was wary of moving forwards and committing himself further, and unable to go back. He was stuck.

It was Dougal who rescued him. Perhaps he'd noticed the wild look in the producer's eyes, or saw him punch the wall that time in reception. Anyway, Dougal led Sebastian out onto the fire escape, filled his pipe with noxious tobacco, and lit up. When the smoke cleared sufficiently to see his face again, Sebastian found Dougal was fixing him with a beady eye. 'Make a decision,' he said. 'It doesn't have to be the right one.' He exhaled a filmy blue cloud and gazed balefully down over the Soho streets, full of tiny scurrying figures. 'D'you suppose theirs are any better?'

Sebastian went back into his office and picked up the phone. He called Trevor William's agent and agreed the terms, with the exception of the five-day weeks and the hotel. He fixed lunch with Helen Quigley and contacted his other star, Jason Prynne. He booked production offices in Acton Studios. He arranged a meeting at Bank Frød. And, with Dougal's help, he added a week to the schedule, rejigged the budget and faxed the topsheet to Brit TV. The writers would just have to rein in their creativity and work to the brief he gave them.

* * *

Sebastian arrived home feeling better than he had for weeks. Even the Cavalier beached on the front lawn, a sight which usually filled him with gloom, couldn't completely dispel his sense of well-being.

'Jemma!'

'Have you seen what they've done now?' Jemma was shaking her red hair like an angry setter.

'Who? What?'

'The bloody council, of course. "Interferes with sight-lines and is in direct contravention of the Town and Country Planning Act 1990."'

'What are you reading?'

'Listen to this. "Complaints of your unauthorised erection distracting drivers on the Bristol Road." Jemma screwed the letter into a tight ball and hurled it at the door. 'It makes me so bloody mad when next door put up a conservatory the size of the Crystal Palace.' Her eyes were sparkling, she was quivering from head to foot.

Like Sebastian, Jemma was a keen gardener. Her latest project was an encampment of willow wigwams, copied from a photo in *Homes and Gardens*, through which she grew sweet peas. One or more of the neighbours must have taken exception to them. She and Sebastian lived in a conservation area, so things sometimes got rough. 'What's so stupid is, these are exactly the sort of plant supports they would have used when these houses were built.' Sebastian decided against correcting her on a point of garden history. 'Which is more than can be said for the patio doors and hot tub at number twelve.' The thought flashed into Sebastian's mind that there was an opening – no more than a crack, perhaps – for a how-to planning permission segment that could be slotted into a garden makeover show. Great planning permission disasters … ten worst boundary disputes … no, it had almost certainly been done already.

'What?'

'I said, there's nothing to eat, so if you want supper you'd better order a takeaway.' That was the downside of Jemma's rages. Now the world would have to be punished, and that included her husband. In fact, he would be top of her list.

'I made a really important decision today. I hired the director.'

'Good for you. Just don't bring him here, will you.' It wasn't quite what Sebastian had been hoping for. Perhaps on balance it was just as well they hadn't so far succeeded in producing any offspring.

'Indian or Chinese?'

'Who cares? So long as they deliver.'

Sebastian laid out the chopsticks and made some green tea for Jemma, knowing she'd be calm again by the time the doorbell rang. In fact she was already bending down to retrieve the crumpled letter. He watched her carefully smooth out the wrinkles before putting it back into the file on the kitchen table.

'We can apply for planning permission.'

'I know.' Jemma sounded weary now, no longer angry. 'It just seems so stupid getting architect's drawings of a wigwam.'

'Well, yes. But in the scale of things …'

'I know. So how was your day?'

'We've got a director.'

'Isn't it up to Albie? After all, he's the one who knows about all that stuff. Where is he, anyway? I thought he was supposed to be back by now.'

'So did I. But he seems to have disappeared off the face of the earth.'

'Oh. Well, so long as he's happy for you to take decisions.'

Sebastian felt an urgent desire to change the subject. 'Choosing the director's a big step forward.'

'And have you chosen the right one?' Jemma had a way of putting her finger on the crux of the thing that could be quite unsettling.

'Well, I hope so. Obviously. It's hard to know.'

'What's your gut feeling?' Now she was doing it too.

'My gut feeling is relief at having made a decision. When my gut comes up with an opinion on Trevor William, you'll be the first to know.'

'Trevor William? Lives in the Black Mountains?'

'You know him?'

'I was reading something about him.'

'Yes? What?'

'I don't know. Something at the hairdresser's.'

'What?'

'I told you, I don't know. He sounds completely mad. Quite a handful, I should think. Still, I'm sure you're on top of it. Is that tea ready?'

Sebastian's gut was coming up with a feeling now, and it wasn't a good one.

8 Schmoozing

At Bank Frød the next morning they sat round the table in silence, apart from the muted roar of the Mayfair traffic that seeped in through the windows. Giles studied his well-manicured fingernails. Keith, the junior account manager, scanned the file in front of him. Sebastian watched and waited.

The door opened at last and a tall, cadaverous man in his fifties walked in. He regarded them sternly – clearly they were all of them half an hour early, which was inexcusable – then shut the door.

'This loan of yours.'

'Yes?'

'Keith tells me you want the first drawdown today.'

'Today's the first day of pre-production.'

'I don't think we can do that. It's very inconvenient.'

Somehow Sebastian had expected Bank Frød to be more exotic. But, beyond the name and a rather poor painting of a geyser in reception, it was indistinguishable from any other merchant bank with interests in the murky world of TV and film financing. Archie Govan, with his three-piece suit and pallid face, would have disappointed anyone hoping for an easygoing Nordic billionaire.

Giles stood up, grasped the hand of the surprised Keith and was halfway through the door before anyone realised he was leaving.

'But not impossible.' Giles paused. 'In fact I'm sure we can manage it. Keith here will just have to pull his finger out.' Everyone turned to look at Keith, who coloured slightly.

In the taxi back to Snipe & Abercrombie, Giles summed up. 'Archie takes the decisions, or if he doesn't then he talks to the people who do, whom we never see. Keith does the donkey-work and takes any blame that's going. You've got your cash flow cheaper than you would have anywhere else, and there's no reason why it shouldn't all work out perfectly well.'

'But?'

'But with these little banks who go in for media lending you just never know. They go in, they pull out. But when you've got to borrow a lot of money for several months at short notice … well …'

'Well?'

'You've got no choice, have you? Drop me off here.'

* * *

In the back of the taxi Sebastian tried to leave financial anxieties behind with Giles and put himself into the right frame of mind for his next meeting. Confident, genial enthusiasm seemed the right target. It was a struggle, but by the time he'd reached Le Chateau d'If he was nearly there.

'Your guests haven't arrived yet. Would you like to order an aperitif while you wait for them?'

'Just water, thank you.' He watched the maître d' beetle away. Sebastian had never met Jason Prynne before, but knew Albie had lunched him at a cheap but funky Moroccan restaurant. He couldn't have got away with it a second time. This time, with the pair of them, Sebastian had been lucky to avoid somewhere ultra-expensive like Ziggurat.

Helen Quigley was the first to arrive, followed so quickly by Jason that Sebastian suspected he'd been hiding across the street, keeping the restaurant under surveillance. They eyed each other warily while the producer made soothing noises, like a zookeeper presiding over two dangerous animals he hoped would collaborate in producing a cub. Helen had dressed up, to the nines or even possibly the tens, in Ghost and Agnès B. Anticipating this rather obvious gambit, Jason had trumped it with ripped jeans and an old surfing T-shirt. Advantage Prynne.

'So how's *Dalston Square* treating you?' Jason sipped his vodka tonic and smiled at Helen. Thirty-love. There were little laughter lines around his very blue, very cold eyes. Contact lenses?

'Oh, you know.' Helen was not going to be intimidated by this actor, even if he had made a couple of movies in Hollywood. She knew he'd started his career as a trainee weatherman, and she wanted him to know she knew. 'But what about you? I heard they cancelled *Harlem Heist.*' This was the American series that was supposed to be making Jason a transatlantic superstar. Audiences, it seemed, had not warmed to him as a Limey cat-burglar.

Deuce.

'Oh, I only did the pilot. I couldn't commit to a series, with all my film work.'

Sebastian blinked. He thought that was exactly what Jason *had* done – on *Rough Diamonds*. Hadn't he? Sebastian made a mental note to check Jason's contract as soon as he got back to the office. He wasn't bothering to keep the score any more.

'Do you two know each other?' Rather belatedly Sebastian remembered that he was the host.

'No.'

'Not really.'

It was a little delicate. Jason would have been playing the lead, had they not flipped gender back in Mel's office all those weeks ago. Now Helen Quigley was the lead, and Jason was the guest lead for the pilot episode. That meant he outranked Helen in the star stakes, but she was queen bee on the show. Sebastian watched nervously to see how they'd handle it. Jason was staring in a God-I'm-so-bored way across the restaurant while Helen jiggled at her little phone-cum-media centre. Then Sebastian realised handling it wasn't their problem. It was his.

'I just want to say how excited I am to be working with you both on the show.'

Jason flicked his blond mane and fixed Sebastian with his famous blue eyes.

'*Rough*, er … *Diamonds*,' Sebastian faltered. Jason snorted.

'When can we meet the director?' Helen looked up from her Motorola.

'And who is it, anyway?'

Sebastian hung on until the waiter had finished serving the *trompettes de mort* and then gave them the good news. 'Trevor William.'

'Who?'

'Never heard of him.'

Their eyes met and then they both turned towards the producer. Sebastian thought of the two contracts sitting on his desk back in the office. Still unsigned.

'What's he done?'

'How old is he?'

'Well, he's young, very up-and-coming. This is his first big production, but he did an award-winning kids' show and a fantastic music video which got nominated for a Golden Plectrum and he's about to be very, very hot.'

There was an almost palpable silence. The waiter took away the starter plates and refilled Jason's empty glass, which he immediately drained. He caught Helen's eye. For the first time they seemed to be bonding. Jason sighed dramatically.

'Okay. Okay okay okay. We'd better meet him. Helen?'

'I agree. But very soon.' The Motorola was halfway out of her bag again, this time suggesting a call to her agent. Jason looked around for a waiter. Sebastian realised they were both about to leave, without even waiting for the *carré d'agneau Grand Guignol*.

'Wait. He's coming here to meet you. Today. Now.'

'He is?'

'Why didn't you say?'

'I thought I did. Would you excuse me for just a moment?'

Leaving them at the table Sebastian raced to the door and pulled out his phone, praying.

'Hello? Who's that? No, this is Sebastian. Listen, Sophie, I need to talk to Daisy now, right now. Okay.' He waited. The office PABX played a dirge-like Nirvana track. Sophie's idea, almost certainly.

'Hello?'

'Daisy, has Trevor William come in to pick up that script?'

'Not yet.'

'When he does, stick him in a taxi and send him to Chateau d'If. No, better, you bring him. As soon as you can. Otherwise we've lost our stars.' Sebastian ended the call and looked through the window into the restaurant. Helen and Jason were leaning together conspiratorially. Or perhaps he was just feeling paranoid. The journey from the office would take Trevor William ten minutes in a cab. But there was no telling when he'd arrive at Brunt Productions – he was on foot, naturally. He might simply refuse to be press-ganged into this unscheduled meeting. Sebastian took a deep breath, put what he hoped was a relaxed smile on his face and stepped back inside to face the music.

* * *

The hour spent waiting for Trevor William in Le Chateau d'If proved to be the longest in Sebastian's life, so far. At least the food gave them something to talk about. The *carré d'agneau Grand Guignol* was black, more or less, and served on a black plate with black rice and aubergine. Helen stuck to unsweetened cranberry juice, while Jason called over the waiter and ordered a second bottle of a rather expensive Corton, although he was the only one drinking. Sebastian was tempted but an instinct for self-preservation kept him on the Badoit. He tried to make conversation but all he got out of Jason was the odd monosyllable.

The two actors, though, were soon chatting away to each other like the best of mates. Perhaps it was an exercise they'd done at drama school: 'Okay, now imagine you two are great actors, major stars, and some wannabe producer who's desperate to have you in his show takes you out to lunch and gets everything wrong. Away you go.' So on they talked, relaxed and animated by turn, in their element, leaving Sebastian to stew.

The tables were thinning, it was twenty-five to three. Sebastian had been through despair, twice considered suicide in the men's lavatory, and was entering the final, manic phase when he looked up and saw Daisy ushering Trevor William through the door. At that moment he could have kissed her trainers. It was impossible to tell from the director's face what was going on his mind.

'Miss Quigley, Mr Prynne, I can't tell you how sorry I am about this. It's all my fault. I sent poor Trevor to the wrong restaurant and I've ruined your lunch. I can't apologise enough.'

If necessary Sebastian would have eaten her shoes. Jason acknowledged the power of a strong performance coupled with charm, a pretty face and a tightly fitting T-shirt. He smiled kindly at Daisy. 'Jason Prynne,' he intoned deeply. 'Delighted to meet you, Miss – ?'

'Just call me Daisy. And now I must hurry back to the office, so if you'll all excuse me …' She smiled again, a special one for Sebastian this time, a smile of triumph, and slipped out of the restaurant. There was a tiny pause. Jason, Helen, Trevor and Sebastian all stood beside the table, where nothing remained but used coffee cups. Sebastian made the introductions. Trevor William shook both actors by the hand, with great solemnity, looking into their eyes with the intensity of Rasputin.

'I am … so … looking forward … to working with you both. I think, together, we're going to achieve something quite … extraordinary.' They gazed at him, deer in a lorry's headlights.

* * *

An hour later, under the bored eyes of their waiter, the maître d' regretfully asked if they could relocate to another establishment and suggested a coffee bar around the corner. But there was no need. The three creative artists all seemed to feel that they'd finished their business. The meeting had been a great success. Director and actors were deeply engaged with one another in a passionate ménage à trois. With a last joke, an arm around the shoulder and a reminder of imminent costume fittings, they parted on the pavement. *Rough Diamonds* was back on the road.

9   Black Denim

Vanessa McTavish's premises were part of a new development carved out of a redundant Baptist church, a scooter-ride from Soho. The high ceilings offered good acoustics, and the other businesses had got used to sudden shouts of 'On your knees, muthafucka!' coming through the walls. Vanessa had a useful sideline casting Brits in small, villainous parts for American movies.

Trevor and Sebastian sat together in the echoing vestibule and chatted about a film they'd both seen recently.

'What did you think?' Trevor fixed Sebastian with his dark, beady eyes through the steam of his cappuccino.

'Oh, you know, pretty good. A bit slow, maybe.'

'Slow?'

'And that business with the reflections. And the tattoos. It seemed rather self-indulgent.'

Trevor blew on his coffee but offered no response. Sebastian went on. 'That actor, the one who was blown up in *Geezers*, funny eyes …'

'Howie Burt.'

'Yeah. Didn't you think he was a bit –'

'Brilliant.'

'Sure, he was brilliant, but didn't you think he was a bit –'

'Trevor! Stephen!'

'Actually it's Sebastian.'

'Come in, welcome, both of you. Come and sit down.' Vanessa was ageless, dressed in black from head to foot. She led them into her small, chic office, which was entirely white. Sebastian began to feel uncomfortably colourful in his dark blue suit. Although Trevor was dressed, as ever, for mountain-walking, Sebastian now noticed that the high-performance fibres he wore were black, too.

They sat down on the white chairs, then Vanessa explained that Sebastian would be in the actors' eyeline. In other words, when they wanted to look at the director they were going to cop him instead. He moved to another chair, in the corner, and away from the action.

'The Producer's Chair,' Vanessa explained, unnecessarily. Sebastian had to stretch uncomfortably to reach the Jaffa cakes.

'Here's the List. I won't bring streams of people in to see you. There's no point, and it's a waste of everyone's time. You'll see I've broken down the script, with the main parts on the left and the rest on the right. They're pretty interchangeable, aren't they?'

'Well, I wouldn't say –'

'So if we see someone who you like but who's not right for, say, the Vicar, then we could consider him for the Detective Inspector or maybe Second Victim.'

Trevor said nothing. He was reading his copy of Vanessa's List and nodding to himself. Sebastian looked down at his own. There wasn't a single name he recognised. He nodded too, hoping he looked sufficiently serious and professional for Vanessa. But she was giving brisk instructions to her 'Girl', a quiet mousy woman well into her thirties, whose job it was to get the actors in and out on time and keep them all primed with coffee, scripts, and of course biscuits.

First up was a sad-faced middle-aged man whose face was immediately familiar. He'd been a policeman in more series than Sebastian could remember – about fourteen, according to the CV efficiently clipped to the back of the List. Sebastian was so used to his glowering, hard-boiled coppers that his own gently lisping voice came as something of a shock. They talked briefly about his recent TV work, his one-man show up in Edinburgh, the tube strike. He offered to read, Trevor said it wouldn't be necessary. Vanessa wondered if there was anything Stephen wanted to ask. Sebastian said he'd liked his performance as the police sergeant with a secret in *Romford Rescue* and the actor replied that it wasn't him. Then Vanessa thanked him, he shook Trevor's hand and left.

'He seemed good,' Sebastian ventured.

'Wanker,' said Trevor.

Vanessa made a note. 'Onwards.'

The rest of the morning was a blur of black denim and unshaven chins. After the first three Sebastian couldn't tell them apart any more and started to make surreptitious notes on his copy of the List: *bald, big ears and stammer, mad eyes*. He was beginning to feel anxious that he wasn't going to be able to hold his own in the end-of-session summing up. As it turned out, this wasn't a problem.

'Well, I haven't seen such a bunch of talentless no-hopers since I did the BBC Directors' Course,' said Trevor, just before the door closed on the last one. 'Where did you find them?'

Sebastian looked at Vanessa. She laughed. 'That, my dear, was … exploratory. Now that I know a little more about your project, I can plan accordingly.' She was busy at her computer, summoning up a new List. 'And they're not so bad, some of them. They're always working.'

'Not on my shows,' said Trevor. His shows? 'I want actors. Real … actors.'

They went for lunch at an Italian restaurant round the corner on Battersea Park Road. The waiters fawned on Vanessa and installed the trio at her regular table. 'We'll start again at two-thirty,' Vanessa said. 'By then, Zadie' – the Girl – 'will have organised a new List.'

Trevor and Vanessa were soon chuckling away together, thick as thieves. All their talk was about who was acting in what, and Sebastian noticed the American blockbuster part of Vanessa's business was getting a lot more coverage than Soltan Dravic's interesting new *Cymbeline* at the Warehouse, or *Inspector Pettigrew*. Or *Rough Diamonds* for that matter.

'So, anyway, Dickie said that he'd rather die than get involved in such a pile of dreck, but when he heard how much they were offering –'

'And shooting in Barbados.'

'Well, of course he accepted. But when he arrived in Barbados they didn't know who he was. They'd wanted Alan, not Dickie at all. His brother.'

'What did he do?'

'He had a very nice holiday in Barbados. They had to pay him. He didn't do a day's work. So I said to him, 'Now you can afford to do that Beckett season at the Playhouse.' And do you know what he said to me?'

'No.'

'"I don't mind being buried up to my neck in shit, and I don't mind having so few lines. I don't even mind doing it for ninety quid a week. But what I do object to is being buried up to my neck in shit in Chester-le-Street." So that was that.'

Trevor laughed his dry laugh and Sebastian grinned too. He hadn't a clue who Dickie was, or Alan for that matter. And he wasn't entirely clear why this actor, whoever he was, got paid although he didn't do any acting. But he could hardly let Vanessa and Trevor know that.

Still, he enjoyed the pasta. When the waiter brought him the bill Sebastian could see why. A hundred and forty quid seemed steepish for what they'd had but Trevor and Vanessa were already out on the street and Sebastian didn't want to get left behind, so he paid up quickly and hurried after them. Trevor was telling Vanessa how the producer on his last job had leant against the set and brought the whole lot down on top of the cast in the middle of a take. There was something about their laughter Sebastian didn't altogether like.

The afternoon proved very different from the morning. They continued to chew their way through plates of chocolate hobnobs, ginger nuts, and Jaffa cakes but the ever-changing occupants of the Actor's Chair (complete with unimpeded sightline to director and casting director) were a different breed. And Trevor had started to read with them. A succession of miniature performances came to life in front of Sebastian's eyes. It was very strange, after all the script discussions with writers, editors, and executives, to hear the same words in the mouth of an actor.

Sebastian felt intoxicated. Maybe that was the lunchtime Pinot Grigio. Either way, the afternoon in Vanessa's office left him light-headed. As the last actor rubbed his stubbly chin, got to his feet and straightened his black jeans, Sebastian felt excitedly that *Rough Diamonds* had taken on a life of its own.

'Ben.'

'Could be the lawyer. Too obvious for the killer.'

'Jude.'

'No. Didn't like him.'

'Hugo.'

'*I* quite liked him. Jude, I mean.' Vanessa looked up at Sebastian from the new List. Trevor stared at his walking boots.

'Did you, Stephen?'

'Sebastian. I thought he had something.'

'For which part?'

'Um … the pathologist?'

'We agreed on Brian Utterley for the pathologist. I thought.'

'Right. Well, maybe one of those other interchangeable parts?'

'We'll put Jude to one side. Hugo?'

'He's too young for second victim. What about man in pub?'

'The one who gets into the fight?' This was script stuff, Sebastian knew about this. He felt he should say something.

'That's second man in pub.'

'There isn't a second man in pub.'

'There is now. I've reworked that scene.'

'Oh.' Sebastian was looking forward to seeing Trevor's redraft of the script.

As they stood up and stretched their legs at the end of the day Sebastian seized the director and said there were things they needed to discuss. He suggested a quick drink. Trevor evaded his arm, saying he was talked out, and Vanessa chimed in that she had to get to Hendon for a performance by an experimental theatre group from Eritrea. Trevor raised his hand in salute without looking back as he set off at a brisk jog-trot, and Sebastian realised that he didn't know where the director was staying in London. Possibly he yomped back to the Black Mountains every night. The man had no mobile phone (at least, if he did, its number was a closely-guarded secret) and no address.

Frustrated, Sebastian wanted to go straight home but instead called in at the office. It was dark except for pools of light around Dougal's desk and Daisy's.

'How's it going?'

'Fine, dear boy. I'm just sorting out a contract for Billy.'

'Billy?'

'Our location manager.'

Sebastian dimly recalled an elderly gent with the same superannuated look – furrowed skin, hair a little too carefully arranged, smile suggesting major restorative dentistry – as Dougal himself. Probably they'd worked together on the Bonds. Number eight, maybe, or nine? Sebastian liked the speed with which he'd heeded the call. But didn't it suggest he was doing nothing better than sitting at home watching repeats of cookery programmes?

'Just come off a big one at Pinewood,' Dougal said. 'Lives round the corner.'

'Oh.'

'I'm taking some extra money out of Travel and Transport and a week off the 2nd AD's prep.'

'Is that a good idea?'

Dougal looked up at him over his glasses, which reflected the lines of his Movie Magic Budgeting from the computer screen. 'Put it this way, dear boy. It's a better idea than not hiring a location manager. If we don't get on with it we're going to come horribly unstuck further down the line.'

'How much are we paying Billy?'

'Thirteen hundred a week.'

'Isn't that rather a lot?'

'It's at the higher end of the scale.'

Sebastian picked up the ruler from Dougal's desk and put it down again. It wasn't easy having this kind of conversation with him. Like asking his dad why he'd drunk the housekeeping money. 'Is Billy so good? I … didn't really take to him that much.'

Dougal took his glasses off altogether. 'Billy,' he began, 'is a top location manager. He was running locations on big movies – I mean, big movies – when you were still in nappies. He was on *Star Wars*!'

'Wasn't that set in a different galaxy?'

'All right, most of it was shot on a stage. Anyway, the point is, there's nothing Billy doesn't know about the job. He's very experienced. He works on features. We're lucky to have him.'

There was a pause. The end of the honeymoon was in sight.

'So … why does he want this job?'

Dougal closed down his computer and stuffed papers into his old leather briefcase. 'Let's talk about this tomorrow, Sebastian,' he said. 'It's been a long day and I'm tired. I don't want to say anything we'll both regret tomorrow.' He picked up the coat on the back of his chair and made for reception.

'Good night, Dougal.'

'Night.' But all Sebastian saw was his back as he disappeared through reception.

He turned round to see Daisy watching him from her lit office. Now she walked over to him.

'I don't think I handled that very well.'

'Oh, Dougal's just tired. I think he's more worried than he likes people to think.'

'Why doesn't that make me feel any better?'

'Isn't that his job, worrying about money?'

'Well, yes, in a way.'

'There you are, then.' This logic seemed to satisfy Daisy.

'How are the scripts coming?'

'Well, there may be a little problem with Phoebe.'

'Phoebe?'

'You know, Phoebe Grolt. Writing episodes two and three.'

'What problem?'

'Well, it's really weird. I briefed her, she went away happy, seemed fine. I know she had a couple of questions, and Sophie helped her out. Now she's delivered this script full of werewolves, vampires, wise professors in libraries, you name it. And the whole thing's tingling with teen sex. I mean, nothing happens, it's fine for pre-watershed, but it's hardly The World of the Series we talked through with Pat Quine. Don't get me wrong, it's great, but …'

'But not what Steve Bung commissioned?'

'Probably not. Why don't you take it home tonight and have a read?'

Sebastian skimmed Phoebe's script on the train back to East Sheen. Where had all this stuff come from? Not that it wasn't good. Even Sebastian could see Phoebe had done a pretty impressive job of reworking *Buffy the Vampire Slayer* for a new setting in Carshalton. If it didn't look much like *Rough Diamonds*, it had certainly taken on board Sophie's script editing notes. And there were things they could use. A teenage girl with special powers … well, that could make an interesting challenge for Helen Quigley/Dan Beatty.

'The strangest thing,' he was saying as he walked in the front door. 'Now we've got a copshow with legions of the undead. Jemma?' There was no answer, no sign of her. The car had been outside, and it wasn't as if there were many places to hide in their house. Sebastian looked in the garden and couldn't see her there either, at least not at first. Then he heard a sort of muffled groan coming from beneath one of the willow wigwams, by now festooned with sweet peas.

'Help me, can't you?'

'Where are you?'

'Here, you idiot!'

'What are you doing in there?'

'I'm stuck of course, what do you think?' Bending down to deadhead the sweet peas with her secateurs, Jemma had caught an earring on one of the metal ties she used to attach the plants to the support. It looked quite painful. Carefully Sebastian rotated the ring and prised it open.

'Aagh! Christ! Can't you be more careful?'

'Sorry. Do you know anything about vampires?'

'Don't be ridiculous. I'm going in to change. Your friends are going to be here any minute.'

'Oh, why?'

'Because you insisted on inviting them to dinner, that's why. What are you cooking?'

This didn't seem like the best moment for a confession, so Sebastian simply said, 'Pasta'.

10   Unavailable and/or Unwilling

When Sebastian stepped into Brunt's reception the next morning he was surprised to find five assorted men and women squeezed onto the leather sofa. Lucy rolled her eyes and then looked pointedly at the office he shared with Dougal. Sebastian gave an all-purpose smile and moved briskly to where Dougal was already hard at work on his laptop.

'Morning, Dougal.'

All he got in reply was a printed list of names and a bundle of CVs. He riffled through them. Location managers.

'Are these the people outside?'

'Every location manager who's available for our dates and willing, in principle at least.'

'When did you check availabilities?'

'Last night. I think you'll find it's comprehensive.' At the bottom of the CVs was another list of names, a much longer one. *Unavailable and/or Unwilling*, it said at the top.

'Must be lots of work around.'

'And most of it better paid. Probably more congenial, too.'

'Listen, Dougal, I'm sorry if I upset you when I said what I said about Billy, it's just that –'

'Don't mention it, it's your right and privilege as producer. Now I suggest we get on with interviewing the candidates waiting outside, and then make an informed decision.'

It was pretty bloody. Even Sebastian, with his limited experience, could see that these guys and gals were not at the top of the tree. As the final candidate zipped up her cagoule and departed, Dougal began violently stuffing his pipe.

'See anyone you fancy?'

'Not really.'

'Quite sure?'

'Sure.'

'What do you want to do next?'

'Hire Billy, I suppose.'

His capitulation was so complete that Dougal relented. 'I know he's not perfect. But he's the pick of the bunch. We're not putting together the dream team here. We're just doing the best we can. Producing is the art of compromise.' Sebastian blinked. 'Do you want me to call him?'

'Yes. Please.'

A light rain was falling as they stood on the fire escape, enveloped in another cloud of aromatic tobacco smoke. Dougal puffed contentedly. It struck Sebastian that the older man actually enjoyed all this.

* * *

'Hello, Stephen, grab a seat.'

'Sebastian.'

'We started without you, that's all right, isn't it? Next is number four, Stuart Craddock.'

'The one outside with no hair and a pierced eyebrow?'

There wasn'y any response, so Sebastian sat down in the corner on the Producer's Chair. Trevor William was engrossed in Stuart Craddock's CV and didn't look up. Vanessa nodded briefly and the Girl brought him a cup of weak coffee that he didn't want. Stuart Craddock shuffled in and shot him a surly look. Perhaps casting wasn't going to be so much fun this time.

'I saw you in *The Changeling*,' said Trevor. 'You were shit.'

Sebastian cringed. Stuart's face broke into a crooked grin.

'It was a shit production.'

'Do you two know each other?' Vanessa looked confused.

'Old mates, aren't we? Ever since Trevor here directed the worst ever production of *The Good Woman of Setzuan* at college. Mind if I smoke?' Without waiting for an answer Stuart lit up a Silk Cut and inhaled deeply. 'I was the Good Woman.'

Sebastian observed Vanessa making a note on her computer. The shadow of a smile crept over Trevor's face – the first he'd ever seen. 'I've been studying your CV. Tell us about … *No Time To Cook*.'

'It's an ad. Frozen turkey-burgers.'

'Good for you?'

'They're okay if you put on plenty of ketchup.'

'What about *Dipshit*?' This was Vanessa, a bid to steer the interview back onto course.

'Yeah, that was all right. Short film, they're still trying to get the money together to finish it. I play a junkie who tops himself with a machete. So, what are you seeing me for today?'

'Didn't you get a script?'

'Yeah.'

'Did you read it?'

'Left it on the train.' Out of the corner of his eye Sebastian could see Vanessa making another note on her computer.

Trevor said, '*Rough Diamonds*. It's a series about a police officer who finds conventional methods don't work and follows a different line which takes her deep into society's dark psychic underbelly.' This was interesting, thought Sebastian. He was looking forward more and more to reading his director's redraft of episode one. 'Babbington is the evil genius behind a series of murders which our heroine has to solve.' Sebastian turned to Trevor.

'But –'

'I'd like you to read a scene now. Sebastian, would you read Dan Beatty?'

'Me?'

They got through it somehow, Stuart snarling and hissing, Sebastian stammering and stumbling under Trevor William's cool gaze. It was very strange. Especially since Babbington was one of the two parts they'd already cast.

Babbington was Jason Prynne.

Eventually Stuart left, after high-fiving Trevor and leering at Vanessa. She and Sebastian both looked at the director. 'I thought,' said Vanessa, 'that you'd already cast that part.'

'Nothing is set in stone,' replied Trevor, looking at Sebastian.

'That was an interesting scene.'

'Just work in progress. It helps me to see it played. Stuart did it well.'

'But Jason Prynne's playing the part.'

'Won't that rather depend on the script? I assume he has script approval.'

'Well, technically.'

'Well, technically, he might not want to play the part of a twenty-two-year-old psychotic paedophile murderer.' Clearly Trevor had been putting a lot of work into that character.

'But, Trevor –'

'We must move on.' Vanessa waved to the Girl to usher in the next actress.

And so it continued. A succession of hints and suggestions from Trevor accumulated slowly but surely into an alarming fact: he was rewriting the script. Totally. Old characters were gone, new ones materialising before their eyes. And Trevor was changing not just the script, but the format too. In his mind, it seemed, Jason was out. Could Helen Quigley be far behind?

* * *

Vanessa stood up as the last actor closed the door. 'Shall we go through them?' But Trevor was already shouldering his pack.

'I've got to be somewhere. Let's do it in the morning.'

'Trevor –'

'See you tomorrow.'

And, like that, he was gone. Vanessa and Sebastian looked at each other. She shrugged, closed down her computer, and reached into a drawer.

'Directors.'

'Is he always like this?'

'No idea, darling, I've never worked with him before.'

'But, I thought … that was why …'

'No, dear. It's a new experience for all of us.'

Out of the drawer she took a gin bottle, by now almost empty.

'Drink, Stephen?'

* * *

The first weeks of pre-production fell into a pattern. Mornings would be spent with Vanessa McTavish, meeting actors and hearing about their triumphs and disappointments, then reading scenes with them. Sebastian's Dan Beatty was becoming so polished, so solid, it was becoming difficult to imagine Helen Quigley in the role. He'd had several important insights into the character that he felt he ought to share with her at some point. Afternoons alternated between scripts and the production team. Every day Sebastian chased Daisy about the scripts, and she assured him they were almost ready. The production office at Acton Studios began to fill up with people, and the walls with memos and Post-it notes.

Sebastian chose a very different director for the second block of filming. Jassy Cox was friendly, open, and straightforward. They met and got on together right away. She had an unusual background – assistant costume designer, picture editor, directing dance documentaries – but seemed efficient and enthusiastic. She wanted the job. Her agent accepted the offer. The whole thing was decided in a day.

Unfortunately, Trevor William wouldn't talk to her. It wasn't a surprise, he didn't talk to anyone much, but Sebastian still felt it was unkind of him to snub Jassy and told him so when they had a rare moment to themselves in Vanessa's office.

'Why won't you meet her?'

He turned slowly and fixed Sebastian with his glowering eyes. 'What would be the point?'

'Well, it would be friendly, for one thing.' No reaction. 'And you might be able to share some ideas ...'

'I don't think so.'

'Why not?'

'I don't need ideas from Jassy Cox. And I don't intend to discuss mine with anyone.'

Sebastian knew from his study of *Directing – a Primer for Producers* that this wasn't the usual approach.

'But isn't collaboration what this whole process is about?'

'No.'

Jassy meanwhile concentrated her efforts on getting hold of scripts for episodes four, five, and six. She didn't start, officially, for another three weeks, but hung around the production office anyway, chatting. One lunchtime Sebastian was holding a dripping sausage-pesto melt over the latest bank statement, which showed money draining out of Brunt Productions with the steady flow of a bath emptying, when he heard Jassy through the plasterboard wall, pleading with Daisy.

'When can I see the script?'

'Once the writers deliver and Sophie's had a chance to go through it with them.'

'Won't that be weeks away?'

'Quite possibly, I'm afraid, because they're writing a double episode, and they want to deliver both halves together.'

This was news to Sebastian. 'Daisy? Would you come in here a moment, please?' She appeared in the doorway, eyeing his lunch with distaste. 'Who told George and Jim they could write a double episode?' George and Jim were an unlikely writing partnership, the latest recruits to the project's ever-expanding creative team.

'I did.'

'Perhaps I'd better talk to them. Would you give me their numbers?'

'George isn't on the phone.'

'Don't be ridiculous.'

'He isn't!'

'Well, Jim's then.'

'I really think it's better if I'm the one who speaks to Jim. I know they're both working flat out on this. We don't want them getting confused by conflicting messages. We agreed that I'd be the conduit.'

'Daisy, I want to talk to the writer! Give me his number.'

Daisy stared at him a moment, then turned on her kitten heels and disappeared. She was back a few moments later with a Post-it note, which she stuck on the desk. An anxious face appeared in the doorway. 'Everything all right?'

'Fine, fine, Jassy. Just chasing up your script.' Sebastian dialled the number – it was a mobile – and waited. The phone at the other end rang and rang. Finally Jim's voice answered.

'Hello?'

'Hello, this is Sebastian Boyle at Brunt Productions.'

'Who?'

'What's that noise?' There was a strange thrumming in the background, quite loud, which was making Jim and Sebastian shout to make their voices heard above it.

'What noise?'

'Where are you?'

'Hang on, I'm going to have to put the phone down for a second.' Jim's voice went off the line but the thrumming continued. Sebastian thought he could hear a burst of static and then some kind of walkie-talkie or radio. Then Jim's voice came back over it.

'Oscar Tango, over and out.' There was a rustle and a thump, then Jim said, 'Are you still there?'

'Jim, where *are* you, exactly?'

'About ten miles from Olney.'

'Olney?'

'In Shropshire. I'm going to have to hang up, I'm starting my approach.'

'What do you mean?'

'I'll call you back.' The line went dead.

'Daisy!' She reappeared, tight-lipped. 'Is Jim the writer by any chance piloting a small plane around the Midlands?'

'I don't know.'

'You told me George and Jim were slaving over a hot keyboard. In fact, George is God knows where and Jim is taxiing down a runway in Shropshire.'

'He's a keen pilot.'

Sebastian opened his mouth to say something, something he would surely have regretted later, as Dougal bounded into the room. 'Excuse me, but I must talk to you urgently, Sebastian.'

'I'll be with you in a minute, Dougal,' he said, trying to shrug off the arm that encircled his shoulder in a friendly hug.

'A minute may be too late,' Dougal hissed, and his bony fingers dug into Sebastian's arm as he steered the producer past Daisy and down the corridor into the washroom.

'What in God's name can be so urgent, Dougal?'

'So, one of the writers flies planes when he should be hard at work. So what? That's why he's a writer. That's what they're like. All the more reason to let Daisy handle him.'

'Right. I suppose you're right.' Sebastian glanced in the line of mirrors over the basins. Every day he seemed to look a little bit more stressed. No tics yet, as far as he could see, but … he splashed water over his face.

'And as it happens there *is* something that requires your urgent attention.'

'Oh?' Sebastian was drying his face on the slimy roller towel.

'The cash has ceased to flow.'

'What?'

'Bank Frød has turned off the tap.'

'What are we going to do?'

'Get them to turn it on again.'

'And if we can't?'

'How big's your mortgage?'

'Oh, God.' A vision of Jemma, angry and implacable, rose before him. 'I'd better talk to Giles.'

Giles Savernake's advice, dispensed in short, pithy, and cost-effective sentences, was that Sebastian should meet Bank Frød and do whatever they asked.

'Legally they haven't got a leg to stand on. But I have to tell you that, by the time you've won a moral victory, you'll be bankrupt. How long can you hold out?'

'In what way?'

'How long can you pay what you have to pay out of your own pocket?'

'We're borrowing from the bank as it is.'

'Well, at least it's a different bank.'

'Two, in fact. Brunt Productions has one overdraft, and I've got another of my own.'

'Excellent. Strength in diversity. Chin up. Call me when you've got an offer.'

A succession of phone calls, faxes, and emails to Archie Govan prompted no response at all. Sebastian rang the other banks in the same business, but the message was always the same – they could handle it, at a price, but they'd need several weeks/months/years to go through due diligence and process their endless documentation. Sebastian would be lucky to get his hands on anything before he was, oh, several weeks into filming. By then expenditure would be running at around … he reached out for the calculator on his desk. Dear God. Sebastian slumped back in his chair and gazed bleakly at the breaker's yard beyond the production office window.

'Sebastian? Are you all right?' It was Daisy.

'Fine.'

'Only … there's something you ought to know.'

'Something else?'

'I'm not sure, but I think Jason Prynne's pulling out.'

11 Staying Afloat

Jeremy Cavendish pinned back his eyelid with one hand and was gently probing with the other for a missing contact lens when the door of the executive washroom at Monopolimedia swooshed open and Bernie Gassman strode in.

'Ah, Bernie.'

Bernie unzipped and began noisily to drill the urinal. Jeremy winced imperceptibly, but continued his search for the missing lens in the mirror.

'I heard an interesting rumour this afternoon, at Caffè Nero.'

'Hmm?'

'It seems that Brunt Productions are experiencing some liquidity problems.'

'Source?' Bernie shook vigorously and moved to the washbasin beside Jeremy.

'Lawyer I play tennis with. Seems Sebastian Boyle went the Bank Frød route. Rather inadvisably, I must say.'

Bernie was now at the basin, washing energetically. And not just his hands. Jeremy affected not to notice.

'So now might be the moment?'

'Got you, you little bastard.' Jeremy slid the offending lens back into place and dabbed at his watery eye. 'Well, not just yet, perhaps. But soon.'

'Let him struggle. Okay.' Bernie zipped up. 'What if he sorts it out?'

'My friend tells me that's unlikely. We just have to wait.'

'Let me know when.' The door swooshed again as Bernie exited.

'I do wish he wouldn't do that,' murmured Jeremy to himself, as he selected a different basin. But of course then he wouldn't be so good.

* * *

Lavinia Hurdle was working the phone. A few quick calls to selected informants produced intelligence that was contra-dictory, vague, but slightly alarming. Her client Helen Quigley was committed, in principle at least, to this *Rough Diamonds* thing, but there were several let-out clauses, should she need to avail herself of them. Helen had script approval, for one thing, and they had yet to see a final draft.

Then there was the director. Helen didn't actually have director approval, but everyone wanted her to be happy. And Lavinia wasn't sure she would be happy with Trevor William. His CV wasn't impressive, and yet there was something about him, the agent reflected. The kind of thing that made you sign someone up. Not talent, though he probably had that too. No, it was more a burning desire, a determination to get what he wanted. That could go either way for an actress. He could make Helen look very good, or he could expose her horribly.

It was tricky. What's more, Lavinia had heard that Brunt had contracted Jassy Cox as the second director. Jassy was nobody, so far as Lavinia could make out. Brunt were making some unexpected choices. She decided it was time for another lunch with Steve Bung at Brit TV.

In the meantime Lavinia called her client to say it was all going terribly well and she'd been promised a script in the next couple of days. The word on it was very, very good.

* * *

Back at the office Daisy was briefing Sebastian. Jason's agent had called with a list of urgent grievances. Jason was still smarting from the humiliating wait for the director at Chateau d'If. He had yet to see a script. And if his part was in any way smaller than originally discussed, he would reluctantly have to withdraw.

'Trevor wants to recast anyway. It really depends on Brit TV. Are they buying Jason and Helen Quigley, or will Helen Quigley be enough on her own?'

'Better ask them, then.'

'I'll try Steve Bung. I've got his direct line.'

So far Sebastian had spent exactly four and a half minutes with the executive who'd committed over three million pounds to his project. Now would be a good moment to cement their relationship.

'People say he works late, and he's very approachable.'

* * *

The phone in Steve Bung's office rang and rang. Sebastian held on for the voicemail, thinking he'd leave an upbeat message to say he'd be calling tomorrow. But before it came on there was an angry voice barking into his ear.

'Do you know what fucking time it is?'

'Hello, is that Steve Bung?'

'Who do you think it is, you're calling my office, aren't you? Who is this?'

'Sebastian Boyle.'

'Who?'

'Sebastian Boyle. From Brunt Productions.'

'Never heard of him.'

'We're making a drama series for you. Called *Rough Diamonds*.' Silence. 'With Helen Quigley.'

'Oh, that. Copshow. What's so urgent it can't wait until tomorrow?'

'Well, it's just … I had a question about casting, and I wanted to run it past you.'

'Jesus on a fucking skateboard. All right. Run it past me.'

'Jason Prynne.'

'Like it. Like it a lot. Get him.'

'No, we've already got him. The thing is … we might not be keeping him.'

'Eh? Why the fuck not?'

'Well, I think he's not keen on playing second fiddle to Helen Quigley.'

'Course he isn't. Make him feel he's the star. He'll be fine.'

'We were wondering about … Stuart Craddock?'

'Who?'

'Very interesting young actor, up and coming.'

'What's he done?'

'Well, er …' He was scrabbling frantically through piles of papers, trying to find Stuart Craddock's CV.

'Hello? You still there?' At last Sebastian pulled it out from beneath a half-drunk cappuccino, sending a scummy tide across his desk. 'Yes, here we are. Cutting-edge theatre in Glasgow –'

'This is television.'

'Yes, of course … *Mister Treacle* … I think that may have been a kids' show …'

There was a contemptuous snort at the other end of the line.

'And, er … something called *Dipshit* –'

'Listen. Sebastian. He sounds a bit low-profile for us.'

'He's on the way up –'

'That was a polite way of saying no. Now I'll say it the other way. Fucking no. All right? Jesus.' The line went dead.

Daisy was packing up at her desk and didn't ask how the conversation had gone. Sebastian wondered whether lip-reading through the window was another of the skills in her burgeoning portfolio.

'Good night, then, Sebastian.'

'See you tomorrow.'

'Oh. Something I meant to mention earlier. My salary hasn't been paid this month.'

'Really?'

'Usually it comes through on the twentieth.'

'Better talk to Munraj in accounts.'

'I did. He said I needed to talk to you.'

'Oh. Well. It must be a technical glitch or something. I'll check tomorrow.'

'Okay.' Daisy headed for the door, but not before giving him an appraising look.

'Sebastian?'

'Yes?'

'Nothing. Good night.' At last she was gone. Now, finally, Sebastian could have his nervous breakdown.

* * *

He awoke the next morning bright and early. At around five-thirty, in fact. Jemma was deeply asleep, splayed out like a rag doll, but it was already light outside and the birds were getting noisily territorial, trying to shout down the clank of bins being emptied behind the flats opposite.

Downstairs Sebastian compiled a handy inventory of things to worry about, then checked his diary and groaned. This was the first day of his health and safety course. Sebastian rooted through the detritus on the coffee table and came up with the course details. Two days at … Biggleswade. Jemma was still asleep when he left the house.

It was halfway through assessing the risks associated with filming in a derelict warehouse made of asbestos and formerly used for biological weapons research that Sebastian's mobile rang. He'd disobeyed the order to surrender his phone and left the room with a muttered apology to the instructor.

'Trevor? Thanks for calling. This is a bit tricky. You know we were talking about maybe recasting Babbington?'

'Who?'

'The Jason Prynne part.'

'Oh. Yes.'

'You said you wanted Stuart Craddock?'

'Stuart?'

'Well, I've spoken to Steve Bung and he won't approve him.'

'Does he have approval of the cast?'

'Of course he does. He has approval of everything. Including you.'

'Well, it's not a problem.'

'You're happy with Jason?'

'I've cut the part.'

'What?' But Trevor had gone. Sebastian checked his messages. There weren't any. With a heavy heart he re-entered the strange parallel universe of health and safety. The instructor, a wild-haired gonk from a seventies disaster movie, was in full flow.

'What I require you to do now is to fill in the risk assessment form in your packs. Identify the risks and for each one rate whether the likelihood of it occurring is low, medium or high. Then judge the severity – low, medium, or high. Then put down the steps you would take to offset the risks, and complete the report.'

The risks of falling through the asbestos roof and into the water potentially contaminated with Weil's disease while collecting anthrax spores along the way were small, but the severity if you did succeed in pulling it off was, undeniably, high. By contrast the risk of Jason Prynne flouncing off, Trevor William disappearing, Daisy going off-message, the scripts being late and not very good, and the lack of cash flow shutting down production seemed in each case high, while the severity was off the scale. Terminal.

Sebastian looked around. The associate producers, line producers, production managers, unit managers, location managers, and the rest of them were working quickly and efficiently through the exercise, like bright well-behaved children doing their GCSEs. It was all too clear that cash with a reluctance to flow was not their problem. It was somebody else's. Why couldn't his problem be someone else's, too? After all, wasn't it all about collaboration? He got up.

'Finished already, Mr Boyle?'

'I just need to make an urgent call.'

'I have explained to you that it's the producer who stands in the dock, on a criminal charge, should there be a fatal accident on your shoot. Have I not?'

'I'll only be a moment.'

Outside Sebastian dialled the office and asked for Dougal. 'Help,' he said. 'Get me out of here, please, Dougal.'

'Where are you?' Sebastian explained. 'Why didn't you say, dear boy? I've got the certificate, you don't need to bother with it. Just walk away.'

'Can I? Really?'

'Of course you can. You're the producer.'

Back at Brunt Productions Sebastian pulled his worry list out of his pocket and started in on Dougal. The associate producer held up a hand.

'The money. Sort out the cash flow, Sebastian. Everything else can wait. Is there any bank, any bank at all, that you haven't tried?'

They went through the list. It seemed very comprehensive.

'What about distributors? An advance against foreign sales?' Not in this case. Sebastian had already learned that British drama, unless it was in frocks, was thought to be dark, gritty, and generally repulsive by the rest of the world's TV buyers, and in the case of *Rough Diamonds* he felt they were probably right. He'd succeeded in making the show unsellable before he'd even started.

'No, Dougal. I don't think so.'

'Well, you've got three choices. One: abandon the production.'

'I can't. You don't know what that would mean.'

'Of course, the broadcaster could sue you for breach of contract. Two: sell or mortgage your house, take out a personal loan, and finance it yourself.'

'The budget's over three million, Dougal. Have you seen my house?'

'Just as a temporary measure, of course. You'd still have to borrow the rest of the money from somewhere.'

'And the third option?'

Dougal was stuffing his pipe methodically. He looked up. 'Take the production to another company. A big independent. One with lots of resources, cash-rich.'

'Such as?'

'Well, of course lots of them are in worse straits than you.' Dougal tamped down the tobacco. 'But there are one or two big enough who might want to pick up a project with Helen Quigley.'

'Is this twenty questions?'

'I'm sure you know much more about the kind of companies that might be interested than I do.'

'I'm not.' Sebastian hardly knew the names of the main players. Most of the drama specialists seemed to live hand to mouth, like Albie, averaging a production every year or two if they were lucky. They didn't have cash reserves. For that you needed a company that was seriously commercial – which meant a big, fat, juicy contract for high volume, low budget programming, stuff to pad out the broadcasters' daytime and early evening schedules. Cooking, gardening, DIY, voyeurism, and humiliation – that's where the money was. There were also a few companies who'd grown rich on sitcoms starring their own board of directors. From time to time they dipped a toe, sometimes a whole foot, into the murky waters of TV drama. Would one of them bail Sebastian out? Who had the dosh and might want to buy into *Rough Diamonds*? What did Sebastian have that anyone would want? And, more importantly, would pay for it, cash up front? It came down to one name.

'Monopolimedia.' Dougal said the word as Sebastian was thinking it. Dougal held out the phone to him, like a gun with one bullet.

Sebastian was instructed to present himself for a meeting at eight the following morning, and to bring his own cappuccino as the runners wouldn't be in that early. Dougal raised his eyebrows as Sebastian put down the phone, then shepherded him out of the office and into The Intrepid Fox a few doors down the street. In no time they were wedged into a corner of the pub beside two online editors discussing their day's work on some pop promo.

'Took me seven hours on Flame.'

'Did you get it all?'

'In the end. I tell you, I'd never have believed such a big star had so much hair in such unexpected places.'

None of Sebastian's reading to date had covered this kind of thing, the expensive repair work that kept the Soho suites humming. Inexplicably it set him thinking about Daisy. He was wondering why when Dougal put a pint and a small whiskey in front of him, and the same for himself. Before long Dougal's pipe had cleared out the editors and Sebastian had enough room to get his drink up to his mouth.

'The thing is, you're still in the game,' shouted Dougal encouragingly.

Sebastian nodded and drank. 'What do you think Monopolimedia will want?'

Dougal's voice cut through the surrounding hubbub. 'Total control,' he yelled back. 'Most of the production fee, if not all. Lion's share of any profits. All the credit.'

This was even worse than Sebastian had expected.

'Look at it this way. We'll slash the production fee, and up your development costs. You said yourself there are no foreign buyers lining up, so profits don't figure. Credit, schmedit.'

'But don't we *need* the production fee?'

Dougal shrugged. 'What's the alternative?'

Sebastian had no answer.

'Got to be going. High tide tonight and I haven't put up my flood boards.' Dougal lived on an island in the Thames somewhere near Shepperton. He drained his glasses one after the other. 'Good luck tomorrow,' he called, as he shouldered his way to the door. 'Don't forget the train strike.'

Sebastian was about to follow when someone clapped him on the arm, sending a wave of beer sluicing out of his glass and over his jacket. 'Sebastian! I haven't seen you in a coon's age. How the hell are you?' He turned to see a muscle-bound homunculus in a weightlifter's vest, no visible neck and hands the size of his combat boots.

'Todd? What are you doing here? I heard you never stop working.' Todd Esterhazy had been a runner on the first ever *Britain in Bud*. Since then he'd left gardening programmes far behind and become a sought-after assistant director.

'Wrapped one this evening, so I'm celebrating the fact that I'll never have to look at that arsehole of a director again.'

'Who was it?'

'Ah, life's too short, mate. Just avoid any director who wears cowboy boots, that's my advice.' Todd threw back his head and tipped a pint of lager down it in one go. 'What you up to?'

'We're prepping a new series. I don't suppose you're free for the next four months?'

Todd belched violently. 'Sorry, mate, got one starting next week. Three months in Sardinia, it's going to be hell.' He grinned. 'Then a movie in Thailand. How come I get all the shit?'

'Oh well. Good for you.'

'Still filming blokes digging holes in the ground?'

'As a matter of fact I'm doing a drama series.'

'How's it going?'

'Can we talk about something else, please?'

'Sure. Listen, I'm meeting Terry.' Terry was his 2nd AD, his right-hand man. 'We're going out, the four of us, why don't you come along?'

Fifteen minutes later Sebastian was clinging onto the back of Todd's race-replica Suzuki, doing well over a hundred on the Westway where it leapt over the roof of Ladbroke Grove. Terry was in front on a lurid green Kawasaki with Gus, their runner, wedged tightly on behind him. A third bike, something red and Italian, brought up the rear – at least until Steve, the 3rd AD, saw his chance and shot past. Todd immediately rose to the challenge and the Suzuki leapt forward, thrumming like a tent in a hurricane.

The big orange lights of the Westway were long gone, and now the bikes were peeling off a brightly-lit bypass and entering a roundabout. They glided round it three or four times, each circuit a little lower, then Steve on the bike in front succeeded in easing his machine so close to the road that it made contact. Instantly a shower of coloured sparks erupted from his knee. Terry did the same thing. Sebastian couldn't see Todd's knee, his eyes were tightly shut, but he was still horribly aware of the tarmac coming up to meet him as a third stream of sparks joined the other two. Todd whooped again and then they were accelerating hard, following the other bikes out of the roundabout and the illuminated zone, and heading into the dark night.

Sebastian saw leaves overhead as they barrelled into blind corners on a twisty country road overhung with trees, using both sides of the carriageway. The machines in front lit up their route, which looked like a bright green tunnel in the fierce halogen. Then Todd opened up the throttle and overtook the red bike and the green one on a corner and screamed into the lead, something Sebastian had been praying wouldn't happen. Corners, road signs (Slow, Caution, Danger) popped up from nowhere and disappeared in an instant. They flicked from leaning one way to leaning the opposite twice a second, or that was how it felt to Sebastian. He shut his eyes again and promised that if only he came back from this ride alive he'd feel nothing but relief and joy at the miracle of life.

When Sebastian dared to look again, Todd was coasting to a halt outside a five-barred gate in the middle of nowhere. 'Whoooo!' Todd pulled off his helmet and Sebastian limped after him.

'What were all those sparks?' Todd pointed to the worn lumps fixed to the knees of his racing leathers. 'Sliders, mate. Titanium. Enjoy the ride?'

'Mostly. Where are we?'

'High Weald.'

'What are we doing here?'

They left the three bikes parked in a neat line just off the road and walked over the gate. A sign read 'Strictly Private'. Todd climbed over it and the rest followed. There was still a glimmer of light in the west, just enough to pick out random flashes from the fluorescent and reflective patches which dotted Todd's biking gear. They were in a wood, with no sign of anything there except trees. Sebastian found himself wondering exactly what Todd and his team did for relaxation apart from racing motorbikes.

Eventually they stopped in a small clearing. 'This is it,' said Todd. The others stood round him, smiling expectantly.

'What is this place?'

'My wood. Bought it last year. Listen.' Sebastian couldn't hear anything, except perhaps the first indications of tinnitus. 'Listen hard.' There was a distant bird-call, a sort of liquid gargling. 'Hear it? Fantastic, isn't it?'

'What is it?'

'Nightingale. That's why I bought it.' The ADs had spread themselves on the ground and were quietly smoking. Todd lay on his back looking up at the trees and listening and smiling to himself, a joint hanging from his lip. Sebastian had never seen anyone look so contented.

After an hour they set off home. The journey back was much less frenetic. This time the pace was fast but not mental, and everything felt just right to Sebastian as they dived in and out of turns and swept up and down the wooded hills.

Todd dropped him off outside his house and bungeed the spare helmet onto the seat behind him. Then with a wave he set off up the road with his team. Sebastian checked the time. It was a quarter to four in the morning. He felt serene, not even slightly tired. But he knew he would, very soon.

12 Paperwork

He woke with a jolt as Jemma banged the door on her way out. Sebastian sensed the last residue of that serene feeling draining away, then slammed upright and grabbed at his watch. It was twenty to eight. Wrenching the duvet off he threw on the first clothes he could find and half-ran, half-fell downstairs. Outside there was a space where the car had been. He remembered the train strike.

Sebastian wheeled Jemma's scooter out of the garage and wobbled, revved, braked, and tooted his way through the gridlock, earning the hatred of every roaduser he met. Even pedestrians regarded him with contempt. He did not get his knee down.

Skidding to a halt outside Monopolimedia at 08.11, Sebastian felt pretty pleased with his time. Eleven minutes (plus, say, five for parking, locking up, stowing embarrassing helmet, negotiating reception and lift, etc.) seemed within the bounds of acceptability for an early business meeting.

Bernie Gassman didn't agree. 'You're late. Bring a coffee?' His eyes gave nothing away as he took in Sebastian's appearance.

'Oh, er, no.'

'Don't want one?'

'Well –'

'Cause if you do you're out of luck.'

He prised the lid off his extra-large cappuccino and took a big bite out of some top-of-the-range viennoiserie.

'What?'

Sebastian was staring at Bernie in a don't-I-know-you? sort of way.

'Nothing.'

'You said you wanted to talk to me about cash-flowing some production of yours.'

'Yes.'

'And why would I want to do that?'

That was it. At The Channel. Bernie had been the man in the black suit giving the receptionist an earful.

'Oh. Well, there are business advantages –'

'Money. That's why. What have you got?'

Even Sebastian knew a little about Bernie Gassman. He was something of a Soho legend, after all. In five years he'd worked his way from the juvenile offenders' court to the boardroom of the fastest-growing media business in the country, and he hadn't made many friends along the way. But there was something else about him, something vaguely familiar, that Sebastian was still struggling to place.

'What could you have that we might conceivably want?' Sebastian gazed at the wall behind Bernie's bullet head, at the framed photos. Bernie Gassman with celebrities, all of them signed. Bernie with pop stars. Bernie with politicians. Bernie with actresses.

'Helen Quigley.' Bernie blinked. Sebastian's guess had been right – Bernie was a people person. Of a sort.

'Why would we need you to get us Helen Quigley?'

'Because when *Rough Diamonds* was greenlit your Helen Quigley project went down the tube. *Dark Thoughts*, wasn't it? And Brit TV are doing a deal that'll take her off the market after this, keep her to themselves. This is your chance to get Helen Quigley. You won't get another.'

Bernie adjusted the Palm Pilot by a few millimetres. 'What do you need?'

'Cash-flowing through pre-production, until we can refinance without Bank Frød.'

'How much exactly?'

'Er –'

'Fax me the spreadsheet.'

There was another pause, as Bernie synchronised the Palm

Pilot with his Rolex. 'By eleven.' He stood up. Sebastian followed suit. Bernie sat down again.

That was it. Interview terminated at eight twenty-three. Sebastian found his own way down to reception and out to the waiting scooter. Soon he was in his own office with his very own cappuccino and a whole bag of croissants. Dougal came in and asked how it had gone.

'Fine. Bernie Gassman's very … direct.'

Dougal peered at him more closely. 'Did you spend all night in that pub?'

'No, I went for a bike ride.'

'Oh? You look a bit rough, that's all. Is that new?'

'No, it's Jemma's.' Sebastian had needed to wear something waterproof on the scooter, and her jacket was the first thing he found. If he didn't mind it being shiny and pink, why should Dougal? 'Anyway, let's get on with this thing for Monopoli. Can you tweak it a bit to get more money up front?'

'You read my mind.' Dougal's long, wrinkled fingers were already twinkling over the keyboard of his computer.

Sebastian wandered over to Daisy's desk and surveyed it. Nothing there except a phone, a computer (password protected), and a copy of *The Knowledge*. The filing cabinet beneath was locked. Sebastian felt it would be demeaning to try and force it.

'Hello, Mister Boyle, don't often see you nowadays.'

'Hello, Grace.' Sebastian watched her empty the waste-baskets in reception. Then he looked down. Sure enough, Daisy's bin was brimming with screwed up balls of paper. Gingerly removing the sandwich wrapper, moist tissues, and a banana skin, Sebastian smoothed out the topmost sheet.

It was the draft of a letter from Daisy to someone called Jake Smith. Sebastian didn't recognise his name but he seemed to be someone's head of drama. Uncrumpling another sheet, Sebastian read a fuller version of the same letter. Jake and Daisy seemed to be on friendly terms. Daisy was proposing that she would do something for him while keeping the 'key talent' (whatever that was) attached and happy. In return, she trusted Jake would honour their agreement to make her – continued on page two. But there was no page two.

Three further crumpled balls revealed nothing more than gradually improving attempts to give notes to Pat Quine in a form he'd find acceptable. The next scrunched-up sheet, though, turned out to be half of a fax to a publicist with strict instructions to sit on 'the information' until Daisy confirmed that the time was ripe. What 'the information' was, the fax didn't say.

'Lost something, have you?' Grace was beside him with her bin-bag and J-cloth, eyeing Sebastian curiously.

'It's a recycling survey I agreed to take part in. '

'You want to recycle these?'

'No, thanks, they're … the wrong type of paper.' Sebastian hurried back to his office. 'Dougal …'

'What did you find in her bin?' Dougal asked, without looking up from his screen.

'I think she's plotting something.'

'Know all, say nothing.'

'What?'

'Sun Tzu. *The Art of War*. Or is it *The Prince*?'

'I never knew you were so Machiavellian, Dougal.'

He chuckled drily. 'I worked on a couple of terrible American movies in the early eighties, out at Pinewood. You pick these things up. Oh look, there's Sophie. She's keen.'

Sophie waved cheerily through the internal window and carried her post through to her cupboard.

'I hope those big Jiffy bags are what I think they are.'

Sophie had hardly arrived before she was off again. Probably she only came in for a bowl of free cereal on the way to her story seminar. Sebastian walked across and found her room empty. Well, not empty – on her desk were two freshly printed scripts. Now at last they had a full set, even if their parentage was a little confused. Sebastian scooped up the new drafts and hurried back to his office to read them.

In Pat Quine's latest, Dan was caught up in a mercy killing disguised as a murder that was really a suicide – or maybe it was a suicide disguised as a mercy killing that was really a murder. Anyway, it kept you guessing right up to the end, and perhaps beyond. Dan's character was developing nicely, there were some warm moments and not too many quirks, and Sebastian thought that with Helen Quigley in the role the audience would love her.

The thing now, thought Sebastian, was to get the script to Helen before she slipped through his fingers. He worked the photocopier and booked a courier, then locked the original in his filing cabinet. It was still only nine o'clock. No Lucy, no Daisy. He started in on George and Jim's monster double episode.

It was nearly eleven when Sebastian reached 'Fade out' and slowly became conscious of people bustling back and forth on the other side of the window. Dougal was speaking quietly on the phone. Sebastian was vaguely aware of Daisy watching him from her desk, out of the corner of her eye.

He had been in a dark place. George and Jim had taken him on a roller-coaster ride. It was all there – excitement, fear, suspense, panic, horror, even humour. A very powerful piece of writing.

'Well?' Dougal raised his eyebrows as Sebastian laid down the script.

'It's a masterpiece.'

'Oh dear.'

'I know. If we were making a movie –'

'We probably wouldn't be here.'

'But as it is … Brit TV have commissioned a long-running series. And this is a signature piece.'

'A what?'

'Something with the author's fingerprints all over it. That's what the broadcasters all say they want. But … they have to be the right fingerprints. And George and Jim are jobbing comedy writers. No one wants their fingerprints all over anything.'

'What will you do?'

'Get them to tone it down, I suppose. Lower their sights a bit. Yes, Daisy?'

She was standing at the door. Sebastian could see her gaze settle on the script, which was lying face-up on his desk.

'Is that George and Jim's script?'

'It certainly is.'

'Did you … I thought …'

'Here. Take it.' Sebastian was in no mood to justify himself to Daisy. 'Read it and we'll meet to discuss in …' He looked at his watch. 'Two hours. Okay?'

'But –'

'Now I've got to fax this cash flow.' He dumped the script in Daisy's arms and closed the door. *Cut the Crap and Shoot your Shit,* an American indie manual he'd recently found behind a radiator in Foyle's, was already paying dividends.

* * *

In the world outside Sebastian's office, meanwhile, the ducks were once again drifting out of line.

Helen Quigley had decided she wouldn't commit until she saw the script, liked it, and heard from her agent, her best friend, and a make-up lady in Ealing she trusted completely that it was right for her. Meanwhile The Channel had come back with a new offer: a beefed-up part on *Dalston Square,* complete with resurrection if required, plus the main story in the Xmas Special, plus another series of her own choosing. And Lavinia her agent had cannily held off signing Brit TV's contract. Not forgetting, of course, that Helen was in mid-fling with a good-looking but untalented actor five years younger than her, and would like to do something for him beyond what she was already doing in the privacy of the Chingford hacienda. The Channel had promised to find something suitable.

Things were looking less rosy for Jason Prynne. His boyish good looks were softening into jowls and flab, his hair-dyeing routine starting to show, the rumours about his coke habit becoming more persistent. More importantly, he'd just made a new series and word was starting leak out that it was a total dog. *Harlem Heist* was a dog, too, but an American one, never shown in the UK and not likely to be, so it didn't count, except for future US co-productions. But a home-grown flop was something else. In another month Steve Bung would be taking his name off lists, not putting it on.

Even Steve Bung, however, was not immune to change. For the last five years his word had been law to anyone wanting to make drama at Brit TV. But one of those sporadic games of executive musical chairs was in the offing. If that happened all deals were off, all green lights went to amber, everyone sat tight and waited to see what happened. The question was, who would replace him if he did go? Or was it all just a scam to enable Steve to renegotiate his already high salary up into the stratosphere?

Trevor William, meanwhile, had not been sighted for over a fortnight. Sebastian called his agent, with the usual dispiriting result. By now Marc Pershore simply gave a bark of amazed laughter when someone asked if he knew where his client could be reached. The absence of the director became more and more noticeable. Everyone needed to talk to him. Then, without warning, he was back – fit, keen, and almost normal. His head had been shaved. His cool grey eyes were the same as ever but overall his face was calm, almost relaxed.

'Everything all right?'

'Well, considering. We've all been wondering where you were.'

'Read this.' The director pushed a crisp, freshly-printed script across the table. *Rough Diamonds* episode one. No writer credit. Sebastian picked it up.

'I'll be with the art department.' And Trevor set off upstairs as Sebastian hurried to his office, turned off the phones and nervously began to read.

13 Balls in the Air

Mel Gioconda told her assistant to hold her calls. Putting on a CD of neo-Gregorian chant she closed the blinds, lit up a herbal cigarette, and lowered herself gently onto the beanbag. She needed to think, or rather, to allow her unconscious mind to let her know what she already thought. Mel placed a good deal of faith in the powers of the unconscious mind. It had got her this far, after all.

To the outside world Mel presented a smooth, calm exterior. Early in her career she'd hit on boundless enthusiasm as a win-win, one-size-fits-all reaction to anyone or anything she met. If the idea or the person proved to be a disappointment, Mel got credit for accentuating the positive and providing much-needed encouragement. The less impressive the idea or individual, the more credit she earned. And if they turned out to be good, then Mel was already streets ahead of her rivals by having responded so well before the general opinion had formed.

By now there were lots of writers, directors, and producers whom Mel had encouraged in the early years, and many felt a debt to her for being their earliest champion. Others whose careers had fallen by the wayside retained a warm corner for Mel, who alone had believed in them, in hearts otherwise filled with rancour. Very few noticed the lack of any direct effort by Mel to promote those she appeared to favour. Instead she left it to others to make the crucial judgments, but was prepared to accept the credit when it was laid at her door.

This method had worked brilliantly at The Channel, where avoidance of judgments and decisions was the central executive activity. Every question was pushed up to the next level, and the next, and action was taken, if at all, amidst a fog of confusion as to who'd instigated it.

Mel and Steve Bung, her opposite number at Brit TV, worked in opposite ways to achieve much the same results. Mel loved, admired, and supported everything; Steve loved, admired, and supported nothing. Both were quite prepared to let the market decide, and then line up behind received opinion. It was a question of which you preferred: Mel's suffocating hugs, or Steve's bracing candour.

Mel's technique had already brought her a long way from a 2:2 in botany at Hull. Now she was considering three offers: move to Los Angeles as head of programming for a new subscription channel; continue doing what she was doing already at The Channel, for an enhanced salary; or replace Steve Bung at Brit TV. Hence the music, the herbal cigarette, and the phone ban.

It was a disaster. No matter how she looked at it, Mel could see no way around making a choice. Worse still, she'd be saying no not just to one person, but to two. It went against every principle she had. At least two individuals, in fact two whole executive boards, were going to love her less as a result of her decision. If the three sets of executives had conspired together to cause her pain and anguish they could hardly have come up with a more effective plan. She came to the end of the CD but was no nearer an answer than when it began.

'Mel?'

'What is it, Michelle? I said to hold all calls, didn't I?'

'Yes, Mel. But –'

'What?'

'It's urgent.'

'I'm busy. It'll have to wait.'

'It's *really* urgent.'

'I'm handling a crisis here, Michelle!'

'But that's why she needs to talk to you.'

'Who does?'

'Molly.'

'Molly van der Post?'

'Yes.'

'Why didn't you say so? Send her in.'

Alongside her work promoting programmes, Molly van der Post looked after personal publicity and PR for a few chosen individuals. Helen Quigley was one. Mel was another. Placing the right story in the right publication at the right time could be crucial in the successful advancement of a career, as Mel was well aware. It was, after all, no coincidence that she'd been appointed to her current job as drama supremo at The Channel shortly after the very public and indeed literal fall of her predecessor, from the vodka bar at the top of the Altiplano Hotel down through the open-plan staircase to the fountain in the dining room below. How unlucky he'd been to be photographed, floundering dazedly among the marble cupids, with that Brazilian rent-boy. And how fortunate that Mel should that same day have been profiled in the same paper and pictured with her sensible teacher husband and three smiling children, all doing well at non-selective state schools, and no trace anywhere of the Filipino servants.

'Hello, Mel, all well?'

'No, bugger it. Sit down.' Molly was perhaps the only person with whom Mel felt completely at ease. There was no need to smile at her, even less to simper.

'Decisions, decisions. What are you going to do?'

'I don't know.'

'You can't say yes to all three.'

'Obviously.'

'Unless …'

'What?'

'Well … you have to say no to two of them only if you say yes to the third.'

'I'm not with you, Molly.'

'But if you don't say yes to any of them, you don't have to

say no to any of them either. Keep them guessing. And loving you, of course. Unless you want to move, that is?'

'Not particularly.'

'Then stay where you are, say 'Yes – maybe' to all three, and keep on smiling. All they can do is admire your integrity and improve their offers to the point where the benefits are so huge you no longer care about putting people's noses out of joint.'

'You are a genius, Molly.'

'That's what you pay me for, darling. I must go now, Helen's in a tizz.'

'Helen Quigley?'

'She's in a similar predicament to yours. When they want something, some people just won't take no for an answer.'

* * *

In her compact office in Acton Studios, Jassy Cox was happily drawing. Now at last she had her scripts, and was absorbed in storyboarding. She tucked a stray lock of hair behind her ear and hummed to herself as she filled in the boxes on her sheets. Each one represented a camera shot she'd later use to tell the story.

This was Jassy's favourite bit of the whole process. She enjoyed working on her own, without the distractions of actors and lights and weather and all the things that stood between her and the finished product. Storyboarding always made Jassy think of happy childhood days spent stretched out on the floor in her bedroom, her Lakeland crayons fanned out on the carpet like a wooden rainbow, as she carefully drew pictures of princesses in a variety of elaborate costumes.

'Cup of tea, Jassy?'

'Yes, please.'

'Earl Grey?'

'Perfect.'

Angel withdrew her head and closed the door softly. Jassy continued drawing. She missed the princesses, really, she thought, as she sketched a shot of a man tied by his hands and feet to a bed. In some ways she'd have preferred to direct children's drama, a nice adaptation like *The Midnight Folk*, but only the Americans spent that kind of money on English classics and naturally they preferred American directors so there just wasn't the work. Carefully she shaded in a close-up of the man's face, eyes closed and mouth open in a scream. George and Jim certainly had a dark imagination. Or one of them did. Which one? Jassy wondered idly as she moved on to another close-up, of the hands this time, with the fingernails missing. She was looking forward to meeting them, but couldn't help feeling a little apprehensive too. Pat Quine's script was something else again. No torture, thank heavens, but Jassy was worried that she didn't altogether understand it and you couldn't just ask a writer what he was on about, it made you look such an idiot. Really, she wished she could have had Phoebe's scripts, at least one of them. She hadn't read them but Phoebe sounded a much more normal person, a girl too, and Jassy felt sure they'd have got on well.

Above her head Jassy could hear music, footsteps, laughter, and the occasional crash from the art department. She knew Trevor William was up there with the designer and his gang, because they were a gang. They had lunch together and often went for a drink together at the pub over the road at the end of the day. They were friendly enough but hadn't asked Jassy to join them and now Trevor was there she guessed they wouldn't. She still hadn't exchanged a single word with her fellow director and when he saw her coming in the corridor he always dived off into another office before they met. It was a bit hurtful.

It hadn't been like this on her last job. Commercials were different, of course. *Sunshine Serial*, the muesli-ad mini-soap, wasn't something Jassy's agent put on her drama CV, naturally.

Picking up the Light Mid Green – this really was a very comprehensive set of crayons – Jassy idly began colouring the fingertips, where the gangrene was beginning to set in. Strictly speaking this wasn't necessary, since the storyboard was only meant to give a rough approximation of the shot – size, angle, that kind of thing. A bit technical really. There were times when Jassy thought it had been a lot more fun helping design costumes than it was directing. But the truth was that she hadn't been very good at designing costumes people could wear in a typical TV drama. Bat-wing sleeves, jewelled girdles, and veils woven from latticed gold thread weren't much in demand on *Deptford Emergency*. Probably commercials made more sense, in the end. With a week to shoot thirty seconds, at least you had just about enough time to do it properly. And, after all, it often did need thirty or forty takes to get the camera move exactly right.

In a few weeks Jassy's best friend and right-hand woman would be joining her. As the continuity supervisor, Bernice got only a week of prep, but Jassy was already phoning her every day to talk through the production. Some of the crews could be very male, and it helped to have someone at your side who understood how it felt to arrive on location looking your best, trying to make a good impression, only to get an inch of mud over your new Prada ankle-boots. For now she had to make do with Olga the production coordinator, who was so quiet it was hard to tell what she was doing, let alone what she was thinking, and her assistant Angel, who was as raucous as a one-woman girl band. Still. No doubt it would all work out fine in the end.

* * *

Lavinia Hurdle was updating her client.

'Helen?'

'Lavinia.' Helen adjusted the volume control on her phone. 'Heard the latest?'

'What?'

'Executive musical chairs.'

'Who's where?'

'We're not sure yet. But it looks as though Jack Fuchs is off to Six, Bill Crapper's being replaced by Steve Bung, and Mel Gioconda's taking his job at Brit TV.'

'Who's replacing Mel?'

'Bill Crapper, I expect.'

'Shit.'

'Exactly. It gives all the bastards the excuse they've been looking for to dump everything they've promised to make and start over with a clean slate.'

'Can't they take projects with them?'

'They can. But only if it suits them.'

'So what'll happen to *Rough Diamonds*?'

'Your guess is as good as mine, sweetie. Well, almost.'

'And the *Dalston Square* offer?'

'I've got calls in. But the last time they did one of these executive shuffles, it was six months before the dust settled.'

'Oh, Christ. I've just exchanged contracts on a timeshare in Fuengirola.'

'I'll call you as soon as I've got some news.'

* * *

Across town the same intelligence was being digested.

'You are fucking joking.'

'I fucking am not.'

Jeremy Cavendish drew deeply on his Marlboro Light. Bernie lit up a Silk Cut. They stared at each other across the chrome table.

'We've got production worth nearly ten million with the pair of them.'

'Tell me about it.'

'What's this going to do to our cash flow?'

'What you did to that work-experience girl.'

'That was a totally unfounded rumour!'

'Who cares? The point is, we're in deep shit.'

'Okay, Bernie. First things first. How reliable is this rumour?'

'Very. Someone I pay a big retainer to, who works in Robin Bygone's office.'

'You've got a mole in Brit TV's business affairs department?'

'Naturally.'

'Don't tell me any more. I play squash with Robin, for Christ's sake.'

'First Tuesday of every month, three-thirty at the Queen's Club.'

Jeremy looked at Bernie narrowly.

'Last week you lost 11-9, 11-3, 11-2.'

'I hope you don't have me under surveillance too?'

'Of course not, Jeremy. Don't be ridiculous.' Bernie inhaled, extracting from his Silk Cut every available milligram of tar, nicotine, and anything else going. 'That would be a waste of money. I see you myself every day.'

'What can we do?'

'I've got our people going through the contracts. Every one we can, we'll nail. Every one we can't, we'll fight. Threaten to pull out our stars. Up the loan facility, it'll be a little while until the bank knows anything. Chase up every invoice.'

'That can send the wrong signal.'

'It's the same signal as always: don't fuck with us. Okay?'

Jeremy paused, dragged unhappily on his Marlboro. 'Okay.' He got up, then paused at the boardroom door. 'What about that Helen Quigley show, *Rough Diamonds*?'

'Whoever's taking over at The Channel will want to keep her. Whoever's at Brit TV will try to take her away. So long as she's attached to this show, we want it.'

* * *

There was excitement and a renewed sense of purpose in Brunt's script department. Sophie had just got back from her story seminar and her head was swimming with intoxicating new ideas.

She couldn't understand why both Sebastian and Daisy seemed to think she'd picked a bad time to go on a three-day course. It just showed how little people understood the art of script editing. Sophie shuddered at the idea of working on these new drafts without knowing what the Inciting Incident was, or where the Act Two Mid-Act Climax should come, or how to identify the Obligatory Scene. It surprised her, when she considered how much experience the *Rough Diamonds* writers had, what elementary mistakes they made. Still, she was confident she could fix the problems.

By now Sophie had the six scripts pasted up page by page on her walls. She found it easier to see the structure that way. Except that she only had four walls. So episode five was on the floor, and although she tried not to walk on it, pages kept getting stuck to her feet. She tried to keep episode six on the ceiling, but even with Blu-tack the pages dropped off, and they'd brought quite a lot of the new paint down with them too.

Blissfully unaware of the latest developments, Sebastian was blocking out the schedule and fine-tuning the budget. Everything seemed in pretty good shape. As soon as he finished Trevor's rewrite of episode one he sent a copy round to Helen Quigley with a note to ignore the previous version, which, he lied, had been sent by mistake. He felt sure the script would clinch it for her. Unfortunately, he couldn't send a copy to Jason – his character, although now back in, had metamorphosed into a four-foot kung fu master. When Sebastian mentioned this to Vanessa she simply rolled her eyes, so he was rather hoping that Trevor had a four-foot actor with special skills in mind.

That, however, didn't solve the problem of Jason Prynne. There hadn't been much ambiguity about Steve Bung's position, so Sebastian would just have to find another part for him somewhere else. And in fact there was a meaty role in the double episode, where George and Jim had come up with a clever reworking of *Alien* set in south-east London. The cyborg was an attention-grabbing part and would suit Jason down to the ground, if only he'd agree to the change. Somehow it had to be presented as an upgrade, which wasn't easy for a character who didn't make an appearance until episode four, and then only when the lead director, the one he'd sat down with, had buggered off and been replaced by another one even more obscure.

Jassy Cox adored Jason and was desperate to have him. Sebastian felt that he wouldn't be able to resist Jassy, and so it proved. He arranged a lunch for the two of them somewhere intimate and not too expensive and Jassy reported back that Jason would be delighted to play this new character under her direction. Sebastian wondered what she'd promised him. He decided it was better not to know.

There was another piece of good news. Todd Esterhazy's Sardinian shoot had collapsed, so he and his team were unexpectedly available. He wouldn't commit to the whole series, and demanded extra payments in cash in brown paper bags, but he did accept the job. Sebastian felt that there was at least one area where he could be confident, especially after he'd seen the look of recognition that flashed between Todd and Trevor William – an unstoppable force taking stock of an immovable object.

That just left the central problem of cash flow and Monopoli. Sebastian hadn't succeeded in turning up any alternative source of finance, and now stories were appearing in the papers about Bank Frød and possible legal action over money laundering. Munraj the production accountant had sat on invoices and salaries for as long as he could and the production urgently needed to come up with some actual money.

There had been no response to the stuff they'd faxed to Monopoli, and Sebastian had said nothing to Daisy about what he'd found in her waste-paper basket. He'd been careful to say nothing in front of her, either, suspicious that it might find its way back to this Jake Smith character. Now he decided to take the bull by the horns and phone Bernie Gassman.

'Hello, Bernie.'

'Yes?'

'It's Sebastian Boyle … Brunt Productions … We met. *Rough Diamonds* …'

Silence.

'I wondered if you received the cash flow?'

'Yes.'

'And … what did you think?'

More silence. Sebastian wondered if it worked on Steve Bung. Steve Bung probably loved it. The two of them probably went bowling together.

'Sorry, what was that, Bernie?'

'Make me an offer.'

'An offer? Well, we thought that in return for cash-flowing the production we could offer you –'

'In writing.' And he hung up. Sebastian was beginning to prefer Archie Govan at Bank Frød – now, sadly, a fugitive from justice, according to Giles.

Sebastian cobbled together something to keep Brunt Productions going. He wondered how much Daisy knew. Surely she must have noticed a certain coolness in the office? If so, she didn't mention it. She read the scripts, made notes on them, dealt with the writers' agents. Whatever was going on behind her bob, he'd find out soon enough. Anyway, he had other fish to fry. Sebastian was off to the South of France.

14 Bunkered

Outside the airport at Nice wind whipped through the palm trees and made the leaves rattle. A few drops spattered down as Sebastian edged his way up the long taxi queue, and then abruptly rain fell in tropical cascades. In less than a minute his new linen suit was soaked through and his summer shoes were sponging up the floodwater. Sopping gangs of sales executives stormed the waiting taxis. Their surly drivers shouted angrily but to no effect, and soon a line of Mercedes, fully laden, was crawling out of the airport and down to the autoroute. That left Sebastian and one other passenger on the now abandoned taxi rank.

'Christ. Is that you in that shitty suit, Sebastian?' It was his lawyer, Giles Savernake. 'Hang on a sec, I'll be right back.'

When Giles returned five minutes later he was followed cortège-style by a white stretched Lincoln limousine, complete with tinted windows and Tunisian driver in uniform. 'Found this next to the Avis stand. A bit dearer but a fuck of a lot more fun, wouldn't you say?'

'You're going to Cannes in that?'

'We, Sebastian. We are going to Cannes in that.'

The interior was packed with the standard accessories – cocktail bar, satellite TV, mirrored coke table; everything except a Corby trouser press. Giles poured champagne, put his feet up on the white leather upholstery and lit a cigar. 'Expenses. Don't worry, not yours. So what brings you to this cesspool?'

'Money. And I've got to make a speech.'

'Planning to see a bit of glamour?'

'If there's time.'

Giles snorted. 'There's no time and no glamour, either. This isn't the film festival. Just a hole in the ground the organisers call The Palace and everyone knows as The Bunker, where they buy and sell everything from porn to pre-school.'

'What about you?'

'Client fancies acquiring a broadcaster. I've come to sort out a few points. Pass me the phone, will you, mine's flat.' Sebastian gave him the on-board handset and he booked a table at Cannes's most expensive restaurant. 'You'll join me, won't you?'

'Thank you, Giles, I'd love to. But it's tonight I'm making my speech.'

'Pity. Come along afterwards if you can.' He slid down further into his overstuffed seat. 'I'm knackered. Wake me up when we get there.' The Lincoln hissed along the autoroute, raindrops clustering on the windows. Sebastian hauled out his sleek new handheld and tried to improve his speech. It wasn't easy. Somehow there didn't seem to be anything worth saying about *Inspector Pettigrew*, especially since he hadn't even worked on it. But the distributors who'd invited him didn't seem to care that it was Albie's credit and not Sebastian's – just so long as they got a speaker to introduce their show. It had been blackmail – a vague promise of investment in *Rough Diamonds*, but only if he helped sell his brother-in-law's series to the Koreans. He needed that investment. Albie would have risen to the occasion and for his sake Sebastian felt he had to try.

What the hell would they make of it in Korea, anyway? Sebastian poured himself another glass of champagne.

By the time they hit the Croisette Sebastian was feeling a lot better. He woke up Giles, thanked him for the lift, and swayed into the Ritz-Carlton-Majestic. Under the harsh stare of the world's most condescending hotel staff he successfully reached the lift and ascended to the fifth floor, and after a struggle with the electronic key burst into his suite. On closer examination it proved to be more in the nature of a bathroom with en suite bed. A thought was nagging at the back of Sebastian's befuddled brain: if he didn't have any luggage, that meant … it had remained in the boot of the Lincoln. His bag, containing the dinner jacket and tie he was planning to wear that night. Where was Giles staying? In his pixillated state Sebastian hadn't thought to ask. And presumably Giles's phone was still flat, so no good trying to call him.

Sebastian looked in the mirror at his suit, now drying rapidly in the heat of the hotel. Okay, so it was wrinkled and creased. But, after all, wasn't that the whole point of linen? And it did seem a size or two smaller than when he'd put it on, but if he wore the trousers as hipsters and undid the jacket buttons it would be absolutely fine. Sebastian felt sure he could carry it off. The best thing now, without a doubt, would be to take a little nap and sleep off the tiring effects of the journey. He slumped onto the narrow bed that almost filled the room and instantly passed out.

It was dark when Sebastian awoke. Someone was digging inside his head with a pruning saw. His suit, now dry, had shrunk a further size and fitted him like a sausage-skin. His shoes were ringed with white tidemarks and his shirt was so crumpled it looked like seersucker. He could see his watch quite plainly without even having to lift a cuff. It was five to eight. He was nearly an hour late.

At least he didn't have far to go. The *Pettigrew* dinner dance was taking place downstairs in the hotel's immense ballroom. This was scattered with tables and a Latino band entertained the buyers while they ate. The helpful girl at the door steered Sebastian to a table right at the front, so most of the diners had ample opportunity to examine his costume at their leisure as he threaded his way through them. Every other man was in black tie except for one, who was in white tie. All the women wore evening dresses. Bravely Sebastian carried off his shrunken duds as best he could, hoping to strike a note of untrammelled creativity or, at worst, mild but engaging eccentricity.

'Jesus, Baz. What's with the fancy dress?'

'Hi, Kerry. My luggage went astray.'

Kerry was a big old blonde, the Australian head of the distributors. She gave Sebastian an assessing look then snapped open her tiny mobile. 'Tracy? Get me a man's dinner suit, chest about forty-two, waist …' – she peered down – 'what, thirty-six? Shortish legs, plus a shirt, tie, socks, shoes, the works. One of the guys must have a spare, or the hotel, see what you can come up with. You've got ten minutes.' Kerry snapped the phone shut. 'Welcome to Cannes, darling. You're on straight after the pavlova.'

All in all it was a night Sebastian would later try hard to forget. The fuchsia cummerbund and matching dickie-bow paired with a magnificently ruffled dress shirt made him look like the victim of a cruel makeover prank. He'd forgotten his handheld and had to give the speech from memory, which led to some oversights and an unfortunate confusion between North and South Korea. Those fifteen minutes at the microphone were the worst in Sebastian's life thus far. At last, stammering and shaking, he was led down from the podium and back to his table. Kerry squeezed his hand reassuringly. 'Don't worry, Baz. I don't think anyone was listening. Have a brandy.'

'No thanks, I'd better not. Listen, about *Rough Diamonds* –'

'Call me when I'm back in Sydney.'

'Right.'

'There was a guy here looking for you earlier. Stick around for the dancing?'

'I don't think so. See you later.' He made his escape and almost ran from the room, slap bang into a familiar face.

'Jason!'

'How are you? Enjoyed the speech.'

'What are you doing here?'

'*Harlem Heist*. Same distributors as yours, they've dragged me here to promote it. They say it needs all the help it can get.'

'Oh. I'm sorry to hear –'

'Forget it. Show's crap. What can you do?' He waved one hand rather wildly, as though swatting away the whole problem like an annoying fly. 'Look at it.' His arm took in the elegant hotel foyer decked with gaudy posters, placards, and flyers for hundreds of indistinguishable television series. High-kicking ninja-women featured strongly.

'A maelstrom of mediocrity. Shit. A shitload of … shit.' Jason staggered and Sebastian grabbed one flailing arm before he keeled over completely.

'Can I help you to your room?'

'You're kidding. Follow me.' And he lurched unstoppably forward, intent on the gold and scarlet of the bar.

Drinking with Jason Prynne was an alcoholic roller coaster ride. By turns angry, funny, charming, foul-mouthed, tearful and wildly aggressive, he seemed to be building up to some sort of spectacular climax, and Sebastian didn't want to be there when he reached it. In the course of an hour he and most of the other people in the bar learned all there was to know about Jason's childhood in rural Shropshire, the expulsions from schools, his early acceptance by RADA, sharing the stage with legendary actors of the seventies, his youthful successes in films, the collapse of his first marriage, the coke, the booze, rehab, telly, more coke, more telly. Prestigious telly first, then high-budget series, then more routine stuff. 'Going … down!' he yelled, maniacally.

'It's been a great evening, Jason, but I do have an early flight tomorrow –'

'Down, down, down!'

'See you back in London.' Sebastian wriggled out of his grasp and stumbled into the foyer. Back in the bar he could Jason's voice rising to a scream.

'DOWN!' There was a terrible crash, then silence. The lift pinged and opened. Sebastian got in without a backward glance, went up to the fifth floor, hung the dinner suit and fuchsia accessories outside his door with a thank you note, and turned off the light.

* * *

The rain followed him back to London, and Sebastian stood with Dougal under an umbrella on the fire escape for their debrief.

'I take it you've heard about Steve Bung?'

'No. What?'

'He's been fired.'

'Seriously?'

'The runner got it from the sandwich delivery girl. Her boyfriend services the photocopiers at Brit TV.'

Well, there was little they could do about it, just carry on as before, Sebastian thought. At least until it was official. Steve Bung might take months to go, if he ever did, and by then they could have finished shooting. Or he might up sticks tomorrow. You could never tell with executives. Top of Sebastian's worry list now were the scripts.

* * *

Sophie felt she'd been working at the speed of sound if not light to get the six episodes into shape. No one was allowed to touch the opening episode, that was understood, because Trevor William's draft was now holy writ. Sophie asked Daisy if she'd told Pat Quine yet his episode had been totally rewritten by the director. Daisy was still working up to it.

To Phoebe, Sophie explained that she'd got her mid-act complications in the wrong place, and she needed to build the power of the counter-idea in order to create a satisfactory resolution of the extra-personal conflict at the climax of the third act. Phoebe nodded a lot and Sophie was pretty sure she understood, but if not Sophie was confident she could easily rejig the scripts herself.

George and Jim proved surprisingly resistant to some of her notes when they came in for a meeting, and Sophie had to remind them that she was the script editor on this show and when it came to the scripts, in the end her word was law. George didn't look very happy, but then he never did. Jim didn't say much either, which was unusual for him.

Sophie went into Sebastian's office to bring him up to speed, but he didn't seem to understand how much progress she'd made. He glared at Daisy and told Sophie to bring all the scripts into his office. Sophie explained this wasn't possible, because they were stuck all over the walls of her office, and one side of the meeting room as well. Daisy came to have a look and then told Sophie very quietly to take them down and reassemble them.

'That's all very well to say, but once they're on the floor it's quite hard to remember where all the pages go, actually, especially when George and Jim don't use page numbers.'

Daisy peeled the pages off the walls and ceiling and said she was going to handle the next stage herself.

Sophie was outraged. 'There's no respect in this industry for script professionals. That's why there are so many duff shows.'

The script debate continued in Sebastian's office.

'She's got to go.'

'She's trying her best. She's still learning.'

'Then let her learn somewhere else, where she can't do any harm.'

They faced each other across the desk. Daisy wasn't going to admit she'd been wrong about Sophie.

'What's the big problem?'

'The big problem is that we have six scripts, as yet unapproved by the broadcaster. Two are about half an hour overlength, one is about a quarter of an hour under. Pat Quine will probably joining Pete Clapp in taking his name off and complaining to the Writers' Guild. George and Jim's agent has demanded they be given someone else to work with. Phoebe phoned me in tears to say she's having a nervous breakdown and she still doesn't understand what an inciting incident is. What is it, by the way?'

Daisy shrugged.

'Just tell me what you need.'

As it turned out, that wasn't necessary. When Sebastian starting reading Monopoli's proposal he was standing by his desk, but by the time he was halfway through he found he was sitting down.

'You all right there, Sebastian?'

'Yes, fine, thanks, Dougal.'

'Only you look a bit pale.'

'Did you read this?'

'Well, I may have glanced over it as I put it on your desk.'

'Bloody hell.' Sebastian skimmed though the rest of the document. It was totally unacceptable. 'What are we going to do?'

'Accept it.'

'What? We're giving up everything!'

'True. But you survive and live to fight another day.'

'What's the alternative?' Sebastian was thinking of Albie, what he'd say when he finally returned.

'Well, you haven't succeeded in raising any more money. I should think we're pretty close to trading insolvently, if we're not there already.'

He put in a call to Giles.

'How's your hangover, Sebastian?'

'I don't have one, thank you, Giles. How was your dinner?'

'Don't ask. It turned out to be one of those places where they don't take any cards or cheques. At all. The bill came to around five hundred quid and I didn't have more than a couple of hundred francs in cash.'

'What happened?'

'They held me hostage while a courier brought a wad of notes. It's out near Grasse, this place, so I was there till about four in the morning.'

'Did your client buy the broadcaster?'

'No.'

'Oh well. Listen, I need your advice on a contract with Monopolimedia.'

'Don't. Not with Monopoli. That's the best advice I can give you.'

'I don't have a choice.'

With a heavy heart he agreed to Bernie's offer. There was one bonus, however. With no scripts to edit, Sophie was, ipso facto, redundant. She left to set up her own production outfit with Bruno, her boyfriend.

15 Your Name Here

At Monopolimedia, meanwhile, Bernie was updating his partner.

'Sorted.'

'So you're saying we've got it, now? This *Rough Diamonds* thing?' Jeremy, perched on the edge of Bernie's desk, swung his legs nervously.

'Jake's ironing out the scripts while I tie up the legals. We'll sign after the read-through.'

'What about Sebastian what's-his-name?'

'He goes. Daisy's the one with the contacts.'

'And how much does Helen Quigley know about this?'

'Nothing, at the moment.'

'But when she finds out we're turning *Rough Diamonds* into another soap …?'

'She'll be over the fucking moon. After all, that's what she's good at.'

* * *

After three days of sitting on a bus, looking at nondescript buildings and roads and eating lunch at Pizza Express, Sebastian was beginning to feel like a pensioner on a budget coach party tour of London's most boring sights. But then, suddenly, the technical recce was over and it was time for the read-through.

They gathered in an army barracks on the King's Road, marshalled by sentries armed with assault rifles, beneath a sign reading 'Alert Status: Amber'. Even the army had to supplement its income as best it could. The actors drifted in and assembled in knots by the coffee urn. Trevor William arrived and immediately annexed the big chair at the head of the table. Todd and his ADs appeared in full racing leathers.

Costume department personnel cast an assessing eye over the actors, guesstimating who could be fitted from stock. Angel distributed copies of the script and chatted up the better-looking actors shamelessly. Jassy smiled shyly at no one in particular. Gradually the room filled up.

Phoebe Grolt was there, dressed in a charity shop man's suit, and more nervous even than Sebastian. He gave her an encouraging smile and she nodded back, setting her ear jewellery into motion. She may have tried to smile, too, but if so her face wasn't working. She sat down as far as she could from everyone else in the room, in a corner behind the coffee urn, ready to accept responsibility for episodes two and three.

Episode one was a bastard, with no one standing up to claim paternity. Of Pete Clapp's work barely a word remained, and Pat Quine was never going to accept a shared credit. His agent had been in touch. Despite his extensive rewrite Trevor William didn't seem keen to take the credit, either. The name on the front of the script, Terri Dulswig, was unfamiliar to everyone – unsurprisingly, since it was an anagram of Writers' Guild. No one asked if Terri would be attending, although one actor claimed to have appeared in a play of hers at the King's Head.

There was a lull as the army-issue clock above Trevor's head passed zero hour. Sebastian glanced at the three empty chairs: Helen Quigley, Rick Todge, and Steve Bung had yet to make an appearance. People refilled their coffee cups. Conversation rose, fell, then died altogether. Faces turned to Sebastian. He looked at Trevor William. Trevor William looked right back. Sebastian cleared his throat and got to his feet.

'Let's make a start, shall we? I'm Sebastian Boyle, the producer, and I want to welcome you all to the *Rough Diamonds* read-through. Let's just go round the table briefly and introduce ourselves.'

They'd got as far as 'Dale Whitney, playing the paedophile sexton' when there was a burst of laughter and shouting outside.

The doors flew open and a column of Monopoli personnel marched in. Sebastian didn't recognise any of them – the head of development, his development executive, or his three script executives. There may have been an executive production executive in there too. They gathered round a subsidiary table and continued talking among themselves, ignoring Angel as she passed round additional copies of the script.

Sebastian's mobile rang with a message: Rick Todge, executive producer, sent his apologies. No news of Steve Bung or Helen Quigley. Sebastian decided to begin, again, and nodded to Trevor William.

If the script survived the read-through, it could survive anything. Most of the actors seemed to make it a point of honour to offer a sort of anti-performance, one that reserved their right to any number of later rethinks. Two or three gave it everything they'd got. The stage directions were read in a flat, deadpan monotone by Todd, his twangy Afrikaans drawl filling the room with vivid evocations of crime scenes and camera moves, while Trevor William gazed pointedly out of the window.

Angel was reading in for Helen Quigley, and giving the big speech in scene twenty the full benefit of her deep, throbbing voice when the door opened and Helen Quigley herself stepped into the room. Everyone looked up except Angel, who was well into character and didn't seem to notice the interruption. Helen Quigley raked her with an icy glance, then offered the company a tight smile and mouthed 'Sorry I'm late' in best panto fashion.

At last Angel stopped, but it seemed she wasn't going to surrender her chance of glory without a fight. The next line scripted for Dan Beatty was voiced simultaneously in Helen Quigley's light alto and Angel's rasping contralto. She looked up, surprised to hear the competition, then blushed violently as she recognised Helen Quigley. Helen gave a shit-eating smile and proceeded with the speech while Angel stared at the table.

They staggered through the first episode and got to the closing scene, where Dan/Helen discovers the body of the baby, and Todd intoned 'The end'. There was a brief lull, then an explosion of chairs scraping, lighters torching cigarettes, nervous laughter, and a stampede for the coffee urn. Sebastian glanced across at the Monopoli table, where the script team sat in a huddle, conferring in undertones. There was no sign of Steve Bung. He grabbed a cup of coffee and took it across to where Helen Quigley was standing, apart from the others.

'No thanks, I don't drink coffee.'

'I'm so glad you could make it, Helen.'

'I've never missed a read-through.'

'Only I wasn't sure you'd got the script.'

'Well, here I am.'

'Yes.' Sebastian noticed the coffee in his hand and drank a mouthful. 'Urgh.'

'That bad? When I said I don't drink coffee, I mean I don't drink the kind you get at read-throughs.' She smiled, for the first time.

'Wise decision.'

'Do you know where Steve Bung is?'

'I'm sure he'll be here soon.'

'Episode two! Episode two now, please, everybody.' Angel had finished laying a new script – still warm from the photo-copier – in front of each place at the table, plus a stack for Monopoli, and was shooing reluctant actors back to their places. Sebastian watched Helen sit down and pick up her copy. He nibbled his thumb nervously. Episode one had been quite a polished piece of work, as it should have been, combining as it did the talents of Pete Clapp, Pat Quine, and Trevor William. Sophie had been kept well away from it. The next two scripts were a different story. Both were written by Phoebe Grolt, with additional input from Sophie, and most recently they'd benefitted from ten days of intensive, cutting-edge script editing by the Monopoli team. Sebastian glanced over at Phoebe behind the coffee urn. He could see her leafing through her script, a look of bewilderment on her face. He was wondering why when Todd began declaiming the opening stage directions, the script supervisor clicked her stopwatch, and they were off.

Very soon Sebastian was nearly as bewildered as Phoebe. He didn't recognise the script, and it was clear she didn't either. Sebastian felt twin lasers burning into his head and looked up to see the director staring across with narrowed eyes. Shaking his head by a few millimetres Sebastian looked across to where the Monopoli personnel were following the reading with every sign of keen enjoyment. Phoebe's vampires had made a comeback, but the tone had shifted considerably. Gothic had been replaced by camp. The dark, violent undertow of the series format and the much-reworked episode one was giving way to a grinning, brainless, pre-watershed pastiche. Where there had been darkness, now there was light. Where there had been grit, now there was whimsy. Episode two was a totally different show.

Helen Quigley faltered, then stopped. She looked up at Sebastian. Before she could speak he stood up quickly and called a ten-minute break, then retreated to the far corner of the room pursued by Trevor William, Helen Quigley, and Phoebe Grolt.

'What is this, Sebastian?'

'What's going on?'

'I didn't write this!'

'Wait. Listen. Somehow the wrong script has been given out. Angel!' She hurried over. 'Where did you get this?'

'Jake Smith brought it with him.'

'Who?'

'Monopoli's head of development.'

Sebastian glanced at Daisy. She avoided his eye. So that was the Jake Smith she'd been writing to.

'I see. Thank you, Angel.' She moved back to the rest of the group.

'If we do this script, I walk.'

'And me.'

'And me!'

'Okay. Just listen. We'll start again, with the right scripts. Maybe by then Steve Bung will have arrived.' He went over to the Monopoli table.

'Hi. Jake Smith? I'm Sebastian.'

'Yeah, I know.' Jake stroked his goatee. 'What's the hold-up?'

'There's a problem with the script.'

'Yeah? What?'

'The writer didn't write it. The director won't direct it. Helen Quigley won't act it. So there'll be a few minutes delay while we get the proper one over here.'

'Says who?'

'Me.'

'And what about the producer?'

'I *am* the producer.'

'Nah. Daisy's the producer. Aren't you, Daisy?' She had sidled up and now stood at Jake Smith's side.

'Well, good luck, Daisy. You've finally got yourself the job title. All you need now is the job to go with it.'

'What do you mean?' She looked anxious and uncertain – just like the face he glimpsed sometimes in the mirror, Sebastian thought.

'This is my production, Daisy.' David O. Selznick would have been proud of him. 'Find your own.'

'But Monopolimedia are in charge now. You did a deal.'

'I haven't signed anything yet. I think all of you had better leave now. You too, Daisy. I hope they've given you an office.'

'Now listen, tosh –' began Jake Smith, when Todd's short but impressive form interposed itself between them.

'Not in here, please, gents. Outside in the car park, by all means, where I'll be delighted to take on anyone who fancies it.'

He gave Jake a shove.

'No? Then off you go.' Jake Smith opened his mouth, closed it again, picked up his bag and strode towards the door, followed after a moment by his entourage.

'Thanks, Todd.'

'No worries. Let's get on with it, shall we?'

They handed out the scripts, Phoebe's this time, and in a few minutes were up to their ears in the authentically dark world of *Rough Diamonds*. For fifty minutes DS Dan Beatty stalked the netherworld of Phoebe's unloosed imagination, here and there reined in by Trevor William's restraining hand. Helen was delivering her penultimate final speech when the door opened again and Steve Bung launched himself into the read-through.

'Fuck! Sorry.' He yanked out a chair and sat down noisily. Everyone turned over the last page of his or her script, Helen did her last line and Todd said 'The end.'

'Late, am I?'

'Hello, Steve. Sebastian Boyle. Producer.'

'I remember. Where's Jason Prynne?'

'He's in the next block.'

'Hello, darling.' This was to Helen, who greeted Steve with a coy smile. 'Couldn't miss your performance.'

'You did, ninety-nine per cent of it.'

'Bloody hard getting out of the office at the moment.'

'We did hear something.'

'Did you?' Steve looked surprised. 'Bloody builders put a new door in and forgot to unlock it first. Turned out they'd left the key in East Molesey. How did you know?'

'Steve, can I get you a cup of coffee? No tea, I'm afraid.'

'Yeah, large cap, no chocolate.'

'Okay. Right.' Sebastian signalled to Gus, resplendent in her partially unzipped Team Honda leathers. She came over and Steve's eyes popped halfway out of his head as he took in the sight.

'Christ on a bike! Who are you playing?'

'I'm Gus. I'm not an actress, I'm a runner.'

'Really?'

'And now I'm going to run for your coffee.' She flashed him a brilliant smile and sashayed to the door.

'Blinder!'

'Very keen girl.' This was Todd. 'Very serious. Pretty fast on the track, too.'

'Yeah, of course. Anyway, how did the read-through go? How was Jason?'

'Jason's not in this block, if you remember –'

'Course I do. And the lovely Helen? Bet she was good!' Helen Quigley adjusted her smile, which had slipped a bit during the Gus incident, and cranked it up a notch or two.

'Brilliant. Wasn't she, Phoebe?' Phoebe had sidled nervously up, and Sebastian steered her towards the executive. 'This is Phoebe Grolt, writer of eps two and three.'

'Hi Phoebe. So Helen, what are you going to wear for this show?'

'Wear? I don't really know yet.'

'Maybe racing leathers? Looks bloody sexy. What do you think, Sebastian?'

'Well, I think Helen would look great in anything –'

'Or nothing! Eh, Helen? Just kidding, go on.'

'But her character doesn't ride a motorbike in the show …'

'Ah, don't be so literal.' He turned to Helen. 'Don't you hate that? Producers can be so unimaginative sometimes. Oh well, your call, of course, Sebastian. So long as it does the business and pulls in ten million we'll be happy, won't we, Helen?' Helen smiled non-committally. 'Anyway, got to go now, got another meeting in town.'

'Do you want to take the scripts with you? They've changed a bit.'

'Nah, bike 'em round to the office, I can't be lugging scripts in and out of taxis. See you soon, darling.' This to Helen. 'Let's do lunch at the Ivy, get Sebastian here to give you the afternoon off. Bye.' And he was gone.

Gus returned with the large cappuccino. She shrugged and handed it to Todd, who popped the top and swigged it down.

'What kind of bike do you ride?' Phoebe asked Gus nervously.

'RC 30.'

'Totally mental classic thoroughbred racer,' Todd explained. 'Half the time it's off the road because she's dropped it on a corner and Gus has to ride on the back of someone else's. Not that they complain.' Gus smiled and turned to Phoebe.

'Do you ride?'

Phoebe blushed. 'Just a scooter.'

'Scooters are cool. Which one?'

Phoebe told her.

'Good choice. I've got to go now, but see you on the shoot, maybe?' Wide-eyed, Phoebe watched Gus walk away.

The room was still full of people, eating the sandwiches Angel had produced and standing in knots, chatting. Trevor William talked intensely to actors while the costume department moved swiftly among them, booking fittings and shopping expeditions. The assistant directors handed out rehearsal time-tables and discussed props. Sebastian smiled. They'd survived the read-through, everyone was doing what they were supposed to be doing. For the moment it was all going fine.

'What did you think, Dougal?'

'Can we talk outside, dear boy? I'm dying to light this thing.'

They walked downstairs to the parade ground and were soon enveloped in a blue haze.

'Went okay, didn't it?'

Dougal sucked at his pipe.

'You're joking, I suppose?'

'Why?'

'Have you perhaps forgotten that in the course of the read-through you de-financed the production?'

'But how could I have done anything else?'

'I hope you've got a Plan B up your sleeve, because as of two hours ago we're broke.'

'We'll just have to ring round all the banks again –'

'Forgive me interrupting, Sebastian, but you've already tried that. You have two options. One, fold the production, at least for the time being. Maybe you can stand everyone down and put it on ice while you come up with something.'

'If we close down we'll never start up again.'

'I agree. Two, you come up with enough yourself to tide us over for at least the next two weeks.' He clamped his jaw on the pipe and puffed grimly. 'By the end of today.'

* * *

As usual Sebastian was struck by how different Jemma looked in her white coat. This time she was wearing protective goggles and a face mask as well. Her appearance was strange and a little intimidating.

'I tried to phone you but they kept saying you were busy.'

'They're right, I'm in the middle of a root canal. What's so urgent?'

'It's the house. Can you take that thing off?'

'What's happened to it?'

'Nothing. Yet. But we may need – is there somewhere else we can discuss this?' Sebastian was painfully conscious of the receptionist, craning forward to catch their conversation.

'Not now, no, I should be back in there, doing Mr Alston. Can't it wait?'

'How long till you're free?'

'Come back at half past two.'

In the meantime Sebastian went round to the bank and explained the position to an assistant manager.

When she heard his plan Jemma wasn't angry. She was incandescent. She said it was completely unfair to pull her out of her work at zero notice to do something that needed to be properly discussed first. It was tantamount to holding a gun to her head. Unfair, unreasonable, unacceptable. Sebastian was a selfish pig. A financial incompetent. Hopeless.

Sebastian agreed. What else could he do? It was all true. But he still needed the money, and her signature to get the loan.

They went to the bank, Jemma signed and returned to her surgery without a word. Sebastian spared a thought for her afternoon patients.

* * *

Back at Brunt Productions Sebastian embarked on an orgy of cheque signing. His wrist was sore by the end and his signature looked like a childish attempt at forgery. As Dougal lit his pipe, Sebastian noticed how the flaring match illuminated his hollow cheeks and eye sockets, making him look about a hundred.

'Are you okay, Dougal?'

'A little tired, dear boy. But at least we're through today. Now all we have to do is make the damned thing.' With a parting wave he set off on the long journey back to his island in the Thames.

'Drink?' It was Trevor William. 'Or are you in a hurry to get home?' Sebastian certainly wasn't. His only hope was to slip in quietly once Jemma was asleep.

'Where shall we go?'

The Mason's Arms was a cavernous place somehow over-looked when the tide of themed drinking-places swept over west London. It retained the sticky red carpet, smoke-stained 3D wallpaper, even a complete set of those cards behind the bar discouraging requests for credit and questioning the sanity of the staff. Eventually the stony-faced barman twitched his chin to indicate he was ready to take their order.

'Tomato juice.'

'Right. A tomato juice and a pint of bitter, please.'

The barman poured the drinks, then pressed a switch beside the till. A barrage of Limp Bizkit broke over their heads.

'Hey! Do we have to have that on?'

'Customers like.'

'We're the only customers in here.'

Sulkily the barman turned the music down a fraction then retreated to the inaccessible end of the bar and began reading a paper. Trevor and Sebastian relocated to the least loud part of the pub.

'Well. Here we go, then. Cheers.' He raised his glass.

'Cheers.' Trevor sipped his tomato juice. 'So what are you going to do?'

'About what?'

'Monopoli.'

'They're out of the picture. It's just us now.'

'And the financing?'

'It's all sorted. Don't worry about the money.'

'I won't.' He finished his tomato juice. 'Couple of question marks over the crew.'

'Who?'

'Locations. Has Billy sorted out the police station?'

'Not yet.'

'He'd better not leave it any longer. And make-up.'

'Katya? She's lovely.'

'I hear she drinks. And bitches. I don't want my actors arriving on set unhappy.'

'Let's see, shall we. Any others?'

'That's it for now.' He picked up his jacket. 'I'll be rehearsing in town so I won't see you for a few days.'

'Oh?'

'Todd knows how to reach me.' Once again he was gone. Sebastian abandoned the rest of his beer, which was sulphurous and flat.

He got home late, but not late enough. Jemma had waited up for him and was now furious she'd been kept up so long, on top of still being furious about the loan. It was very discouraging, arguing with someone so completely in the right. Finally they were both too tired to go round the circuit once more and went to bed instead, with a last bout of duvet-tugging and angry sighs.

Sebastian lay on his back in the dark and watched the lights from the night bus sweep across the bedroom ceiling.

16   Don't Take This the Wrong Way

The next morning was Saturday, and Sebastian slept in. By the time he got up, Jemma had already disappeared into her own weekend schedule. Slobbing down to the kitchen in his dressing gown, Sebastian rooted around for something to eat, without success.

On his way back from the faux-French café with some reasonably authentic fake croissants Sebastian noticed the lilac car, and the girl in the driver's seat. She got out. It was Daisy.

'Can I come in?'

Sebastian looked at her. Daisy's eyes were red and puffy. He held open the front door and followed her inside.

Once they were in the kitchen Daisy began to sob. Sebastian got her to sit down at the table and made them both some coffee.

'I'm sorry, I shouldn't have come.'

'Have a tissue. No, probably not. Why did you?'

'I had to talk to you. I've been so stupid, those people at Monopoli are such shits.'

'Didn't you guess they would be? Besides, you haven't exactly behaved like a flower fairy yourself.'

Daisy blew her nose, noisily. 'You're right, go on, I deserve it. It's all such a mess.'

'Why did you do it, Daisy?'

'They promised me I could produce it.'

'What about loyalty?'

'They said they'd back me up.'

'I meant, loyalty to me.'

'Oh. Well, I thought you owed some to me, too. I could do it, you know. Producing.'

'I'm sure you could. But not by stealing someone else's show.'

'But that's exactly what *you've* done.'

'What do you mean?'

'*Rough Diamonds* is Albie's project, after all. You're just –'

'Just what?'

'Well, you make gardening programmes, don't you? I mean, I'm sure they're very good, I wouldn't know, I don't have a garden.'

Sebastian could see her point.

'Look, you've helped a lot, and I do feel sorry for you. But no one ever said you could produce *Rough Diamonds*.'

'I thought you'd see it was a good idea.'

'No. I'm sorry.' He poured out the coffee. 'So what are you going to do now?'

'I want to come back and work at Brunt Productions again.'

'Full marks for chutzpah.'

'You know how much I can help you.'

'But can I trust you?'

'Yes.' She fixed Sebastian with her eyes, which for the first time he noticed were a striking blue-green colour.

'Have you got new contact lenses?'

'And I'll be your script editor again. And do whatever you say.' Daisy hadn't shifted her gaze.

'Well, I do really need a script editor at the moment, as it happens.'

'Where are you going?'

Sebastian returned with a memo from Brit TV's executive producer. Rick Todge had faxed to say he was unhappy with the script situation. He was instructing Sebastian to postpone the shoot.

Daisy put down the sheet of paper. 'But why now?'

'God knows. Because he's only just read the scripts, I expect.'

'It's that Gothic thing again. Jake kept banging on about that. How it wasn't Brit TV, and they'd never wear it. Though I think he was really more concerned about the foreign sales. You know, too dark and gritty to make money abroad.'

'You think Monopoli are behind this?'

'For some reason they really seem to have it in for you.'

Out in the hall the front door banged open, and a heavy gym bag hit the floor. Jemma came to the kitchen door and looked at Sebastian enquiringly.

'This is Daisy. Daisy, my wife Jemma.' They exchanged a guarded hello. Daisy was still dabbing at her nose with a tissue, while Jemma glowed pinkly from the oxygenated blood coursing around her body.

'Well, I'll leave you two to work out whatever crisis you're in the middle of,' Jemma said. She climbed the stairs.

'Let's sort this out on Monday. We can't do anything until we get the notes, anyway.'

'You mean I can have my job back?'

'Your script editing job, yes.'

Daisy threw her arms around Sebastian and kissed him. Her eyes, he noticed, really were a most extraordinary colour. He squeezed her back and she smiled. 'See you on Monday, then,' she said, as she left the kitchen. Jemma was watching from the stairs as the front door closed.

'Daisy's my script editor.'

'I know. You've often mentioned her.'

'And I had to let her go but now I've taken her back.'

'So I see. I'm going to have my bath now.'

'What time should we leave for the play?'

But there was no answer.

After her bath Jemma went out again and Sebastian didn't see her until it was time to leave for the National. The Cavalier had been resurrected by the local garage and they drove there in silence, finding a parking space right behind the theatre, which meant they'd arrived too early. They stood at the bar while the Venezuelan cabaret band did their worst. Eventually Jemma put down her white wine and turned to face her husband.

'It's been years since we've seen *Three Sisters*,' he said.

'We've got to talk.'

'I've said I'm sorry. I wouldn't have taken out the loan if there was any other way, I'm going to pay it back in the next fortnight.'

'It's not that.'

'You can't seriously be jealous of Daisy. You know how she's been giving me the runaround. In a work way, I mean.'

'Not that, either.'

'What, then? That near miss at the lights?'

'I'm seeing someone.'

'What?'

'He's called Graham. He's an orthodontist.'

'Hang on. You mean –'

'Sebastian!' An arm snaked around his shoulders and gripped him tightly. 'I didn't have you pegged as a theatregoer. Who's this?' Jason Prynne lurched towards Jemma with a louche smile. 'Your lovely wife?'

'Jemma, Jason Prynne.'

'How do you do.'

'I do okay, actually, I really do. I'm afraid your husband and I got up to some tricks together down in the South of France.'

Jemma gave him a startled look.

'Yeah, up till all hours, boozing and gossiping, got into a fight with this Korean guy –'

'I think I'd left by then.'

'Really? No, I distinctly remember you braining him with that bottle of Cointreau.'

Jemma was staring at Sebastian in alarm.

'I think I'd have remembered that. Are you performing tonight?'

'What, here? That's a laugh. I haven't been asked onto a stage in London for ten years at least.'

'Oh. I thought perhaps –'

'They can't handle it, y'see. Want everything tidy, predictable.

Commuter belt drama, don't frighten the horses. What are you going to see?'

'*Three Sisters*.'

'Christ! How can you bear it?'

'I happen to like Chekhov,' put in Jemma, crisply. By now she'd completed her assessment: drunk ... egomaniac ... man.

'Chekhov, sure. But what about those Blackwells?' he shouted. In this production each sister was a member of the same acting family. 'Christ, it's grisly!' Several people had by now paused in their chatting and G&T-sipping to watch this exchange. Possibly one or two recognised Jason's face, or were fans of *Danger!* from the Eighties or even, God help them, *Harlem Heist* (by now available on low-rent cable).

'We were just going in,' Sebastian said.

'The bell hasn't even rung yet, have another drink.' Jason dug him in the ribs. 'I seem to remember you know how to put it away.'

'You must be mixing me up with someone else.'

'Whatever you say. Same again?' He elbowed his way through to the bar waving a fifty-pound note and calling 'Make way for a thirsty actor!'

'What did you get up to in Cannes?'

'I told you, I made a bad speech, tried to stop Jason drinking himself to death, and had an early night. Maybe I should have left him to it. Anyway, never mind that, what were you saying?'

'I'll tell you later.'

'I think you should tell me now.'

'Well, well, well. What have we here? Who's unlucky enough to have his pearls scattered before you tonight?'

'I beg your pardon?' Jemma looked through narrowed eyes at the figure in stonewashed denim. Sebastian felt it was really too much for one night. He didn't even like the theatre, it was Jemma who was on the mailing list.

'Jemma, this is Pete Clapp. A writer.'

'Really. What do you write?'

'Drama. Something television and the people who work in it don't have much time for. Isn't that right, Sebastian? So you come here for it instead.'

'Pete wrote for *Rough Diamonds.*'

'I created *Rough Diamonds.* Before Sebastian here had me thrown off. What was it he said? "Not enough light and shade, more like dark and shade."'

'Shall we talk about this later?'

'How does Chekhov measure up to your standards, Sebastian?'

'Well, it was Jemma's choice, really, but –'

'Would he get a commission from Mel Gioconda? Or Steve Bung?'

'I think you'd have to ask them.'

'Here you go, mate.' Jason shoved what looked like a triple vodka into Sebastian's hand, and drained the one in his own. 'Who's this?'

'Pete Clapp, writer. Jason Prynne, actor. Listen, we've got to go in now, maybe we can meet up in the interval.' He grabbed Jemma and almost threw her into the auditorium, but not before Jason took his glass and drained that too. The last Sebastian saw as he disappeared into the stalls was Jason clasping Pete Clapp in a bear hug.

It was hard to discuss Jemma's news inside the theatre, surrounded as they were by tweed-jacketed Chekhovians, up like them from the suburbs, so Sebastian buried himself in his programme and waited for the lights to go down. First, though, there was an expectant hush as a man appeared in front of the curtains. 'We regret that, due to indisposition, the part of Olga will be played by Cornelia Smith.' Ripple of consternation. 'The part of Masha will be played by Bryony Teitelbaum.' Mutterings of disappointment. 'And we are very grateful to Alice

Toaster for stepping into the part of Irina at such short notice.'
Rumble of rebellious anger.

'I paid to see *Three Sisters*, not three understudies,' someone
shouted from the back of the stalls. The man on the stage
glared. The muttering subsided, and the house lights went
down. The audience settled back unhappily in its seats.

Probably Sebastian wouldn't have remembered much
anyway, even if the entire cast had comprised nothing but
Blackwells. As it was he found it hard to concentrate on the
lacklustre production. What exactly had Jemma said about the
orthodontist? Graham, was it? To add to his distraction Sebastian
could hear muffled shouts from the foyer. He imagined Pete
Clapp and Jason Prynne pounding one another with a whole
range of liqueur bottles and the thought gave him more
satisfaction than anything that was happening onstage.

As the lights came up for the interval Sebastian whispered
to Jemma 'Let's go,' and she nodded. They took the emergency
exit that avoided the bar, and after exploring various concrete
staircases blocked by alarmed fire doors at last found their way
out of the building. They sat in the dark car and talked.

'I don't want to go into any details. I just wanted you to
know.'

'How long's it been going on? Are you going to live with
him? Why?'

'I said, I don't want to discuss the details.'

'What do we do, then? Just go on as usual?'

'I suppose so.'

'But – how can we? What's going to happen to us?'

'I don't know.'

Sebastian drove home, and his driving was unusually careful
and considerate, as though he was on his test. He slowed to let
a gang of drunk teenagers stagger across Battersea Rise. He
used his mirror and indicators with exemplary thoroughness. He
really was in a bad way.

At home Jemma undressed in the bathroom, having locked the door first. By the time Sebastian came to bed she'd already switched off the light. They wished each other goodnight, politely. Sebastian thought to himself, quite distinctly, 'My marriage is over.' It sounded peculiar in his head. Then he thought 'Fuck those Blackwells. And Pete Clapp. And Jason Prynne. And Graham, whoever he is. And the rest of them.'

Then he went straight to sleep.

* * *

It was still dark when Sebastian woke. He got up quietly, took his clothes and dressed in the bathroom. Leaving a note for Jemma he drove to work.

At six o'clock on Sunday morning the roads were empty and slick with dew. Fifteen minutes later he was parking in Acton Studios. He fired up the computer in his office and started on the pile of scripts. Once it got to nine o'clock he phoned Daisy and asked if she wanted to join him.

Reading the scripts with Rick Todge's memo in front of him, Sebastian couldn't help noticing how often the word 'dark' seemed to come up. He was on the edge of losing his nerve by the time Daisy arrived.

She was wearing clothes Sebastian had never seen her in before, old jeans that made her seem much younger than the focused, ambitious woman he was used to. She was carrying two large cappuccinos from the place across the road and a bag of doughnuts. They picnicked on the floor in a sea of script pages.

'What did you think of the Monopoli version?'

'Not as good.'

'But all the same you were prepared to go with it?'

Daisy shrugged. 'I thought we could change some of it back. But in a way, you know, they're right.'

'What way?'

'Well, at the moment the series is a turn-off. Isn't that what Rick Todge's memo is about?'

'It's original.'

'Same thing.'

'Too cynical. I don't think you believe that. It's Jake Smith talking.'

Daisy smiled. 'Well, as he would say, you're making it for the audience, not yourself.'

'Yes, but he's not making it for the audience. He really *is* making it for himself – and not as a viewer, or even as a producer clocking up credits he feels proud of. Jake Smith and Bernie Gassman and the whole lot of them are churning out stuff for themselves as shareholders and highly-paid executives of a media company. To them it's just product.'

'Oh, please. I sense a speech about The Golden Age of Television can't be far off.'

'Okay. You're right. After all, I'm no different, except that I'm much less good at it than they are.'

'That's right, go on, now the self-pity.'

'God, Daisy. Why are you being so tough on me?'

'When you're being so nice you me, you mean? Would you rather I nodded and agreed and thought to myself, "What a tosser"?'

'No.'

'Well then. It's just that I've heard so many times from so many people how television isn't what it used to be, the heart's gone out of it, it's no fun any more, there's no creativity, it's all about ratings and bums on seats and profits. And always from people in their thirties, or forties, or fifties. It's almost as if you don't want anyone else to enjoy working in TV. And I do enjoy it. When I'm middle-aged it'll be my turn to say how exciting it all was at the end of the twentieth century, when we made such great stuff and got off on doing it. Don't you see? There's a never-ending golden age and a never-ending age of crud and they're both now. You decide which one you live in.'

Sebastian looked at her carefully. 'So which one does *Rough Diamonds* belong to?'

'We can't know that. We can only do the best we can. The rest isn't our business.'

'Let's get on with it, then.'

Daisy and Sebastian worked right through Sunday. They phoned for pizza and again around ten o'clock for kebabs from the Greek joint over the road, and drank a bottle of Demestica. It was quite festive – certainly a lot more fun than Saturday night at the National Theatre. Possibly it was the effect of the Greek red but Sebastian began to feel Daisy might have a point about fun and telly and the golden age and crud. They summed up over a shared sheftalia and the dregs of the wine.

'We like what Phoebe's done. But we can't ignore Brit TV. So these changes address their concerns without undermining what's good about the scripts. Agreed?' Daisy's finger was poised above the computer keyboard.

'Agreed.'

Daisy clicked on *Accept all*. There was a brief rattle from the hard disk as it did its work. Then Daisy clicked again and the laser printer began squirting fresh script pages into its hopper.

'Thanks for helping today, Daisy.'

'It's the least I could do. In the circumstances.'

'Thanks anyway.'

It was empty and silent again by the time Sebastian arrived back in East Sheen, almost like a continuation of the early morning journey. He felt as though a day had been stolen from him. No, that wasn't it: more as if he'd been given an extra one, a day apart. Sebastian realised with surprise it was the first time he'd actually enjoyed himself since the project had begun. Driving through the slick streets he'd felt sure there was a lesson here to be learned, but as he locked the Cavalier and lumbered up to the front door of his dark house he was still struggling to work out what it might be.

17 Trust Me

The rehearsal room was large and nondescript. One wall was lined with metal-framed windows overlooking a busy four-lane highway. Fluorescent lights. No furniture except for a battered old wooden table and six stacking metal chairs in one corner. On the table were scripts, pencils, disposable coffee cups.

Helen Quigley, expensively dressed, stood reading a script. Trevor William, dark and small, sprawled in one of the chairs, watching her. The light from the windows was low. It was late in the day.

The door banged as the last young actor in ripped jeans exited. Helen walked to the window and stood there smoking, looking out at the rush-hour traffic. There was a long silence.

'So there you are.' She blew out smoke and looked out of the window. 'That's how I feel.'

'It's up to you.'

'You saw how they treated me. So what if I've never played any part beside Rikki? It's not as though I've had no offers. I went to drama school, same as them. I just got lucky straight off, and never looked back.'

'They're jealous.'

'Too bloody right they are. That little tosser Stuart would tear his own arm off for a part in *Dalston Square*.'

'And they've only seen you in that one role, so how can they tell what you can do?'

'I've done all sorts with Rikki, anyone'll tell you. She's had two abortions, a break-in at the shop, road rage, a lesbian affair with Charlene, a baby, suspected ovarian cysts, attempted rape, been framed for Delroy's murder, accessory after the fact to shoplifting and mugged twice, to say nothing of two marriages and a teenage boyfriend and the crack episode they never showed. There's not much can happen to a woman hasn't happened to Rikki.'

'You could try speaking slower.'

'What?'

'Speak slower. Take your time.'

'What's wrong with the way I talk?'

'Nothing. But it's not *Dalston Square*. You can ease up. The audience will stay with you.'

'I don't think much of that Stuart, as a matter of fact.'

'He'll be fine.'

'Will he? I'll kill him if he tries popping his eyes like that at me during a take.'

'He won't.'

'How do you know?'

'Trust me.'

'That's just it, isn't it? I've got to. You're the director. And it's single camera, I know what that means, even if I haven't done any before. You can make me look like shit if you want to.'

'Why would I want to?'

'Or you can help.'

'Yes, I can.'

'Don't do me from underneath, okay? It makes my neck look fat.'

'You'll be fine, and you'll look great.'

'Yeah, I bet you say that to everyone. How you going to make that Colin look great?'

'You don't know how I'm going to shoot it yet.'

* * *

Back in Acton Studios Dougal was humming like a top. He was on the phone all day long, barking and cajoling, while his fingers did their rapid dance over the computer keyboard. A map on the wall showed the production base in Acton and fanning out from it clusters of coloured marker-pins, one for each location, like fallout from a dirty bomb.

'Nearly there, dear boy, nearly there.'

'Have you got a list?'

'A list? No.'

'Could you ask Billy to do one, please – what locations we've found, what we're still looking for, how much we're paying.'

'I'm sure he has it in hand.'

It was a delicate area, but Sebastian's earlier reservations about Billy and his cast-iron hair and smile had been reactivated by something Daisy had said. 'Jake Smith was happy to leave most of the crew alone, when he took over, except for Billy. Apparently he did a job for Monopoli in the early days and it didn't work out.' It was a concern Todd shared.

'Billy Locations is a flake, yes or no?'

'I don't know, Todd. What do you think?'

'Flake. Definite. Where's our police station?'

'I thought you'd seen it.'

'No way. Day after the recce, he said. Been asking every day since. Have you tried to get the man on his mobile? Funny how wherever he is there's no signal.'

Sebastian tried Billy's phone. He got the 'Please try again later' message.

'Dougal. When did you last speak to Billy?'

'I left a message for him only yesterday, dear boy. Why?'

'But when did you actually speak to him?'

No one had seen Billy since the recce. Dougal looked a little shaken.

'Leave it to me, I know where to find him.'

Sebastian was wondering how to break the news to Phoebe of a particularly bold script change Trevor William was proposing when Dougal asked to have a word. Sebastian went back into the office and Dougal closed the door.

'He's in Jamaica.'

'What?'

'Billy is working on a feature film. In Jamaica.'

'Oh my God.'

'I'm sorry, it's my fault.'

'He's just left us high and dry? Didn't even bother to tell us?'

'He said something about not having been paid. Not that that's any excuse, of course.'

'And his locations? His deals?'

'I'm starting to go through them now.'

An hour later Dougal looked, if anything, worse. The locations were flapping in the wind. And *Rough Diamonds* was now three days away from shooting in the first one.

'Jesus Christ, Dougal. This is a disaster.'

'Up to a point, dear boy. Better to think of it as an opportunity to exercise our crisis management skills.'

'Dougal –'

'I know. It's my responsibility. I'll sort it out, pull in some favours if I have to.'

Sebastian left him busy on the phone. Locations, locations, locations. As he stepped out of the office Daisy wordlessly handed him a trade magazine.

BUNG BUSTED

DRAMA CHIEF QUIZZED IN SHARE SCANDAL

TV drama's Mr Big is at home on "gardening leave" following allegations of illicit share dealing.

Reporters investigating for Channel programme *Where's the Wonga?* claim to have uncovered the dumping of shares by TV executives hours before the release of an internal report which downgraded Brit TV's advertising revenue forecasts by more than 30%.

Allegedly, by far the biggest seller was Steve Bung, Brit TV's controller of drama. A larger-than-life figure, Bung has contradicted the stereotype of the grey management suit. Parties thrown on his private yacht have become legendary in the business, along with a reputation for fast decisions and slow lunches. His wife Samantha, 26, is the latest in a line of comely blondes who have succumbed to Bung's charms.

Widely regarded as the industry's best drama head, Bung is known for not pulling his punches. Last month his description of The Channel's autumn schedule as "a bargain-basement bunch of bollocks" was widely quoted in the trade press.

Although his job at Brit TV is believed to be highly paid, Bung owes his wealth more to an early investment in a mobile phone company in his native Australia that netted him several million pounds, as well as a substantial stake in an online betting service.

Brit TV are refusing to comment on the allegations, and Bung himself has not returned calls. In his absence drama decisions are being made by his acting deputy, Richard Todge.

Sebastian had barely finished reading the article when the phone rang.

'Hello, Rick.'

'Richard to you.'

'Hello, Richard.'

'Never mind that. What about these scripts?'

'What about them? Richard.'

'Don't get lairy with me. Where are the changes I ordered?'

'You've got them.'

'No I haven't.'

'We biked them round first thing on Monday.'

'Well, I haven't seen them.'

'Okay, we'll bike round another set now.'

'You just do that, then we'll talk again.' And he hung up. Already Sebastian was missing Steve Bung, badly. He just had time to shout for Daisy when the phone went again. This time it was Jemma.

'We need to talk.'

'Yes, we do. Can it be this evening?'

'I'm out at my yoga class.'

'Oh. Yes. Well, when you get back?'

'I think we should meet now. It's almost lunchtime. Can you come over?'

'It's a bit tricky.'

'I understand, this is only your marriage, what's that compared to a TV programme?'

'We're in the middle of a crisis at the moment.'

'This is the problem, you see, Sebastian.'

'Two crises, actually.'

'Three. Your marriage is in crisis as well, in case you hadn't noticed. I'm giving you the chance to do something about it. If you'd rather get on with making more pap for the illiterate masses, go ahead.' Sebastian had been about to say that it wasn't pap for the masses, *Rough Diamonds* was shaping up to be a groundbreaking piece of drama, but it was too late. She'd hung up.

He arrived at the surgery only five minutes late, and the receptionist had a message for him. Sebastian was to meet 'them' at the café up the street. Did she smirk slightly as she delivered it, or was it just his paranoia, sharpened by recent events? However confusing Sebastian's marriage was to him, to a dental receptionist in East Sheen it was an open book.

A tall man with a puzzled frown stood up as Sebastian threaded his way towards Jemma's table at the back of the café.

'This is Graham. Graham, Sebastian.'

'Hi.' He held out his hand. It seemed churlish not to take it. Sebastian muttered something all-purpose.

'I thought you two should meet.'

'Why? Are we going to play poker for you?' Jemma sighed with irritation. Graham pushed his glasses further up the bridge of his nose. 'Sorry. So, Graham. Jemma tells me you're an orthodontist.'

'That's right.'

'And that you're having an affair.' Jemma closed her eyes. Graham looked startled.

'We are?'

'According to Jemma. Romance between the root canals.'

'Really?'

Jemma decided to intervene. 'Graham's a friend. He knows we've been having some problems. I asked him to come and meet you because I didn't want there to be any misunderstandings.'

'A friend?'

'A friend.'

'Well, I think I've already got more misunderstandings than I came with. What kind of friend, exactly?'

'The kind you can talk to. The kind you can discuss your problems with.'

'Oh. Not the kind you go to bed with, then.'

An old lady at the next table turned slowly round, cup held in mid-air, and scanned the table thoroughly before returning to her own friend to share her delight at this unlooked-for entertainment.

'One can lead to the other.'

'Of course.'

'Can I say something?'

'I think you should, Graham.'

'I just want to say I've heard all about you.'

'I bet.'

'Jemma's told me what you do.'

'Uh-huh.'

'And I just want to say how much I enjoyed *Inspector Pettigrew*.'

'Oh for Christ's sake, Graham!'

'No, really, Jemma. These things should be said. Men don't talk about their feelings enough.'

'I think you could be the exception that proves the rule, Graham,' Jemma said, rather coldly.

'Well, thank you, Graham. Although of course I didn't produce that, it was my brother-in-law, Albie.'

'You both did a great job. And, speaking for myself, I'm hoping very much that my friendship with Jemma will develop into a full-blown affair.'

'Ah.'

'Thank you for sharing, Graham. Now you can stop. Be a man, keep your feelings to yourself for a change.'

'I just think it's better to be honest. Get things out in the open.'

'Well, some things are better not out in the open.'

'I can't lie to you, Jemma.'

'Perhaps you should practise.'

Sebastian began to feel as though he were the lover and Graham the husband. He even looked like a husband. Was that the way it worked now? Or was it just that any man over thirty without piercings and a Versace wardrobe looked like a husband? Perhaps it was Graham's glasses and earnest, please-don't-misunderstand-me manner? Sebastian hadn't a clue, but found he was longing to get back to the relative clarity of his other crises.

'Come on then, Jemma. Why were you so anxious for me to be here?' Whatever he'd been expecting, it wasn't a male bonding exercise.

'Graham takes me seriously.'

'Graham takes his feelings about you seriously. Is that fair, Graham? There's a difference, Jemma.'

'I don't know what my feelings for you are, Sebastian.'

'Fair enough. I'm not too sure what mine are for you at the moment. I think Graham's streets ahead of both of us.'

'Would you two like some space?'

'No, Graham, that's very kind of you but at home we get more space than you can probably imagine. You hang in there and I'll get back to work, which frankly isn't going very well at this particular moment.'

'I'm sorry to hear that. What are you working on now?'

'Well, it's a copshow with a twist. Starring Helen Quigley.'

'Oh! I love her. I didn't know she'd left *Dalston Square*.'

'Well, she hasn't yet. Not officially. This is strictly confidential. If the tabloids get hold of it …'

'I understand. So, who's she playing in your new programme?'

'Well, she's a detective sergeant who – Jemma?'

But Jemma didn't even pause in her headlong run for the door. Sebastian looked at Graham. He shrugged.

'So, this is more of a leading role for her, I suppose?'

Sebastian nodded. 'Listen, Graham, could we …?'

'Sure, I've got to get back to the surgery too. Why don't we meet up one evening for a drink? You could tell me all about your new – what's it called?'

'*Rough Diamonds.*'

'Is that the title?'

'Yes. Why?'

'Nothing, it just sounds a bit … don't you need the word murder in there somewhere?'

'Not necessarily.'

'Well, it's none of my business. All about *Rough Diamonds.* Tell you what, I'll get Adrienne to come along.'

'Who's Adrienne?'

'In reception, you must have seen her. She wants to train as a hygienist.'

'Well –'

'How about next Friday?'

'I don't know, Graham.'

'I'll call you. Okay? Bye, Sebastian!'

Sebastian saw a taxi at the lights and sprinted for it.

* * *

When he stepped back into the production office Dougal was wreathed in smiles. 'Meet Janine.'

'Hi, Janine'.

'Janine is our new location manager.'

She was young but serious, her hair yanked together in a no-nonsense ponytail. 'Dougal's explained the situation.'

Dougal took Sebastian by the arm and guided him firmly back into their office. 'She's gold dust.'

'Where did you find her?'

'Designer on *Boys in Blue*. Owes me a favour. Says she's the best they've had.'

'So how come she's available?'

Dougal shot him a look. 'You're becoming more and more like a producer.'

'Dougal, now is not a good time for us to fall out. Especially when for once you're in the wrong.'

He gave Sebastian an icy look, then laughed. 'You're right.' Taking his pipe from his pocket Dougal began to dig around in it with a penknife. 'Technically she's got two more weeks on *Boys in Blue*, wrapping it up. In practice she's done and dusted, and she can start right away.'

'I should talk to the producer. Who is it?'

'Benjamin Prike.'

'God. I thought he'd retired.'

'At his age? He's only sixty-six.'

Sebastian was on the point of asking Dougal how old *he* was, but thought better of it. 'Do you know him, then?'

'He used to be my assistant. In the old days. Here, I've got his number.'

There was nothing for it but to call him. Sebastian didn't want to tell Dougal that Benjamin Prike had sacked him from his first ever job in television.

'Yes?' The voice in Sebastian ear sounded as if it were coming from a long way away, emanating from the flies of a theatre or possibly the lady chapel of a large cathedral.

'I'd like to speak to Benjamin Prike, please.'

'This is he.'

'My name's Sebastian, um, Boyle.'

'Did you say Boyle?'

'Yes.'

'Tell me, Sebastian. Did you or did you not work as an assistant on an industrial video for, let me see, British Gas?'

There was an uncomfortable pause. Sebastian could hear breathing, rasping and uneven, down the phone.

'Why do you ask?'

'Humour an old man, Sebastian. If I may call you Sebastian?'

'You may.'

'Thank you. Was it you, Sebastian?'

'It was.'

His pedantic manner was catching.

There was a slow exhalation at the other end of the line. 'I thought so. Now, what can I do for you, Sebastian?'

'I wanted to ask you about a location manager called Janine –'

He looked at Dougal. Dougal mouthed back.

'Banton? Bunton. Janine Bunton.'

'Her work is excellent. Tell me, Sebastian, since we are speaking, did you ever encounter again your erstwhile colleague?'

'Who?'

'Your fellow worker on our little effort outlining the many benefits of North Sea gas?'

'I don't remember any fellow worker. Unless you mean the one on day-release from the young offenders' institute.'

'That is exactly whom I mean.'

At the back of Sebastian's mind something stirred uneasily.

'Not so far as I know.'

'Interesting. Well, I mustn't keep you chatting. Good luck with whatever it is that requires Miss Bunton's services.'

'Thank you, Benjamin.'

'Please don't mention it, Sebastian.'

He hung up.

'Do you know Ben?'

'A bit.'

Sebastian was straining to remember a cold, wet shoot on a gasholder in Staines, nine years earlier. He recalled a long day of constant rain and no tea breaks, Benjamin Prike beneath an umbrella. There was a director/cameraman fuming over the failing light, a hunched sound man who never spoke. And then that runner –

'Thumbs up?'

Sebastian nodded.

'That's settled, then. She starts tomorrow. Today. I'll have to pay her more than Billy, of course.'

'But you said we had to pay top dollar for Billy because of his features experience.'

'I know, dear boy. And now we have to pay top dollar plus for Janine, even though she's only worked on long-running series.'

'But why?'

'Because we're desperate, dear boy. Or hadn't you noticed?'

Now Sebastian came to think of it, there was something vaguely familiar about that runner.

'Sorry, Dougal, what was that?'

'I said, Benjamin Prike always was a prick. Even in his twenties he looked like a bishop and talked like Noel Coward. Now you could put him in a museum. I'm going out for a smoke.'

Dougal opened the window and climbed through it out of the office, which was on the ground floor of Acton Studios. Sebastian watched him drift away among the skips and prop wagons, sucking through his pipe at a lighted match he sheltered with a cupped hand.

In the production office two industrial-strength photocopiers were churning out the tons of paperwork that help to fuel a late-twentieth-century shoot. Sebastian put in a call to Rick Todge at Brit TV, shouting over the din, and was told he'd gone to his villa in Umbria.

Sebastian had one more meeting before the end of Friday. Tite Bros was one of the City's oldest merchant banks and had been in business since the time when it was done in coffee houses, and a gentleman's word was his bond. In the nineties a thirty-page contract was his bond, even for Tite Bros, but they clung to their pedigree, keenly aware it was the only thing to separate them from the riff-raff who nowadays made the running in financial circles. Sebastian climbed up a mahogany staircase in a narrow City alley so darkened with age it might have been hewn from basalt. Unused to the byways of the square mile, he was surprised such places still existed. At the first floor landing was a dull engraved brass plaque, and as instructed he knocked and entered.

Sebastian had expected morning coats and pinstriped trousers, but he was disappointed. The room might have been more than two centuries old, and the furnishings, but the people were the same ones who tried to elbow past him in the theatre bar or clipped him with their trolleys in Waitrose on Saturday mornings. A tall, middle-aged man dressed in blue chalkstripe inclined his slightly stooping frame towards Sebastian and held out his hand.

'Mr Boyle? Let's go into the partners' room, where we can talk in comfort.' He ushered the producer through a doorway into another area of his heritage theme park – the Private Bank Experience – and invited him to sit down among the smell of rich old leather and beeswaxed floorboards.

'Now, how is it we may help you?'

'I need to borrow money.'

'I see, I see.' Ralph was serious and responsible, a family doctor or lawyer of the old school. 'I hope we can be of service. And what, if I may enquire, is to be the purpose of the loan?'

It was Daisy who'd steered Sebastian towards Tite Bros, having heard their name mentioned several times in the hyper-contemporary offices of Monopoli. 'Are you sure?', he'd asked her. Oh yes, Daisy was quite sure, she thought Monopoli were in some kind of crisis themselves and she heard Bernie Gassman say he was going to a meeting at Tite Bros. They certainly weren't on the commonplace media-money map, and theirs wasn't a name that came up in the Soho clubs, at least not in the ones that Sebastian had succeeded in penetrating. He felt he was stealing a march on his competitors and at the same time sticking two fingers up at Bernie and his all-devouring company by filling his boots from the same discreet treasure chest as them.

'Television production cash-flowing. I understand you've done some work in this line before?'

Ralph smiled equivocally. 'You will understand, of course, that I am not at liberty to discuss the affairs of other clients, Mr Boyle. But it is true to say that Tite Bros are not complete strangers to the media. Now, would you care to run through the details of the loan?'

When he emerged into the alley near St Paul's the streets were slippery with rain and City commuters crouched beneath their umbrellas as they were swept like a flood of dirty water into the wide drain of Bank station. In an hour Sebastian had learned a lot about the City, and why Tite Bros was still flourishing after two hundred and fifty years in business. Their terms were far harsher than Bank Frød's, their penalties stricter, their sanctions more enforceable. They were more expensive. And yet there was something oddly reassuring about the whole set-up which left him with a feeling of acceptance, almost contentment. At those rates there was no earthly reason for them not to take the business. So long as he paid the interest charges and arrangement fee and all the rest of it, Tite Bros had no incentive to fail him.

In addition they'd wanted him to move his personal account there – which, given their lack of cashpoints, interest-bearing accounts and all the other usual banking services might have seemed unattractive. However, Sebastian had been won over by the highly desirable chequebook with which Ralph had presented him.

He'd murmured that George V had had one just like it.

18 Top Team

Sebastian opened the front door. He and Jemma hadn't planned anything for the evening, although Friday was their usual night for going out. Sometimes they just stayed in and watched a video with a takeaway. Neither option seemed likely on this occasion. He stepped into the house, wondering what to expect.

What he got was a note, a short one – just the single word 'Gone', plus a J for Jemma underneath. No indication of where to, for how long, with whom, or whether temporarily or permanently. Never had Sebastian felt so keenly the lack of prepositions. She hadn't said why, either, but he didn't feel that needed explaining. He went to the fridge and opened a beer, and the phone rang.

'Hello?'

'Sebastian?'

'Yes?'

'It's Graham here.'

'Oh.'

'I was wondering if you want to come out for a drink, maybe get a bite to eat.'

'Is –'

'I'm on my own, so I thought maybe tonight would be a good night. Like we arranged. You could tell me more about *Rough Diamonds*.'

'I'd love to, Graham, only I'm a bit busy, what with starting a shoot on Monday and Jemma leaving me.'

'Of course, I understand. Perhaps next week, then?'

'Perhaps. Bye.' Sebastian put the phone down. He felt he hadn't so much lost a wife as gained a boyfriend.

He turned on the TV. There was nothing on.

Maybe journalists never found anything to read in the papers, and bus drivers waited for hours at bus stops for buses that never came. Or maybe it was just Sebastian. Or maybe there really wasn't anything to watch on Friday nights, and it was the broadcasters' way of letting him know he was a sad bastard who deserved to be punished for staying in when all decent people were out having a good time, eating and drinking and dancing and watching films and plays and going to concerts and doing all the other things that made life worth living. Television was fundamentally different, wasn't it? For all the executive blather about appointment viewing and signature pieces the truth was that telly was more like a utility than entertainment or, for God's sake, art. It belonged with gas and electricity and water. People didn't think of it in terms of the unique and the important, more as a continuous supply, to be turned on and off at will. In the end it might be just too close to life to be, well, entertaining.

So, naturally, Sebastian watched anyway. He watched *Dalston Square* and *Boys in Blue* and *Gotcha!* and *Telly's Stupidest Cock-Ups* and a sort of documentary about a woman who designed inflatable sex toys. He drank more beer. He ordered a takeaway curry and ate it in front of a film – based on a true story – about a Texan who raced giant combine harvesters but lost his eleven-year-old daughter in a tug-of-love to his deadliest rival, a mountain-man survivalist from Arkansas planning a pipe-bomb attack on the federal headquarters in Amarillo. Sebastian was so impressed by its awfulness he looked it up in his old hard-copy film guide, but *Freakin' A* must have sneaked under the radar because there was no mention of it.

By the time it was over there were no more beers in the fridge, so Sebastian had to drink them warm. It was an hour or so after midnight and the world defined by his sofa and the TV screen, the only light on in the house, had become a strange place. Wow. There were programmes here he never even knew existed, not on terrestrial. They must have been seeping through from cable. No-budget factual entertainment shows with teenage presenters on work experience, free film clips, and public domain graphics. Assemblies of out-takes from home videos (the best must have already been used in prime time). Weird documentaries about musicians unknown outside their local pub, shot and edited in a drummer's Hartlepool bedroom. Whole series devoted to G-strings and peephole bras. People like Albie used to say people only got the best of American TV so they couldn't judge what it was really like. Well, checking out some of the channels with the higher numbers round about four in the morning, Sebastian was gaining a broader picture. He goggled and laughed and drank more warm beer. What a great, great thing television was, after all. He rolled into bed just before it got light, feeling proud and happy to be part of it all.

Saturday morning brought a new perspective. He'd forgotten to draw the curtains so pale grey light washed into the bedroom early, but Sebastian didn't wake up until a crash close to his ear suddenly made him sit bolt upright. A moment later his head went off like the clapper of a bell, just as Jemma said 'You look awful.' She was dressed for gym, in a tracksuit, and looked as though nothing stronger than yoghurt had ever passed her lips.

'You had a party, then, last night?' She was rooting in the wardrobe, pulling open drawers.

'Quiet night in.'

'Really. Whoever you had it with was sick over the sofa.'

'I think you'll find that's chicken dopiaza. Mine.'

'You mean you emptied all those bottles by yourself? No wonder you look terrible.'

'I'll tidy up later.'

'If you like. It really makes no difference to me.'

He levered himself up onto one elbow. 'What are you doing, Jemma?'

'Just picking up a few things I need.'

'Why?' His brain seemed to be working at quarter-speed. 'Where were you last night?'

'If I want anything else I'll let you know.'

'You weren't with Graham. Were you?'

'Goodbye, Sebastian.' She was gone. Sebastian heard the front door click and that was that. He got up, took three Paracetamol and ran a bath. In the fog of biliousness, nostalgia, and genuine sadness it was impossible to tell where one ended and the others began.

After his bath he bagged the bottles and tidied the house. When Sebastian took the rubbish outside to the dustbin he noticed something different about the garden. Jemma's wigwams were gone. For some reason this affected him more than anything else. Climbing roses lay stretched out on the ground. Sebastian uprooted up a handful of couch grass, wondering where Jemma's wigwams were now.

Dougal called from the production office, where he was double-checking everything ready for the start of the shoot while Janine touched locations with her magic wand. Everything was set for Monday. Sebastian pottered around at home, experienced the novelty of housework, then went out for a long walk in the park. He saw two setters and a red deer, all of which made him think of Jemma.

Arriving back at the house, Sebastian spotted a familiar lilac car parked outside. Daisy said she'd just arrived and had decided to hang on for five minutes in case he turned up.

'Dougal said you were in.'

Daisy had brought Dougal's update on the locations.

'You could have emailed it.'

'Oh well.' He noticed her hair was different. It looked nice. She smiled at him over her tea. 'How's Jemma?'

'Fine. Fine, but ... gone.'

Did he detect a tiny glint in Daisy's eye?

'Oh, I'm sorry, Sebastian. Have I just put my foot in it?'

'Not at all.'

He thanked her for the location list and watched the lilac Nissan move off towards the South Circular.

At six-thirty next morning Sebastian's production car arrived. By seven he'd been disgorged at the unit base, somewhere off Tottenham Court Road. Everywhere men and women dressed in extreme weather gear stood around holding Styrofoam cups of tea and coffee and chatting. Sebastian went around shaking hands.

'Hi, Todd. Where's Trevor?'

'On set.'

Sebastian walked to the grungy café where the first scene was to be shot. The art director was strewing litter on the floor with an expression of great concentration, while a prop-boy squeezed a puddle of brown sauce onto a table-top to his direction.

'Seen Trevor?'

Without taking his attention from the litter or the sauce the art director jerked his head towards the door to the kitchen. Sebastian could hear voices inside.

'You sick bastard. Look what you've done.'

'Okay. Do you want to try it without the meat cleaver this time?'

Sebastian went in.

'Hello, Trevor.'

Sebastian smiled. The figure in paramilitary black looked up sharply.

'What?'

'Just saying hello.'

'I'm rehearsing my actors.'

'Oh. Right. Sorry.'

Sebastian retreated.

'Mind my litter!'

'Sorry.'

The funny thing was, Sebastian didn't remember anything about a meat cleaver in that scene. He decided to see what was for breakfast. Dougal, spurning all-weather gear in favour of his regulation tweed jacket and cord trousers, was enjoying an early pipe in the open air where no one could complain about it. He steered Sebastian towards the catering wagon.

'Fat Bob, this is Sebastian. He's the producer.' A spherical cockney geezer straight out of a light entertainment sketch stuck out a meaty paw.

'Pleased to meet you, Sebastian, what'll it be?'

'What is there?'

'Sausage bacon fried scrambled black pudding tinned tomaters fresh tomaters hash browns mushrooms haddock kippers fried slice bubble toast and beans.'

'Oh well, a bit of everything, I suppose.'

Dougal grinned wolfishly.

'Except the kippers. I didn't cook yesterday.'

'Daisy find you okay?'

'Yes.'

'Did she sort you out?'

'What do you mean?'

'With the locations.'

'Oh. Yes, she brought the list. How's Janine doing?'

'Fine.' Dougal nodded at an anoraked figure deep in conversation with a huge troll. 'There she is, you can ask her.'

'Who's that she's talking to?'

'That is a living legend. That's Coneman the Barbarian.'

'What does he do?'

'Ask him.'

The troll detached himself from Janine and lurched down the street swinging an oversized traffic cone from each hand. He kept moving, head down, avoiding eye contact. Sebastian stepped in front of him.

'Hello. I'm Sebastian.'

Stopping dead in his tracks, the troll stared at Sebastian.

'Who are you?'

No answer.

'What do you do?'

The troll regarded Sebastian with stunned incredulity.

'What do I do?' he rumbled. 'That's a laugh. I do probably the most important fucking job on the whole fucking unit, but do I ever get so much as a fucking thank you? Do I fuck.'

'I didn't –' Sebastian began, but Coneman hadn't finished.

'Have you ever wondered how it is that a unit gets its vehicles where it wants them? Eh? Or how they keep the whole street clear for that shot where they don't want no cars in the way, and there's a school at one end of the street and Sainsbury's at the other, and the residents' sodding association is made up of retired men from the council with a GCSE in complaining and time on their hands? Well, have you? Course you ain't. Why should you care? So long as it's done. But if there's so much as one motor parked where the director wants to shoot then they're all over me, why didn't you do this, why didn't you do that, why didn't you do the fucking other. Well I tell you, if I didn't do it, it's because it can't be fucking done. No matter what some cunt says.'

'Well, I –'

'Take a typical street. Unrestricted parking, right, no fucking lines or nothing, it ain't so fucking easy. The location manager sticks hundreds of polite letters through people's letter-boxes, and some people move their cars, and some want money to move their cars, and get it, but some people won't do it. Just won't fucking do it. See?'

'Yes, but I really –'

'So what I do is I go in early and wait. Soon as some cunt moves his car I whip in with the van, cone it all out, and I'm talking serious cones here, I don't mean one or two of something eighteen inches high you could pick up with one finger. I mean a fucking *cone*. Three feet tall, concrete in the bottom, some cunt tries shifting one and fucks his back just like that. And I really line 'em up. Touching, they are. Ten of 'em to a car-sized space. You don't fuck with cones like that.'

Sebastian, eyes glazed, just shook his head.

'Ready to rehearse, into the van they go, job done. Unit manager takes over, I'm off to the next location. So that's what I do. Work them fucking cones. It ain't easy, but if it were, every fucker'd be at it. Some cunt's got to do it. And if it you want it done right, that cunt had better be me. How about you?'

'Me? I'm the producer.'

Coneman regarded him for a moment with pity, then turned on his heel and stumped off towards an ancient Bedford pick-up. Sebastian turned round to see Dougal bent double, sides heaving, his face purple with suppressed guffaws. It seemed a good moment to inspect the costume and make-up facilities.

First Sebastian visited Anastasia in the costume trailer. Seeing her from the other side of the unit base people would mistake Anastasia for a young trainee: long blonde hair, svelte figure. Closer up they were in for a shock: Stasi wasn't a day under fifty-five, rarely smiled (there was no point, since the facelift nothing moved any more), chain-smoked, and talked like a duchess. She must have been interested in clothes – surely? – but no one ever saw her wear anything that wasn't black. She was thin, certainly, but also rather macabre.

'Hello, darling,' she drawled. 'Ready for the off?'

'Be good to get going at last. How's the trailer?'

'Frankly darling it's pretty bloody poky. Have you seen the condensation? It's dripping off the ceiling. How am I going to keep my rails dry?'

'I'm sure you'll think of something.'

'Have to, won't I?'

Sebastian smiled and kept moving. Katya, in make-up, was

more welcoming. Generously proportioned and dressed in flowing, shapeless clothes, she smiled invitingly.

'There's no one in the chair, come in and have a chat.' She shut the flimsy aluminium door with a perfectly executed kick and treated him to a complicit smile. 'Isn't she a sight? Frankly I prefer not to have to look at her if I can help it. If she gets her face done one more time it'll split in half.'

'There's enough Botox in her forehead to make working in the same trailer a health hazard. I'm Howard, by the way, Kattie's assistant.' Howard held out a boneless hand. 'We should really insist on a cordon sanitaire.'

'Have you and Anastasia worked together before?'

Katya guffawed. 'I should think not. Have you seen her CV?'

Sebastian had. It seemed perfectly all right to him, in fact slightly more impressive than Katya's own.

'Ah well, it hasn't been easy for her since the hysterectomy.'

'She used to be worse,' Howard chipped in.

'Yes, the hormone treatment must be doing some good. So tell me, Sebastian, when are we going to get our proper make-up trailer?'

'I don't follow you.'

'Well, obviously this is a stop-gap, I wondered when the proper one's turning up?'

'This is it, as far as I know.'

'You're joking. Aren't you? Sebastian, have you seen the facilities? How can I wash Jason Prynne's hair in that?'

'You may not need to. He's not in the first block.' And, Sebastian was thinking, you may not be in the second. 'You'll have more to do with Helen Quigley, I expect.'

'Oh, her. It'll be fine for her.'

'Not a fan, then?'

'She's all right in *Dalston Square*. If you like that sort of thing,' sniffed Howard. 'But hardly what you'd call a star, is she?'

Sebastian decided to put his foot down. 'That's what we'll

be doing on *Rough Diamonds*,' he said. 'Making her a star. And I hope you'll be giving her all the support you can.'

Katya and Howard exchanged a look, then said together, 'Oh yes, of course.'

As he left the trailer Sebastian wondered whether it was better to fire them both straight away or wait until tomorrow. He separated Dougal from the focus puller, who was in the middle of a long story about his National Insurance, and put the question to him. Dougal frowned.

'What's wrong with make-up?'

'That Katya's a complete bitch, and Howard's poisonous. We can't let them get their hands on our cast.'

'Katya's a pretty good designer.'

'Trevor William warned me about her, but I didn't think it was worth mentioning. I can see now he's right. We've got to get rid of her.'

'Hold your horses, dear boy. And ask yourself this: if Katya's not the top of the heap, then why is she working on this show?'

'Because we made a mistake?'

'Because the better ones turned us down. And there are worse, believe me. Much worse. Okay, say you get rid of Katya. Who do you get to take her place?'

'I don't know.'

'Exactly. There has to be someone better. And there isn't.' Dougal took a step closer. Sebastian could smell the tarry smoke on his breath. 'Do you think I didn't try? But let's face it, Sebastian, we're not offering people the job of their dreams here. Six-day weeks, average to bad money, directors no one's heard of, and no stars worth mentioning. Plus a novice producer. Now, Katya can do the job very well and if she isn't the easiest one to get along with you just have to remember, that's why she was available.'

'But isn't it really important that the actors leave make-up to go onto set in a good frame of mind?'

'Not as important as them being there on time, ready to shoot. It's make-up, Sebastian. Not psychotherapy.'

Sebastian peered at him more closely. 'Are you all right?'

'Of course. Why?'

'You just look a bit shagged.'

Dougal sighed. 'I didn't get much sleep last night. My ait flooded.'

'Your what?'

'Ait. My island. Freak tide or something. I didn't have the boards up and I got up in the middle of the night to find an inch of water on the floor.'

'What do you do?'

'Oh, the usual, dear boy, baled and pumped. It's not the first time. But the rabbits are missing.'

'Rabbits?'

'Bond and Moneypenny. Their hutch must have floated away.'

Sebastian didn't know what to say, so he just put a consoling arm tentatively around Dougal's shoulder. The old man took out a handkerchief and blew his nose noisily.

'I'm fine. Got to get on, sort out the sparks.' Sebastian watched him stride away towards a knot of grotesques who looked like something out of Breughel. The lighting electricians, presumably. He left Dougal to it.

Over by the set Todd Esterhazy was marshalling his troops, a walkie-talkie in one hand and a giant bacon roll in the other. It was eight o'clock, call time. In less than a minute the crew had assembled around the café. Sparks began to put big lamps onto stands and lay cables. The sound guys were unpacking microphones and poles, and connecting up their mixer and recorders. Under the stern gaze of the director of photography, Ludi Schiaparelli, the camera was being attached to a dolly while the grip laid track.

This DoP was a dark horse. Trevor William had been keen – no, had absolutely insisted – on Ludi. His credits were impressive, but there was something about him that was just a little bit too … cinematic. His hair was long and grey, he wore a huge black coat that reached to his ankles, and held his light meter like a talisman. His team were also dressed in black and worked in silence, like a cross between a SWAT team and a closed order of monks.

'Cool, aren't they?' a voice whispered in Sebastian's ear. Todd was standing beside him. 'Met Ludi yet? And if you like the camera boys, you'll love the clapper board.'

'Why?'

'You'll see.' Todd raised his voice. 'Okay, everyone. Very quiet and still now for rehearsal.' He took up a position close to the camera but not too close to where Trevor William and Ludi Schiaparelli were standing. He looked to Trevor. Trevor looked to Ludi. Ludi closed his eyes and almost imperceptibly inclined his head. Trevor said, in a voice at once quiet and carrying, 'Action.'

Stuart walked into the café.

'Cut.'

Ludi made some cryptic signal to the lighting gaffer. Trevor had a private word with Stuart. Sound changed their mind about the best way to get the boom around the camera without fouling the shot. The art director looked through the camera viewfinder and rushed out to move a Coke tin by three inches. Then the same was repeated again. And again.

Finally Trevor pronounced himself satisfied with the rehearsal and Stuart was led off to costume and make-up by the Ducati-riding 3rd AD, while all the various departments busied themselves about their work.

Fifteen minutes later Stuart was in costume, made up (although he looked just the same to Sebastian), and ready to shoot. Todd asked if everyone was set. Ludi and Trevor signified their assent. The black-clad clapper loader prepared the board.

'Stand by for a take.' Todd waited a moment for complete silence.

'Turn over.' Red lights on the camera began to flash and the magazine whirred as the first film stock ran through the gate.

'Board.'

The clapper loader stood in front of the camera and said '*Rough Diamonds*, slate one, take one,' and snapped down the clapper.

'And … action.'

Everyone focused on Stuart walking towards the café door. Everyone except Sebastian. In his head there was one burning question, and he couldn't ask it until the magic word 'Cut' was heard and speech became legal again. Who on God's earth was Trefor ap Gwyllm? That was the name on the clapper board, right below *Rough Diamonds*, in the space reserved for the director. Sebastian fumbled in his pocket, located an extra strong mint, and started to suck it, hard.

19 One of Those

The director moved briskly from Stuart entering the café to the argument scene – now known as the meat cleaver scene – leaving no room for conversation. He was constantly engaged with the actors, with Ludi, with the other heads of department. Sebastian could hardly complain. After all, that was his job. All the same, he couldn't help noticing that on the two or three occasions when Trevor was standing by himself, silently brooding, he quickly moved away when he saw the producer approaching.

'Did you order the stunt arranger for this scene?'

'No, Dougal. I thought you did.'

Dougal shook his head. 'Nor the stunt performer. Nor the armourer.'

'Armourer?'

'For the meat cleaver.'

'Ah.'

The two stood in silence for a few moments, each with his own thoughts.

'Do you know,' said Dougal at last, 'I think we may just be in for a very *memorable* shoot.' And he went off to see about the honeywagons.

The crew were all looking very chipper, especially the ones with mortgages who hadn't worked much lately. Trevor – or Trefor – had the bit between his teeth and a nasty gleam in his eyes, rather like Jack Nicholson in *The Shining*.

The first day quickly fell into a pattern: rehearse, shoot, shoot again, and again, and again. And again. By lunchtime only two of the twelve short scenes scheduled for the day had been completed.

'How's it looking?' Dougal sat opposite Sebastian in a double-decker bus converted for use as a mobile canteen. Each had a plated heaped with green chicken curry in front him. The bus was parked in a London square, now full of office workers who gawped in through the windows to watch them eating. From time to time one of them joined the queue in the hope of getting a free meal.

'Haven't seen anything yet. Is it just me or is this curry incredibly hot?'

'How do you mean, you haven't seen anything?'

'Pass the water, please. I mean there's no monitor and Ludi doesn't like idle spectators looking through his eyepiece.'

'Idle spectators such as the producer.'

'Exactly.'

'Where is Ludi, by the way?'

'Probably lying down in his coffin. He said he needed to rest during lunch.'

'Oh?'

'I expect the sunlight gets too much for him. He'll be fine on the night shoots.'

'Hmm.' Dougal forked up a mouthful of curry. 'This is rather good.'

'If this is their green curry, what's the red curry like?'

'Hot. You'll find out tomorrow, I expect.'

'Do they always cook curry?'

'Quite often, yes.'

Sebastian looked around the bus. 'Have you seen Trevor?'

'I think he's eating in the production office with the ADs.'

On the way over he met Todd again. 'How are we doing?'

'Well, put it this way. If it was nine-thirty, we'd be motoring. But it's ten to two.'

'Are we going to complete today?'

'Only if Clark Kent goes into a phone box and comes out as Superman.'

'Have you talked to him?'

'Yeah.'

'And?'

'As far as he's concerned he's Superman already.'

At two they left the square and went to the next location, a few streets away. Ludi was examining the sky through a monocle of smoked glass. He shook his head in disgust and strode away from the camera. The black-clad crew folded their arms. Todd came over to Sebastian.

'What's the problem?'

'Sun's not right.'

'How come?'

'Trevor wants shade.'

'For God's sake. On this schedule it is what it is.'

'Tell *him*.'

But when Sebastian approached Trevor, he hadn't opened his mouth before the director turned on his heel and followed Ludi off the set.

'You'd better go after him, mate. Or this shoot's over before it's begun.'

Sebastian followed Trevor round the corner and caught up with him as he arrived back at the caravan that was doing duty as the production office.

'Trevor –'

'I can't talk now.'

'You've got to. We're half a day in and almost half a day behind.'

'I can't help the weather.'

'You can compromise.'

Trevor turned slowly to face him. 'Compromise?'

'Yes. You know –' The caravan door opened and Ludi's shaman-like features appeared.

'Cloud.'

Without another word Trevor pushed past the producer and followed Ludi back towards the set. Dougal was waiting for him.

'That went well.'

'At least he's shooting again.'

'For now. What happens next time?'

Dougal stuffed his pipe before answering. 'Just take it a day at a time, dear boy,' he advised. 'It's going to be one of those shoots.'

At the end of the day Sebastian stood with Dougal as Todd called a wrap. 'No point in going over on the first day.' It was seven o'clock. They'd completed four scenes, totalling a page and a half of script of the four pages scheduled. Daisy appeared from the production base and walked over to join them.

'How'd it go?'

'Slowly.'

'Did he do the café scene?'

'I think you mean the meat cleaver scene.'

'What meat cleaver?'

'I suppose he feels he's rewritten the script so much it hardly matters.'

'How's that going to tie in with the scene at the end where Carmichael confesses?'

'Your guess is as good as mine, Daisy. Better, I hope.'

Daisy looked at them and made a decision. 'Come on,' she said. 'I'm taking you both out for a drink.'

* * *

The pub, however, failed to raise their spirits.

'What about Bill Block? I don't suppose he's still free?'

'No. I already checked.'

'Who else is there?'

'No one.'

'What about Jonathan Krankie?'

Dougal just gave him a look.

'Okay, okay. So what do we do?'

'We just have to make it work as it is.' Dougal drained his Guinness. 'I've got to pick up James Bond from the vet's.'

'Oh, they turned up, then?'

'In Sunbury. The hutch floated onto someone's garden and got snagged on a gnome. Moneypenny coped all right but James Bond's in shock.'

'Well, I'm glad they're safe now.' Dougal smiled back and set off homewards.

'What would you do, Daisy? If you were the producer?'

'Just what I was wondering myself.'

'Really.'

'I think on balance you're better off holding onto Trevor William, and finding some way of keeping him under control. What about his agent?

'Useless.'

'Well, what does Trevor want that we've got?'

'Film stock.'

'Okay, so ration it.'

'It's getting him to shoot anything at all that's the problem. He rehearsed Stuart Craddock walking through a door thirteen times. Then there was a re-light. At this rate episode one will be about four minutes long.'

'We'll have to sleep on it.' Daisy got up and took her coat from the chair. 'Can I give you a lift home?'

'Are you going my way?'

'I certainly can.'

'Oh. Right, then. Thanks very much.' Sebastian followed her out of the pub to the car park, and they got into the lilac two-seater.

'This is quite flash. Snug, though.'

'It's perfect for two. The seats go right back, too. Flat. Like a bed.'

'Oh. That's … handy.'

Daisy started the car and they shot out into the traffic.

She drove like a man – badly, but in a confident, assertive way, nosing through the evening traffic and squirting the car into the small gaps which opened from time to time in the one-way system through Wandsworth and the South Circular. She pushed a CD into the player.

'What's the plan for tomorrow?' Daisy dropped a gear and shot into a quiet residential street, part of her customised rat-run.

'I don't know. Try and keep my nerve, I suppose.'

'I meant, for Trevor.'

Sebastian didn't have an answer.

Daisy switched lanes without indicating and hauled round Clapham Common. 'I wish you'd let me help you, Sebastian.' She pulled up at the lights. Red. Daisy turned to face him. 'There must be something I can do.'

Her face seemed very close. In the warmth of the car she'd taken off her jacket. Sebastian swallowed.

'You can drop me off here.'

'Are you sure?'

'Yeah, sure. I need to pick up some shopping.' He fumbled with the passenger door. 'You coming on set tomorrow?'

'I've got some work to do with George in the morning.'

'George?'

'And Jim. The writers. They're still working on episodes four and five, remember?'

'Of course I do.'

'Well then. I'm going through the script with George and Jim and Jassy. You should be there too. I'll come out in the afternoon and see how things are going.'

'Thanks for the lift.'

Sebastian slammed the door shut and trudged past the shops. He did need to buy things but he had no intention of shopping now. He'd order a pizza when he got home. He felt strange – relieved and disappointed at the same time, he didn't know why.

Maybe he'd make that a Chinese.

* * *

When Sebastian woke up on Tuesday he went straight to the cutting room. While the crew had sunk gratefully into well-earned sleep, or lain awake miserably worrying about their careers and love lives, the film lab had been processing all those hundreds of feet of film that had passed through Ludi's camera during the day. By morning the truth was out there.

Sebastian said hello to Taki the editor, who made room for him in front of the monitor. Taki turned down the lights in the cutting room and ran the rushes tape.

A chart and a grey scale. Then the board: Cam, L. Schiaparelli. Dir, Trefor ap Gwyllm. Then …

A sinister-looking young man, shadows emphasising his hollow cheeks and sunken eyes, hesitated outside a door. He grasped the handle and went inside. The picture cut, there was another slate, and the action was repeated. Twelve times. Then a close-up, his hand on a doorknob. Again and again. Seven takes, in fact. Then another close-up, the eyes this time, deep pools of blackness, haunted. Six takes. Sebastian shifted restlessly in his chair. Now they were inside the building. It was a café. The camera darted about the empty room, flicking from one side to another, searching for something, before alighting on a dull gleam in the corner. It pushed in towards it. A meat cleaver. A hand emerged and fingers closed around the handle. Seven takes. Each one indistinguishable, to Sebastian, from the rest. Then the picture disappeared to be replaced by a snowstorm of slash on the videotape. Taki stopped the player and put up the lights. He waited for Sebastian to make the first comment.

'Lot of takes.'

'Yeah.'

'How many minutes?'

'Just under one. One and a bit pages of script.'

'What do you think?'

Taki shrugged. He was young for a film editor, late twenties, and Sebastian had heard his reputation was growing fast. This might be his last TV job. That was true of many of those working on *Rough Diamonds*, as it turned out, but in Taki's case it was because he was on his way to better things, big movies, Hollywood. He ran his hand over the shaved smoothness of his scalp.

'Good. It's very good.'

'Not much of it.'

'No. We'll get this sunk up pretty quick. Who's that actor?'

'Stuart Craddock.'

But Sebastian knew what he meant. He'd hardly recognised the surly young bloke Sebastian had seen loafing about the set the previous day. Stuart, the café, even the door … it had all been transformed.

'What's he shooting on, a fifty?'

'I've absolutely no idea, Taki. Do you want me to find out?'

'It'll be on the camera sheet. Don't worry.'

'Right. I'll be on my way, then.'

'See you.' Taki was already spooling back the tape. Sebastian let himself out and called Dougal.

'How's it going on set?'

'Hang on, I'll go somewhere I can talk.' Sound of footsteps. 'Slowly.'

'Where are you up to?'

'Still setting up the first shot.'

'You're joking.'

'I am not.'

'Okay, I'm coming over. I'll cancel the writers.'

'No, don't do that, dear boy, it smacks of panic. Leave it till lunchtime. Red Thai curry on the menu today.' Sebastian's stomach heaved slightly. 'I'll keep things moving along in the meantime.'

'See you later, then.'

Either the writers were early or Sebastian was late because they were already installed in the meeting room at Brunt Productions when he arrived. Through the big window he watched them wistfully with their cappuccinos in tall, ruffled paper cups, their script pages fanned out on their knees, already sprinkled with flakes of croissant. The scene made Sebastian long for the tranquil days of development hell. He pulled himself together and went in.

'Hi, Sebastian.' Jassy was there too, toying nervily with a paperclip. 'How's the shoot going?'

'Very well. Rushes are terrific.'

'Producers always say that,' remarked Jim.

'But these are.'

'They always say that, too.'

'Sebastian, I hope you don't mind,' Daisy cut in. 'I thought we should get started.'

'Am I late?'

'About an hour,' said Jim.

'Don't worry, Daisy explained you had to view rushes,' Jassy reassured him.

'Which, as we know, are terrific.' Was he imagining it, or was there something of an atmosphere in the room? 'Unlike our script, apparently.'

Sebastian looked at Jim, seething on the sofa, then at George, who blinked unhappily. 'Daisy, can you fill me in?'

'We were just talking about the problem of the double episode. Did you get my text message?'

'What text message?'

'Rick Todge isn't happy with the scripts.'

'Has anyone spoken to him?'

'Still in Umbria. He's flying from there straight to Banff for a symposium on TV violence.'

'I see.'

'So I thought the best idea might be to compress the existing double into the first episode, and then start afresh with the second.'

'And then,' Jassy took up the story, 'we might find there's not enough room for some of the more graphic moments –'

'She hates the fingernails,' Jim cut in. 'Never mind that they're pivotal to the whole fucking story! Just take them out and stick in a car chase, whatever.'

'We can't afford a car chase.'

'Well, a chat with the desk sergeant, then. I take it the budget will run to that?'

'Only if you can write it well enough. I don't know. Can you?'

Jim went white. Jassy put her face in her hands. There was a palpable silence, and then Daisy stepped in.

'I don't think Sebastian meant –'

'We'll rewrite it.'

'What?' Jim stared at George in amazement. They all did. It was the first time he'd spoken.

'I wasn't happy with it anyway.'

'Are you sure? How can we do it in the time?'

George turned to Jim. 'What do you mean, "we"?'

Jim went whiter. 'Think what you're saying, mate.'

'Why don't you go and put in a few flying hours?'

'What, now?'

'Yes. Now.'

They all studied the carpet as Jim gathered up his papers and walked in silence to the door, where he turned to George for one final appeal.

'What shall I tell Colum?' Colum was their agent.

'Tell him to make the cheques out to me from now on.'

Jim opened his mouth to say something, thought better of it, and closed the door after him. A moment later George got up.

'Are you going too?'

'I've noted your comments. I'll have a new draft done in … three days.'

'That's not possible,' breathed Jassy. 'Is it?'

'I wrote this one in two.'

'Two days? But that was with Jim.' Daisy was finding this hard to take in as well.

'He was in Lanzarote. On holiday.' George got up. 'I'll email it to you.'

'I thought – Jim said you couldn't use a telephone.'

'I can't. He's right. It's a – well, never mind. But I *can* email.'

Without another word George pushed through the door, strode through reception, and disappeared from the office.

'Well.' Jassy was agog.

'What do you think, Daisy?'

'George is the writer, we always knew that. It's possible he works that fast. Just. We'll have to wait and see. Sorry you've had a wasted morning.'

'I wouldn't call that wasted. And with luck I've missed the red curry.'

'What?'

'Never mind. Do you want a lift to the set?'

'I've already booked us a car. It should be downstairs.'

They said goodbye to Jassy and walked down to the street. 'Daisy, did we really need a limo?'

'It was cheaper, they gave me a deal. Cottisham, please.' The uniformed driver nodded and pulled out. 'Moment of truth, then.'

'What is?'

'This afternoon. Helen Quigley on set for the first time. I can't wait. How were the rushes – really?'

'Really – they were very good. There just weren't many of them.'

'What are you going to do about it?'

'Well … what are you doing?'

'Changing. I don't want to turn up in a ploughed field looking like some silly script chick in fuck-me shoes.'

'Daisy!'

'That's the great thing about a limo, there's room to do pretty much anything and no one can see in.'

'This isn't you!'

'Isn't it?' She slid off her dress and pulled a pair of jeans out of her bag. 'How do you know?'

Sebastian tried to concentrate on the view through the window – tattoo studios, takeaways, legal aid solicitors – but the tinted window threw back an image of Daisy working the tight denim up her legs that he found disconcerting.

'For God's sake, Daisy, how long does it take to put on a pair of jeans?'

'Nearly there. Do my knickers show through these?'

'I'm sure they don't. Now what are you doing?'

'Just changing my top. Don't you find it hot in here?'

'I'll tell the driver to turn up the air-con.'

'Don't worry. Can you help me with this?' The limo sank to a halt at red lights. Outside, a man in a suit was vomiting copiously into a litter-bin. 'I can't reach it.'

Reluctantly he stretched over to do up Daisy's buttons. There were tiny golden hairs on the nape of her neck, and her skin felt warm. Sebastian tried to concentrate on the drunk man. He was wiping strings of goo from his mouth with a crushed tissue, then he was sick a little bit more. That seemed to do the trick.

20 Special Stipulations

Helen Quigley was making herself as comfortable as someone can in a muddy Surrey field. Her mobile trilled and she picked it up.

'How are you, sweetie?'

Helen re-positioned the phone a few inches from her ear. 'Alive, anyway.'

'How are they treating you?'

'Well, I have to say, Lavinia, it's not what I expected.'

'Problems, dear?'

'They've given me a poky little dressing room in a caravan, it's nothing like my usual dressing room.'

'Difficult on location, sweetie. But have you got a shower?'

'I don't need a shower.'

'That's not the point. Have you got one?'

'I don't think so.'

'I particularly asked for a shower. It's in the special stips.'

'The what?'

'The special stipulations, sweetie, in your contract. Here, I've got it in front of me. 'Spacious private accommodation with personal toilet and shower'. You have got a loo, I take it?'

'Yeah, got that.'

'But no shower?'

'No shower.'

'Right. I'm calling the producer.'

'Hang on a tick, Lavinia. I don't give a stuff about the shower.'

'But I do, Helen. This is something I have negotiated for you.'

'Why's it so important?'

'Because Jason Prynne has a shower.'

'Then I want one.'

'Exactly, sweetie. I'll call Sebastian right now.'

'Hang on. There's something else I want.'

'What?'

'Something Jason Prynne hasn't got.'

'Ah, you're catching on. Let's see. Fruit basket?'

'Got that.'

'Flowers?'

'Got that.'

'Television and video?'

'Got them and all.'

'I know. Bed.'

'Bed?'

'For relaxation. Between scenes.'

'There won't be room in here!'

'Perfect. They'll have to give you a larger dressing room. A caravan to yourself, even. Is yours English or American?'

'Is my what English or American?'

'Your three-way.'

'Hey?'

'Your trailer, dear.'

'I don't know.'

'Never mind, we'll ask for the bed. As compensation.'

'Compensation for what?'

'The lack of a shower.'

'All right, then. Lavinia –'

'Yes, dear? Anything else?'

'I'm not sure about this script. It keeps changing. And the director's a bit peculiar.'

'They all are, sweetie. Now it's much better if I call about one thing at a time. Shall we concentrate on the bed for now and deal with the director later?'

'Go on, then.'

'Right, dear. I'll call you back.'

* * *

Sebastian felt rather self-conscious stepping out of the limo at the location base. Scurrying figures in thermals and anoraks threw him and Daisy sidelong glances as they picked their way through the mud to the mobile production office. The lengthy black car did look a long way from Soho as it nosed its way back down the little country lane. Sebastian was feeling grateful Trevor William wasn't there to see it when he felt someone staring at him and turned round.

'Like the pimpmobile.'

'Hi, Trevor. How's it going?'

'Is that meant to impress us or is it just to annoy Helen Quigley, who was brought out here in a minicab?'

Sebastian began to explain about Daisy's deal but Trevor had already turned on his heel. He couldn't help noticing that Daisy in her jeans was now blending in very effectively with what Dougal called the oily rags while he was dressed for a long lunch at Quaglino's. Gritting his teeth, Sebastian made his way towards make-up to find Helen Quigley. He knocked on the flimsy trailer door.

'Come in!'

'Hello, Katya. Is Helen about?'

'Still in with the wicked witch of the west.'

'Or should that be the wicked bitch in the vest?'

'Hello, Howard. I'll go over and see.'

Sebastian trudged through the churned mud to the costume trailer and knocked again.

'Who is it?'

'Sebastian.'

'Just a tick, darling, we're not quite decent.' He stood and waited.

'Shall I come back?'

'Just a sec.' A fine drizzle began to fall. He'd forgotten to bring his waterproofs, or even an umbrella. 'Okay, come in.'

'Hello, Helen, you look wonderful.' What on earth was

Anastasia thinking of? Policewomen don't run to Armani separates. Neither did Sebastian's costume budget.

'Suits her, doesn't it?'

'Fantastic. But isn't it a bit … well, upmarket for the character?'

Anastasia smiled icily. 'You don't imagine I'd chosen this, I hope,' she hissed. 'We haven't started changing her yet.'

'Oh. Well, very stylish, Helen.' Sebastian smiled at his leading actress. She regarded him coolly. 'Everything all right?'

'You might be getting a call from Lavinia.'

'Oh. I see. Anything I can help with now?'

'Talk to Lavinia.' And she turned back to Anastasia. 'Can I look through my rail again, Stasi? Is there time?'

'Of course, darling. Take all the time you want.' He closed the door.

'Sorry to disturb you, Sebastian.' Gus treated him to one of her ravishing smiles. 'Trevor asked if you'd join him on set.'

'I'll come in a minute.'

'Now, he said. Don't shoot me, I'm just the messenger.'

'Okay, tell him I'm on my way.'

Gus murmured into the mouthpiece of her walkie-talkie as she stood aside to let him come down the steps. Sebastian followed her towards the knot of people around the camera.

'Did you know about this?' Trevor demanded angrily. The crew watched with interest.

'Know about what?'

'This … diktat. About stock.'

'Shall we discuss this in private, Trevor?'

The director began reading out a memo. Sebastian recognised it as one Dougal had written, to him, about the shooting ratio.

'Well?'

'I cannot function in these conditions. How can I direct a film without being able to shoot as I think fit?' Sebastian glared at the camera crew, who busied themselves with urgent maintenance.

'A film?'

'I demand a retraction.'

'Trevor, I think you'll find that memo was addressed to me. How did you get it?'

'Let me know when this is resolved. I'll be in my trailer.' He stalked off the set.

Since when did Trevor have a trailer?

'Gus, would you find Dougal and ask him to come over, please?'

Todd stepped up. 'Nine-twenty, Sebastian. We haven't had an artist on set yet.'

'Okay, Todd.'

He lowered his voice. 'Have you considered firing the bastard?'

'Is there anything useful the crew can do for half an hour?'

'Phone around for another job?'

'Come on, Todd, a bit of support would be nice.'

'We'll bring forward the restaurant. It's a big lighting job in there.'

Sebastian saw Dougal bearing down on him and drew him to one side, away from the men in black.

'It's a ploy, dear boy,' said Dougal, once Sebastian had explained. 'You've got to call his bluff.'

'How?'

'Make this a second unit day. Send him home. Get Todd to direct.'

'Isn't that rather a high risk strategy?'

Dougal rubbed his hands together and re-lit his pipe. 'Just like the good old days at Pinewood,' he said tenderly. 'When Cubby stepped out of his office you always knew there was going to be trouble. Just do it, and watch what happens.'

'And tell Trevor that's what we're doing?'

'Better still, don't. He'll find out soon enough.'

A few minutes later Todd was announcing the reschedule

over the walkie-talkies. Before he'd finished Trevor was back on set demanding to know why the cast and crew weren't ready for him. He looked straight through Sebastian and talked to Ludi. There was no more discussion of the shooting ratio. Sebastian made a tactical withdrawal and left the set to him.

* * *

Five minutes later Helen Quigley was in front of the camera and they were turning over on her first scene. Trevor William seemed determined to prove something. By lunchtime more than half the day's schedule had been completed, and the director instructed Todd to come up with scenes that could be pulled forward from the next day's call sheet. The crew returned from lunch and within ten minutes they were turning over again. By the time they wrapped, ten minutes early, Trevor had completed the unshot scenes from the previous day, all of that day's call sheet and half of the next day's. He'd proved he could shoot fast as well as slow. But was it good? Sebastian would have to wait until he saw the rushes.

He called in on the costume trailer to see Helen. There was an open bottle of Chardonnay on the ironing board. She and Anastasia were hooting with laughter at something. They made an unlikely pair.

'How did it go today, Helen?'

She put down her glass and turned to face her producer. 'That man is a – genius,' she breathed. 'Where did you find him?'

'Oh, er, I, you know … we put a lot of thought into these decisions, as you can imagine …'

'To be perfectly honest, Sebastian, I thought he was going to be a disaster,' she continued, after another gulp of wine. Anastasia topped her up. 'A bit of a fucking nightmare. But he's not. He just … understands. You know. What it is. We do. Actors.' She emptied the glass in one. 'You don't know what it's like to work with a director who's just there to massage his own ego, who doesn't give a shit about anyone else.'

'Well …'

'And I've had to put up with so many of them. Ah well. Fuck 'em. Eh? I'm off home.' She pitched off her chair. Anastasia caught her in a hug and steadied her until Helen could regain her balance. 'Goodnight, Sebastian dear,' she said, planting a big kiss on his cheek. 'See you tomorrow!' Anastasia guided her towards the car and helped her in before returning to the trailer, and he waved from the steps.

'Is it a good idea getting her drunk?'

'She was frightfully nervous, poor thing,' drawled Anastasia, lighting up a Silk Cut. 'First time on a proper set, hardly knew where to put herself. Now she's lost her cherry she'll be fine. I always keep a bottle in the fridge for when they get off.'

'Just for them?'

'That's right, darling. Earl Grey for me. My liver was shot to hell years ago.'

'Well, goodnight, then. Thanks for looking after her.'

'That's what it's all about.'

Sebastian closed the trailer door and went looking for his own car back to town. There wasn't one. In the end he got a lift on the back of Todd's bike. There weren't any spare gloves, and by the time Sebastian got home his hands were blue.

On his answering machine he found a message from one of the slower agents, still trying to place his assorted clients on the *Rough Diamonds* shoot. Then he heard Graham's voice. Sebastian was about to cut him off, in fact to disconnect the machine altogether, when he heard him say 'You're really going to want to hear what I've got to tell you. You think I'm having an affair with Jemma, but I'm not. We really are friends! But … I do know who she's with. Call me.' Sebastian scrabbled through his bag and finally teased Graham's number out of his handheld.

Graham was out. Sebastian didn't leave a message. In fact, he felt disgusted with himself, and with Graham too. Why was he so avid to thresh about in Sebastian's dirty laundry? And Jemma's? Sod him.

Sebastian felt tired and hungry. Tired won on points and he settled for a banana. There was no question of cooking and even a takeaway seemed to demand more energy than he had available. He finished the banana in about five seconds and went to bed.

Next morning he took the train in from Mortlake and walked from Oxford Circus to the cutting room in Lexington Street. Taki and his assistant were sitting side by side at the Lightworks, working through the previous day's rushes.

'Sorry, Sebastian, but I can't send Ringo out for coffees, he's got too much on here.'

'Yeah, we shot a lot yesterday.'

'Seventeen and a half minutes, according to the camera sheets. What did you do, hold a gun to his head?'

'He's a director. He doesn't like to be predictable.'

'He's certainly not that. Have a look at what we've sunk up so far.'

Ringo loaded a tape and vacated the seat for Sebastian. Helen Quigley swam onto the screen through a fog.

'What's that?'

'Smoke, probably, plus diff filters. What's it say on the sheets?'

'Never mind.' However it was caused, the effect was eerie and unsettling. Helen Quigley was unrecognisable. Gone were the bright lipstick, the blonde hair, and the big jewellery familiar from *Dalston Square*, and indeed from real life. Helen had become wraithlike, a pale figure with deeply shadowed, haunted eyes. 'Bloody hell, this looks incredible. What's it like when she talks?'

Ringo reached over and spun the tape on to another set-up. It was the scene where Dan searches an empty warehouse looking for her chief suspect, and meets the caretaker (who turns out to be the suspect in disguise, having murdered the caretaker and stolen his coat and mop and bucket). The scene was shot on a fire escape that looked like a staircase in hell, with no top and no bottom.

'How did he do that?'

'What?'

'Make it look like he's solid, but she's almost a ghost.'

Taki shrugged. Now Helen was talking, asking directions, questions, and getting riddling answers from the killer. Her voice was thin, faltering. Her eyes darted left and right as she spoke, like a frightened animal. Beside the thuggish young man with his mock-polite talk she seemed very vulnerable. Sebastian watched, amazed.

'Who's this actress?' asked Ringo.

'Helen Quigley.'

'What, Rikki?'

'That's her.'

'Blimey. I'd never have recognised her.'

Well, no. Nor would anyone else. It was many miles from *Dalston Square*. They all were. Possibly too many, Sebastian thought, a little uncomfortably, for Steve Bung and Brit TV. On the other hand, they wanted to develop Helen away from soaps, and this was certainly … not a soap. Gothic was back, and in a big way.

'I like it. And he's given me plenty of shots to work with. I can really cut this.'

'Good.'

'Have you seen enough for now? Only we've got a lot to log.'

Taki was still intent on the fitful image on his screen.

21 Casualties

'Well, how is it?' Dougal raised his bushy eyebrows and shielded the burning match from the wind. Today they were on a hillside somewhere in Buckinghamshire.

'Interesting. Pretty good, actually.'

'Enough cover?'

'Taki seems happy. I think Trevor's making sure we'll have choices in the cutting room.'

'Or *he* will.'

'How's he going today?'

'Still setting up the stunt.'

'Stunt?'

'The pile-up. The one Dan walks away from.'

'Last time I looked it was a near miss.'

'He told me you two had discussed it.'

'And you believed him? Dougal. I'm surprised at you.'

'Actually I didn't believe him. But he seems to know when I'm not going to be able to get hold of you to check.'

'With instincts like that I suppose he had to become a director.'

* * *

Back at Brunt Productions it was Lucy in reception who first drew his attention to the news. 'Oh, Sebastian. There's a message from someone called Graham who said it was urgent, about Jemma. Your wife's name is Jemma, isn't it?'

'Yes. Why?'

'There's a piece in the paper you might want to read.'

'Later, Lucy.' Reluctantly he keyed Graham's number, then shut the door of his office.

'He's with a patient at the moment. Shall I take a message?'

'No, could you just say Sebastian returned his call.'

'Oh. Is that Sebastian Boyle?'

'Yes.'

'He did ask to be told if you rang, Mr Boyle. Would you hold on just one moment?'

'Okay.' He waited, imagining Graham in mask and blood-spattered overalls, working away at a tooth with shiny pliers.

'Hello, Sebastian?' He sounded a little out of breath. The effort of his struggle with the tooth, or had he run to the phone in his excitement? 'Have you seen the paper?'

'Why does everyone want to know if I've read the paper?'

'Because of Jemma.'

He went on. Sebastian listened. Mechanically he thanked Graham, in a monotone, and put down the phone. He stared vacantly out of the window. All he could think of was that ghastly trip to the National Theatre, when he went with Jemma to see *Three Sisters*. Their last night together.

Sebastian picked up the phone and made another call.

* * *

They met in a Japanese fast-food eatery where a procession of dishes circulated on a conveyor belt, like a culinary M25. The crunchy noodles Sebastian had spotted never made it to their end of the table. Instead he picked at some raw fish while keeping an eye on the belt in case his luck changed and a plucky noodle fought its way through.

'I don't know what to say.'

'No, it is strange.' Jemma looked down at the table, the curtain of hair obscuring her face.

'Why him, of all the men in the world?'

'I don't know.'

'He's everything you hate!'

'Well, he isn't you.' Sebastian blinked. 'Sorry. I didn't mean that.'

'I didn't realise you actually … hated …'

'I don't. Of course I don't. It's just – everything's different.'

'So how did it happen? He just called you up, what?'

'He tracked me down. Quite flattering, really.'

'Or he got someone in his office to do it.'

'It's the thought that counts.'

'And then you met him again?'

'Yes.'

'Christ. Graham's having kittens. It's more than he can cope with, the thought of you and Jason Prynne together among the drills and mouth-rinse.'

'We've never met in my surgery!'

'Don't tell Graham that. This is the best sex he's ever had.'

'Graham's been a good friend to me.'

'Sure. And Jason Prynne is going to treat you with courtesy and respect.'

'Perhaps I don't want him to treat me like that.'

'How's the drinking?'

'He's stopped that.'

'Jemma, I almost feel sorry for you. Almost. Still, at least now I know where you've put up your wigwams.'

'Oh, I dumped those. Jason's got a flat, he doesn't have a garden. It's very nice, in Holland Park –'

'Tell Graham, he lives for those details.' He got up.

'Maybe it wasn't a good idea, meeting.'

'Better than reading about it in the paper. But I've already done that. Good luck.'

Sebastian left. What else could he do?

* * *

The alarm went off. Day four of the shoot. Sebastian reviewed the scorecard in his head. Losses so far: one brother-in-law, one wife, one location manager, two commissioning editors, peace of mind, possibly his sanity. Gains to date: one second mortgage, about five kilos (he put that down to the location catering), minor palpitations, more room in the bed. On balance: well, too early to say. You had to play the long game.

He got up. What would Trevor William do today? Sebastian wondered as he shaved. Whatever it was, it couldn't be a surprise after one atrocious day, one excellent day, and one – he realised he still didn't know how yesterday had gone. Outside a horn blared. Sebastian rubbed a porthole in the steamed-up bathroom window and peered out. That low-slung vintage Granada could only be his minicab. Tinted windows made sure the driver's identity remained strictly on a need-to-know basis. The horn blared again, a good five seconds' worth of twin air klaxons shaking the dustbin lids and making the cats cringe. It was six-fifteen in the morning. Sebastian got down as quickly as he could before the driver could do it again.

'Where are we going?'

'Uxbridge, innit.'

He settled back into the velour-covered seat. Uxbridge was fine by Sebastian. He had vague memories of a sequence on an allotment they'd scheduled to shoot there. Somewhere in his bag was a call sheet which provided every detail anyone could possibly want, but he felt in no hurry to take it out. Jemma kept pushing her way back into his consciousness. And Jason. Jemma'n'Jason – it had a ring. He couldn't help wondering at which point it had been that the two Js had clicked. The moment the three of them met in the Lyttleton bar? When Jason slagged off the Blackwell clan? The fateful meeting with Pete Clapp?

However he looked at it, Jemma's behaviour made little sense. She'd been getting herself ready to tell Sebastian about her dalliance with Graham the amorous orthodontist. By the end of the evening she'd dumped him, and Graham as well.

How desperate Jemma must have felt to clutch at Graham, an emotional straw if ever there was one. Jason was spectacularly unsuitable, but presumably that was the point of him. With a sudden lurch Sebastian saw how unhappy Jemma must be. A large part of that – most, perhaps, if not all – was due to him. It was almost a relief to yank his thoughts away from his conjugal failings and back to his professional ones.

Sebastian remembered driving down a long straight tree-lined road in Northern France one summer, the bars of sunlight hitting him faster and faster between the pools of shade until it was going light-shade-light-shade-light-shade like a strobe. After a while his eyes had given up trying to adjust and just went slack and he'd been whanging down this empty road faster and faster without really being able to see where he was going. That was pretty much what this shoot felt like. He'd started off trying to be organised and in control and then he'd felt himself pushed back against the seat barely able to move. By the end Sebastian knew he'd be hanging on by his fingernails while everything around him was just a blur.

* * *

Out of that blur a few events stood out clearly. The next day was one of them. They'd just arrived at the hundredth slate, traditionally marked on a film set by champagne. The crew insisted this celebration was also traditional in TV shots, but Sebastian didn't believe they'd seen much Veuve Clicquot on *Boys in Blue*. Nonetheless he'd agreed to have a bottle of Caterers' Non-Vintage out of the fridge to show willing when slate ninety-nine was completed. The heavy green bottle with its pretentious label duly went onto the set together with a pack of plastic cups.

It was received in silence. Trevor William turned on his heel and stalked off. Everyone waited, uncertain what to do. Before

Todd had made up his mind what to call, Trevor was back, staggering under the weight of a cardboard box. Behind him Gus was carrying another. In them were twenty-four bottles of Bollinger, and a vintage one at that. They were chilled, and there were champagne flutes to go with them. Todd summoned the sparks, standby craftsmen, and other outlying or skiving crew members so that all could partake.

The Caterers' Non-Vintage stood, shamed, on a camera box while all around it corks popped and glasses were filled. Sebastian caught Fat Bob's eye. Fat Bob removed the spurned bottle, but didn't refuse the flute of Bollinger that Trevor William held out to him. The standby chippy toasted the director before seizing the spurned Caterers' NV from Fat Bob, shaking it wildly and then showering the crew with it as the cork flew out, racing driver style. In a few moments the whole crew seemed to be drinking, shouting, singing. Even Ludi downed a glass and almost smiled.

It was at this moment that executive producer Rick Todge arrived to visit the set.

'What the *fuck* is going on here?'

'Oh. Hello, Rick –'

'Richard. You in charge of this shower? Sebastian, right?'

'We met in Steve's office.'

'Well it's my office now and I don't like being taken for a cunt. Okay?' Rick jammed his face into Sebastian's. Gus came up and offered him a flute of champagne.

'This is Richard Todge. Executive producer,' Sebastian added, trying to infuse the words with as much menace as possible. But, to the crew, executive producer meant much the same as writer or commissioning editor or development executive or trainee shelf stacker or refuse removal operative. They were all quite simply non-jobs, so far as production personnel were concerned.

'Champagne?' Gus pursued, innocently.

'Fuck off, girlie,' Rick Todge snarled. He turned to Sebastian. 'I saw your progress report,' he growled. 'Ninety-eight seconds of screen time in a day. Are you taking the piss?'

'Have you seen day two yet?'

'And now this. I come out on location and find you've given Thresher's a thrashing. Who's paying for this lot?'

'The director, as it happens.'

'Well, I want to see the receipts. And what about the lost time, eh? Who's paying for *that*? Fucking us, that's who!'

Rick had come for a showdown. Finally he'd read the scripts, made his notes, come to a decision. He'd moved into Steve Bung's office, and he wanted everyone to know it. He wanted to close *Rough Diamonds* down. All this he made very clear to Sebastian when they met later, upstairs in the dining bus. Sebastian and his team had sown the wind with their unprofessional behaviour and would reap a whirlwind of P45s.

Rick Todge's threat, however, was never carried out. The next day Sebastian received an email from Mel Gioconda to say she'd been asked to take over from Steve Bung and was delighted that they'd be working together after all. Rick Todge would be reporting to her. And she had some notes on the scripts.

Sebastian took her out to lunch (Xeno's, new and fashionable, very expensive). Mel was charming. Why shouldn't she be? For all Mel knew, *Rough Diamonds* might turn out to be a massive hit. If so, as controller of drama, the credit was hers. If it bombed, the blame lay for all to see on Steve Bung's broad shoulders. After all, he'd commissioned it – and Mel had already turned it down once at The Channel. If she was still fuming over Sebastian's last-minute defection to Brit TV, she didn't show it. Anyway, she was a defector herself now. Mel smiled at Sebastian like the cat with its own dairy.

* * *

Shooting day followed shooting day, and occasionally a rest day intervened – just enough time for the crew to get up late, fill the washing machine, dry their combats, and have an early night before it all kicked off again.

As the rushes were progressively assembled by Taki's machines a number of things were becoming clear to Sebastian. *Rough Diamonds* was changing. The tone had grown darker, more complex, richer. Better, in fact; but less commercial. Secondly, Helen Quigley was working very well in her new role, and demonstrating ability that Sebastian for one had certainly never suspected. So far, so good.

Thirdly, however, he had a growing suspicion that Trevor William was putting all his eggs – all Sebastian's eggs, too – into one basket. He'd ransacked the resources of episode two and episode three and put everything into episode one. If ever there was a crane shot (and there were several) Sebastian could be sure it was destined for the first episode, whatever it said on the call sheet or in the script. Episode one had a bigger and more expensive cast, more locations, more shooting time, more Steadicam, more cracked-oil smoke, more wind machines, more rain effects, more stunts, more action vehicles. More story. It had more of everything. In fact, it had most of everything.

'This is terrific.'

'What do you mean?'

'Episode one. It isn't telly – it's a movie.'

Sebastian turned to look at Taki. The editor hadn't said it with a sneer, as Dougal might have done. He meant it as the sincerest compliment to the work, to Trevor. At last Sebastian understood what Trevor William was up to.

Suddenly he felt very sick. This was worse, much worse, than he'd feared. He checked the call sheet. They were shooting scene eight today, somewhere the other side of Sevenoaks.

* * *

What looked at first sight like a small lake turned out to be an old quarry, dug out long ago and now filled with greenish water and used as a reservoir.

Sebastian found the crew huddled around an old pontoon, where a small boat was being launched from a trailer. Behind the unit riggers were assembling a camera crane, a smaller (but not much smaller) version of the ones used to build skyscrapers, as well as other equipment he couldn't even identify. It looked very much like what he'd expected – a budget-blowing extravaganza of director toys.

He was just wondering 'Where's the helicopter?' when he heard the thudding beat of the rotors overhead. That just left underwater photography. Was that a frogman holding a submersible camera next to the pontoon? Sebastian did a quick cost calculation, but lacked both the courage and the capacity for mental arithmetic to pursue it as far as the total.

'Drop me here, please.' Getting out of the taxi behind a little wooden clubhouse, he picked his way through ranks of sailing dinghies down towards the shore. No one had noticed his arrival. Sebastian scanned the group for Dougal, then called him on his mobile. He watched the older man move away from the knot of people around the director to answer.

'Hello?'

'Meet me behind the clubhouse.'

They sat among the stowed sails and lifejackets where they could talk in privacy.

'How's the budget?'

Dougal shrugged. 'Fine, so far. A bit over on stock and camera equipment, but nothing to worry about.'

'What about this lot?'

'Ludi did a very good deal on it.'

'Ludi? You mean it's all his?'

'Most of it.'

'And the underwater gear? And the helicopter?'

'Well, not the helicopter, obviously. But there's a company he has a good relationship with.'

'That's more than you can say for us. Where's all the money for this coming from?'

'Don't worry, Trevor understands the limitations. He's robbing Peter to pay Paul.'

'That's exactly what does worry me.'

'He's putting extra resources into the pilot episode, that's sensible, and he'll balance it with savings in eps two and three.'

'He's never going to make eps two and three.'

'What?'

'Don't you see? Everything he's shot so far – whatever it said on the call sheet – he's using in the first episode. It's complete, except for this sequence today. But he hasn't shot anything else.'

'But – he's shot scenes from all three …'

'No. He hasn't. Ignore the scene numbers, look at what he's actually shot, and what have we got? A very impressive one-hour movie, and some bits and pieces.'

'Oh … my … God.'

'Trevor William has made himself a very good calling card. At our expense. And we have two hours of screen time to fill with his leftovers. That's why he kept the script so close to his chest. Why he seemed so relaxed about the other two. Jesus! I can't believe he could be *so* … ruthless. Dougal?'

Dougal had slumped forward on the wooden bench. He looked pale, grey almost, and his breath came in rasping snorts.

'Dougal? Are you okay?' But Sebastian could see he wasn't. He fumbled for his phone and dialled the emergency number, then realised it would be quicker just to grab a car.

An hour later Sebastian left casualty with Gus. Dougal had been admitted and now lay in intensive care with a suspected heart attack. They'd been told to phone later for news, but it didn't look encouraging.

'Who'll feed Bond and Moneypenny?'

'Sorry?'

'And what happens if there's a high tide?'

'I'm afraid you've lost me, Sebastian.'

'Rabbits. Flood boards. Don't worry. We'd better get back to the set.'

Gus drove the Previa back in silence. He thought how well she did it. She was beautiful, efficient, probably talented too.

'What do want to do, Gus? Eventually, I mean.'

She flashed him one of her smiles. 'Direct.'

'Of course.'

They didn't speak again.

22 Super-Deluxe

'Hello, Sebastian. How's the shoot?'

'Hi Mel. It's going really, really well. How are you enjoying Brit TV?'

'A bit of a culture shock.'

'I expect you're coping.'

'Oh yes, I think I can get used to this. Anyway, tell me about *Rough Diamonds*.'

'Well, it's looking terrific. And I think you're going to find Helen Quigley's performance a revelation.'

'Stick something on a tape and bike it over.'

'Why don't you come over, and I'll screen it for you.'

The last thing Sebastian wanted was his one and only trump card playing unwatched on the telly in her office while Mel chatted on the phone to her life coach. Better to make it an event. Involve them in the adventure of production. Above all, get them out of the office, where they're safe, where they're on their own turf. Expose them to the pressures of the process.

'It's very much a work in progress. Better to see it in the right environment.'

'O … kay.'

Mel's diary hadn't caught up with her new job yet and, to be perfectly honest, there was a lot of Brit TV's output that she wouldn't go near without a full hazmat suit.

'How about tomorrow afternoon? I'll get Michelle to set it up.'

Sebastian switched off his phone and stepped out of the bathroom. It was the only room in his house that wasn't strewn with cables, boxes, stacks of tapes, VCRs, and monitors. Ringo the assistant editor shuffled through from the kitchen carrying a pile of videocassettes. They two-stepped around each other as he made for the sitting-cum-cutting-room and Sebastian squeezed past an edit controller to reach the kettle.

'Coffee?'

'Yeah.'

'Please!' Taki's ears were finely tuned.

Sebastian was holding *Rough Diamonds* hostage. Having forced the editors out of Wardour Street, where the director could get at them, he'd moved all post-production into his semi in East Sheen. In the circumstances, making coffee for Taki and Ringo was the least he could do. Besides, they had to cut the first episode into a watchable state within twenty-four hours. They didn't have time to make coffee. They barely had time to drink it.

'Yeugh!'

'Hallo, Daisy. I wasn't expecting you so soon.'

'What's that smell?'

'Ringo burnt his Welsh rarebit. Come in.'

He'd asked Daisy round for a council of war. She surveyed the cables underfoot, the editing equipment stacked in the sitting room.

'Don't worry, we can go upstairs.'

She looked at him.

'There's more room.'

'Okay.'

Daisy followed Sebastian up to the main bedroom. The bed was made – even men can shake out a duvet – and Daisy sat down on it and drew her knees up to her chin.

'How's Dougal?' she asked.

'No change. I don't think they really know yet. Either way he's not going to be back with us for weeks. If at all.'

Daisy regarded him with her blue-green eyes, more green at the moment in the subdued light. 'So it's just me and you, then?'

'Looks like it.' There was a pause.

'I feel we could achieve so much more if we had a more collaborative relationship.'

'You're probably right.'

'How much longer are they going to be working downstairs?'

'As long as it takes. We've got to show this to Mel Gioconda tomorrow.'

She leant forward an inch or two. 'Well, what can we do to speed things up?'

He reached out and touched Daisy's knee as the door opened and Ringo's shaggy head appeared.

'Scuse me, where do you keep the Lea & Perrins?'

'I'll find it.' Sebastian got up and followed Ringo down to the smoke-filled kitchen, where his second attempt at Welsh rarebit was laid out on the table. He scrabbled about at the back of the cupboard for the Worcestershire sauce.

'Not the same without it.'

'No. How's it going?'

'Nearly done now. Just need a little twist of black pepper.'

'I meant the editing.'

'Oh, Taki's finished. He's just dumping it off onto tape.'

Sebastian went through to the sitting room and there was Helen Quigley, flickering eerily across four monitors. Taki was sorting through tapes and smoking a joint.

'Looking good, eh? Sound's not perfect, but I've done what I can. And the music – have a listen.'

He turned up the sound and a haunting, pared-down tune filled the room.

'What is it?'

'Baltasar Musa.'

'Who's he?'

'Latvian composer. Not very well known.' Taki inhaled deeply. 'What does Trevor think about all this?'

'Have you spoken to him?'

Taki shook his head.

'To be honest, I don't know yet. But –'

Sebastian was cut off by the doorbell. Ringo stumped down the hallway and they heard the front door open.

'Who are you?' It was Jemma's voice. 'And what on earth are you eating?'

A moment later she was gazing in horror at the improvised editing suite.

'Hi, Jemma.'

'What in God's name is going on here?'

'Just brought some work home. This is Taki … Ringo …'

They nodded, friendly but puzzled.

'I was hoping we could have a chat. In private.'

Jemma looked around her and glowered at the sink heaving with dirty plates, the scarred paintwork, the fluff gathering in corners.

'I'm going upstairs.'

'Right. No, wait.'

Sebastian jumped up and started to follow her, but Jemma was up the stairs like a greyhound. He made a swift decision and headed for the kitchen instead. It wasn't long before Jemma joined him.

'There's a girl in our bedroom.'

'Daisy.'

'In our bed.'

'Is she? What's she doing there?'

'You tell me, Sebastian.'

'Perhaps she was tired.'

'She didn't look tired to me.'

'What, actually in the bed?'

'Actually in the bed. Undressed and in the bed, to be precise.'

'Bloody hell.'

'I came here tonight because I thought we might be able to find some way … some way …'

Her shoulders heaved and Jemma gave vent to a great sob. Sebastian went to put his arms round her. She hit him, quite hard, with the flat of her hand. The doorbell rang again.

'Jesus Christ, what now?'

From the hallway he could hear Ringo say 'He's in there, mate,' and a second later Trevor William had joined Jemma and Sebastian between the cooker and the kitchen table.

'Give me my film back.' His dark eyes were blazing, his small frame quivered with anger.

'Who are you?' Jemma rubbed at her eyes and looked at Trevor with distaste. Trevor ignored her completely. 'You have no right to steal my work.'

'Trevor, I don't think this is the time or the place –'

'I want my film.'

'Hello, everybody.' Daisy joined them in the kitchen. She seemed completely relaxed and normal, and as far as Sebastian could tell she was also wearing all her clothes.

'How's Jason?'

'I don't want to talk about it.'

'Did you hear what I said, Sebastian? I want my film back.'

'It isn't your film, Trevor. It's my programme.'

'Listen, if you think –'

'Let's talk about this tomorrow.'

'I won't be there tomorrow.'

'I think you'll find you signed a contract, Trevor.'

'I think you'll find I didn't.'

Sebastian darted a look at Daisy. Almost imperceptibly she shook her head. 'Well, in that case it certainly isn't your film. I'll see you on set tomorrow.'

'No you won't.'

'Then another director will take over.'

'We'll see what the Guild has to say about that!'

'They'll probably say you should have signed your contract. Goodnight.' He eased Trevor gently but firmly towards the door.

'Who was that?'

'That, Jemma, was the director formerly known as Trevor William.'

'Why have you taken his film?'

'It's not his film. Shall we talk upstairs?'

'Certainly not, I'm leaving.' Jemma grabbed her bag, tripped over a video cable and recovered herself.

'Give Jason my best.'

The door slammed and she was gone. In the sudden silence Sebastian could hear Taki slowly exhale before passing the joint to Ringo. He turned to Daisy.

'Was that true? Were you really – ?'

'No, of course not,' Daisy replied, briskly. 'We'd better talk about directors.'

'We'll be off, then. Back here tomorrow, nine-ish?'

'Fine. Thanks for working late.'

'No problem,' said Ringo, and opened the front door.

Taki hesitated on the threshold. 'Is Trevor really off the show?'

'Looks like it.'

'Shame. He's really got something.'

'He has. Unfortunately it's a different something from the something we need.'

Taki shrugged and followed Ringo down the drive. Sebastian closed the door and turned to Daisy. She wasn't there. 'Daisy?'

'Upstairs.'

He went into the bedroom. This time there was no ambiguity. Daisy was lying on the bed. Fully clothed, going through *The Knowledge*.

'What about Bill Block?'

Sebastian sighed. 'I suppose we can re-check him,' he said.

* * *

The viewing with Mel presented a problem. If she didn't like what she saw she might pull the plug altogether. If she did, Sebastian would have to break the news that she couldn't have any more of it. He and Daisy stood on the slightly sticky carpet in the Super-Deluxe Preview Theatre, drinking sour coffee from the machine, and waited.

Mel arrived twenty minutes late in a cloud of Nina Ricci. They followed her into the tiny auditorium and sat down in the overstuffed armchairs. It was like watching the in-flight movie in Business Class. Once Mel was settled Sebastian stood up and waved in the direction of the projection booth. The lights dimmed slightly then abruptly went off. A snatch of colour bars, then a countdown leader with diminishing numbers. Sebastian tried to relax as the soundtrack popped and they set off on their journey into *Rough Diamonds – The Movie*.

* * *

'I recognised right away that Trefor ap Gwyllm was a major talent,' said Mel Gioconda afterwards, smiling at the reporter from the film magazine. 'You have to remember that at that time he was still more or less completely unknown. If I'd been commissioning at one of the niche channels, or programming a film festival, I'd have been over the moon about *Rough Diamonds*.'

'This was for Brit TV?'

Mel nodded. 'Unfortunately. It was all about audiences, ratings, share. I was being asked to slaughter *Me and my Pig* on the other side, not discover the next Sundance winner.'

'Difficult.'

'Poor Sebastian. I hardly knew what to say to him. It was a mystery to me why Steve Bung ever commissioned it. Of course, he never reads scripts and he'd never have heard of Trefor.'

'So what did you do?'

'I forget now exactly what I said to Sebastian. I tried to let him down as gently as I could. But, at the end of the day, there was never the slightest chance that Brit TV was going to accept a prime time police series about a vampire detective you can barely see. I had to be honest with him.'

* * *

But that was months later. Immediately after the screening Daisy and Sebastian were installed at the nearest cappuccino bar, gabbling excitedly.

'Well, that seemed to go pretty well.'

'She loved that bit where the traffic warden rises from the dead.'

'Did you see? She actually clapped at the end.'

'She seemed to pick up the *Buffy* resonances.'

'Do you think she really meant what she said about getting it the Monday night slot?'

'It certainly sounded like it. And what about the other thing?'

'"Bucketful of BAFTAs"! Wow.'

They sipped their cappuccinos and chattered on gleefully. It was the first feedback they'd had, and the first time for as long as Sebastian could remember that something had at last gone right. Mel Gioconda adored *Rough Diamonds*. That much was clear. As for the rest, Sebastian had fudged the director situation, telling her that Trefor (she loved that) was being pursued by Hollywood, but he, Sebastian, had other, equally mould-breaking talents at his disposal. She was so enthusiastic she agreed to everything. Sebastian was overwhelmed by a warm tide of approval. Mel even okayed an extra week of filming, which Sebastian calculated was just enough to get them back on track. Now all they had to do was find a replacement for their wayward genius. Bill Block was forgotten, again. Sebastian was intent on securing only the most interesting, outside-the-box talents available. Damien Spent was mentioned again, even Jonathan Krankie.

Daisy and Sebastian finished their coffees and hurried back to the Brunt Productions office to develop their battle plan. Lucy in reception wasn't in reception. Sebastian supposed she'd taken an early lunch, or perhaps she didn't work mornings now that he wasn't around to notice. He and Daisy sat down with their phones and *The Knowledge* and started work on a new list.

Afterwards, Sebastian could never get it clear in his mind exactly how it happened. He'd gone to the tape store with the idea that they had something directed by Damien Spent which was worth a look and started rooting around. Daisy joined him, probably to help look for the tape, and then the door shut and somehow the light got turned off. And then Daisy was standing very close to him. And then – well, they must both have felt pretty exhilarated by the screening and Mel's enthusiasm. There was the feeling of all the weight being lifted at last, and the two of them had become quite close in the previous few days, what with Dougal's heart attack and Trevor's treachery and that incident with Jemma in the bedroom. And Daisy's eyes going from blue to green like that. It was inevitable, really.

When they emerged from the tape store Daisy and Sebastian were co-producers. Lucy had mysteriously reappeared, or arrived, and looked at them oddly as Sebastian closed the door after them. He pulled his shirt straight and leafed through *The Knowledge* while Daisy went to the washroom. Red setters kept coming into his head. He had that sick feeling in the pit of his stomach again but tried not to think about it. Daisy came back in and smiled at him in a way Sebastian found hard to interpret. Affection? Triumph? Contempt?

He wrenched his mind back to their project, one already on its way – according to Mel Gioconda – to televisual history.

'Daisy, did we remember to bring back the tape with us?'

* * *

Back in his booth the projectionist was running *Rough Diamonds – The Movie* for a second time. Once again there were three people in the audience. He was used to this sort of malarkey, it didn't bother him how many times he ran it or how few people watched it, so long as they paid.

This time, he could see from his little window, there was a short dark-haired bloke dressed in a black anorak and two fat guys in suits. The money. They were always easy to recognise. And these two had already been in twice this week to watch other stuff. Bunny and Max Arakhanian, they were called. God knows why they wanted to see all this rubbish. It was amazing what people spent their time and money making. He supposed there must be something in it. Max and Bunny were a serious-looking pair. Americans.

He could see that one of them – Bunny? Or Max? – was still talking on his mobile. The short guy in black kept turning round to look at him. Get used to it, kid! This wasn't the National Film Theatre, all reverential silence as the Douglas Sirk retrospective unspooled. It wasn't telly, either. This was the movie business.

* * *

Trevor William stood outside the Super-Deluxe with his phone to his ear.

'Marc. Speak to me.'

'I've been trying to reach you. You showed them the film?'

'Yes.'

'I thought you couldn't get hold of it. How did you manage that?'

'Never mind. Have you heard anything yet?'

'I've just come off the phone with Bunny.'

'Bunny? I thought Max did the deals.'

'It may have been Max. They both sound the same.'

'And?'

'They want you.'

'They'll fully fund my film?'

'The whole budget, cash-flow it, the lot.'

'How soon can we start?'

'Don't you have to finish *Rough Diamonds* first?'

'Do the deal to start as soon as possible. We'll begin prep right away.'

'You're in the middle of a production!'

'I've finished.'

'But what about *Rough Diamonds*?'

Trevor watched as the Arakhanian brothers squeezed into a black cab.

'What about it?'

23 Storyboarding

Back at Brunt Productions, Daisy was phoning agents, setting up meeting with directors, and generally doing a good job of talking up the project, and herself in the process. Sebastian had to admire the speed with which she'd settled into the role of co-producer. Daisy had even drafted a letter agreement covering her new job title, screen credit requirement, and salary increase. Possibly she saw him hesitate as he took all this in, because she came over and nuzzled Sebastian's neck.

'Problem?'

'No. No, it's just a bit – sudden. That's all.'

'Sudden can be fun. Can't it? Remember the tape store?'

He remembered.

'Well then. When shall we meet these directors?'

Sebastian wanted to go to Acton Studios and tell Jassy what was going on. But there was something he had to do first.

He went wrong several times, and lost track of which bank of the Thames he's on. The river snaked about on its way out of London, and the south shore became the west and even, briefly, the north. At last Sebastian found his way to Alibert's Ait. He had to leave his car and haul himself by hand on a miniature chain ferry that crossed the few yards of water between the shore and the island. On the other side the ait was a suburban toytown of shaved lawns, tiny bungalows and neat paths. There were no roads and no cars. A spinster sailed past on a bicycle with a wicker basket, and gave him a cheery wave. He followed in her wake and found his way to The Moorings, a weatherboarded building like a boathouse with a small front door set in one side. He pulled the handle beside it and could hear inside the faint clang of a ship's bell.

'There's no one in, you know.'

He turned to see the cyclist outside Safe Haven next door.

'He's in hospital, poor chap. Can I help?'

Sebastian explained that he was working with Dougal, and that he'd been concerned about his rabbits.

'Oh, I've been feeding Bond and Moneypenny, although, just between us, I have to say that Moneypenny is rather a fat rabbit and as for Bond he'll be wearing a corset soon, if Dougal isn't careful.'

'And the flood boards?'

'Don't you worry about that. We have a rota.'

'Well, I'd better be getting back, then.'

He made a quick call while he was pulling himself back to the mainland on the ferry and sent flowers to Dougal in hospital. Then he keyed in another number.

'Jassy? How are you? Good, good. Listen, I've got *great* news. We're going to pull your dates forward. What? No, it's excellent, means you don't have to kick your heels in Acton, you can get out and start shooting. How are your locations? Well, I'm sure we can pin down the rest in a week. I'm on my way over now, we'll go through it then. Okay. Bye.' Sometimes the art of conversation is not to let the other person speak. At all.

That just left the scripts.

George, unleashed now from whatever psychic shackles had bound him to Jim, was a new man. Voluble, opinionated, focused possibly to the point of monomania, he seemed to be channelling the whole of his existence into *Rough Diamonds*. His proposals for rewriting Pat Quine's script seemed to Sebastian nothing short of brilliant, upping the Gothic quota by several notches and launching prime time television drama into virgin territory. Jassy was excited by the scripts – terrified, perhaps – and nodded excitedly with a fixed and slightly manic grin to any question posed to her. Sebastian was just delighted she wasn't fighting every inch of the way, like Trevor William. Anyway, he had plenty of other things to worry about, such as his membership applications for BAFTA and a couple of Soho clubs.

Leaving Jassy storyboarding the evisceration scene, Daisy and Sebastian made the trek into Soho where the editors had settled comfortably back into their cappuccino ways. It wasn't as bad as Sebastian had feared. Putting together everything not already in the opening episode – it was good enough not to interfere with, however annoying that might be – they had over seventy minutes of material. Nearly enough for an episode and a half. The only problem now was trying to turn it into a story.

'What *is* this stuff?'

Taki shrugged. 'Some of it's scripted scenes from the two episodes. Some of it must have been shot for the opening film but not used. There's stuff here that's pretty good, actually.'

'Yes, but – what's going on?' There were scenes shot in slo-mo, huge close-ups of lips and eyeballs, fragments of this and that, and things they couldn't even recognise, filmed entirely in red or green.

Taki shrugged again, but this time had nothing to add.

'Why don't we get Phoebe in to have a look?' Daisy was looking at him.

'Because she'll have a fit. And probably collapse. Then she won't be any use to us at all.'

'Maybe it'll give her ideas. She's not a bad writer, you know.'

So they called a meeting. While Jassy coloured in her storyboard, Daisy and Taki and Sebastian sat with Phoebe in the darkened cutting room watching what seemed more and more like a random assortment of scenes, or an unsuccessful try-out by a minor surrealist film-maker. At last the tape stopped and Ringo put the lights back up.

'Wow,' breathed Phoebe. 'It's just … beautiful.'

They waited.

'To be honest I wasn't mad about what I'd written, I was just waiting for the director to say he needed it all changed. And I was dreading it, because I didn't really know what to change it into. But this … it's so … haunting.'

They waited, again, but it seemed Phoebe had finished. After half a minute or so of rapt silence, Sebastian asked, 'Can you fill in the gaps, Phoebe? Turn it into a story?' She nodded. 'Really? Right, then. Good.'

It was hardly conventional, almost certainly not the way they worked up a storyline on *Boys in Blue*, but what the hell, Sebastian and Daisy and the rest of them were headed for stardom and a bucketful of BAFTAs. They were creative people. They could do whatever they bloody well pleased.

* * *

Back in Acton Studios Bernice the script supervisor frowned and sucked her pencil. She clicked her stopwatch, a massive old-fashioned chrome job, and checked the hands. She made a note and frowned again. The script was more than thirty minutes too long. Jassy had told her not to worry but Bernice *did* worry, she knew that Jassy was a sweet girl but technical matters weren't her long suit, and she knew too how Jassy depended on her to sort it all out.

Bernice was old school. Once, long ago, she'd been a teacher. Now Jassy was her favourite pupil, the one who remembered her birthday and brought her flowers or made her a card. Her favourite pupil but not, sadly, top of the class. Still, ever since they worked together on that directing course Jassy had asked for Bernice to be her script supervisor, and Bernice had always been available and always said yes. The truth was, without these jobs from Jassy Bernice wouldn't have worked at all in the last three years, which would make her either non-employed or retired, according to your point of view.

Bernice was no spring chicken.

She put down the stopwatch and stared out of the window at the man emptying rubbish into a skip at the back of Acton Studios. Jassy understood little about the nuts and bolts of production. Worse, she didn't seem to think they even mattered. Somehow she knew no more now than when Bernice had first met her. Really, it would have been better if she'd gone to film school, despite Bernice's contempt for those arrogant young men who came out talking about shooting everything on long lenses and using the same colour palette as mid-period Capra. They might spout rubbish half the time but at least they did understand the basics. Jassy was always falling in love with actors and letting them do whatever they wanted, changing a line here and a gesture there, which played merry hell with the continuity. Time and again Bernice had explained that if the doctor enters the house from the outside with his bag in his right hand, then appears in the hallway in the matching interior with it in his left, it was going to jump when you put the two together. Can't we fix it in the edit? was what Jassy invariably said. Patiently Bernice would explain, all over again, why that wasn't possible.

Bernice had resorted to pictures, so Jassy would understand why the camera mustn't cross the line. What line? she'd asked. *The* line, Bernice had answered, drawing another picture. If you cross it the actors jump from one side of the screen to the other. Jassy had listened with interest and folded the drawing carefully in half and put it in her handbag. The next time Bernice had seen it was at lunch two days later. Jassy had embellished the little stick figures, coloured them in and given one a beard and the other a twirly moustache. But the same day Jassy had repeated the same mistake. The cameraman had looked at the director oddly. Bernice had had to step in and rescue her, explaining it all over again behind the prop store while the crew had taken an unscheduled tea break.

Jassy was out of her depth – further from the shore than she'd ever been before. She was terrified of the first director, who did sound horrid, and shy of the producer, who seemed to know barely more than Jassy did. She didn't understand the script and was afraid to ask the writer what he meant. Jassy found the production team intimidating and the whole project made her so anxious that she wasn't sleeping properly and had started to come out in a lumpy rash.

All this Bernice saw quite clearly. She herself didn't like the script, by George Thingummy, but she felt she understood it well enough and saw it would be difficult for Jassy to make a success of it. It was all about mood, and atmosphere, and intrigue, and nameless dread, and underneath it was a sort of horror story that didn't add up to a hill of beans, in Bernice's opinion. Jassy's talents, such as they were, suited long conversations between nice-looking actors in attractively-furnished interiors. Bernice could help her with those. Master shot, two-shot, go in for matching singles, she would whisper in Jassy's ear, and that was how it worked. It wasn't the most exciting style but at least they could sort it out in the cutting room. Bernice closed her eyes involuntarily at the thought of what the editor might be getting in a few weeks' time.

And now this. Bringing it all forward. Of course, the poor girl was petrified but she wouldn't say boo to a goose and so the production office had just ridden roughshod over her. It was very clear to Bernice that they needed at least another month to get the scripts right. They were all over the shop. A double-length episode, massively overlong, with no story you could put your finger on, and another, more or less normal, which she's just heard George Thingummy was going to rewrite, so that would be back to square one as well.

Bernice wondered what to do for the best. Outside, the man was heaving an entire bathroom into the skip, a rather nicer one than Bernice had at home. Some set they'd finished with on Stage Two, she supposed. Really, this was such a wasteful business, it was wicked.

* * *

Sebastian and his team plunged into another read-through. George's scripts were brought to life by a cast of beautiful young men whom Jassy had been interviewing intensively for the past few weeks. Many of them were more or less unknown, a bold move that made Sebastian wonder if he shouldn't have taken a closer interest in the casting. Mel Gioconda couldn't make it but promised to visit the set early in the shoot to see Helen Quigley in action. Jason Prynne would be joining her at last for the double episode. His character, the cyborg of the original draft, had experienced many metamorphoses but still remained defiantly subhuman.

Sebastian was glad Jason didn't come to the read-through. There'd been no more from Jemma about the progress of their affair but Graham had been considerate enough to send a long and detailed email updating Sebastian on recent developments. He probably ran a Jason Prynne fansite.

Once they'd struggled to the end of the last script Sebastian visited Dougal in hospital. He'd been warned not to agitate the patient. Sitting up in bed in his striped pyjamas Dougal looked old and frail, a survivor from the far-off days when Roger Moore had been box-office gold.

'How's that director getting on?'

'He's gone.'

'Didn't finish the shoot?'

'No.'

'What about the new one?'

Sebastian had been trying not to think about Jassy.

'She'll be fine.'

He wasn't going to tell Dougal that the director had refused to get off the recce bus because she was wearing her new Donna Karan leather coat and the rain would mark it. Instead they'd viewed the locations through steamed-up windows.

'Heard anything from your brother-in-law?'

Sebastian shook his head.

'What about Monopoli?'

'They're suing us.' Sebastian had received the writ that morning. 'Giles says it often happens, it's nothing to worry about.'

Dougal's eyebrows climbed half-heartedly up his forehead, then gave up the struggle and relapsed to their default position. 'By the way, can you bring me my laptop? I ought to update the budget and look at the rest of the schedule.'

'No, Dougal. I can't. You mustn't.'

He looked at the producer bitterly. 'So you can manage without me now, can you?'

'The doctor says you have to rest.'

'How do you think you've got this far?'

'I'm not a total incompetent, you know.'

Dougal snorted. 'And how's it going with that little schemer?'

'Who?'

'Daisy.'

'Oh. Fine.'

'Watch her.'

'You said.'

Sebastian walked across the hospital car park. He thought of Dougal, discharged, back on Alibert's Ait. He'd budget the occasional show, something that would never be made, and watch the ducks swim past his window in the rain.

'What's the matter with you?' Daisy was waiting for him in the car.

'Nothing.'

'How is he?'

'Okay. But his shooting days are over.'

'He's had his share. Anyway, it's the future that matters now.'

Sebastian put his paw over her hand and squeezed it affectionately.

'Not when I'm driving. Did he say anything about me?'

'No.'

They drove back to Acton Studios in unaccustomed silence.

* * *

Rehearsals began. Jason Prynne turned up, at last, and rapid bonding took place. Helen Quigley seemed puzzled and uncomfortable. Everything was different from last time, and she felt herself sinking back into the glutinous unreality of *Dalston Square*, something that Trevor William had made her feel she'd left behind for ever.

All too soon the first day of shooting arrived. Now it was Jassy's name on the slate beneath Ludi Schiaparelli's, and her name at the top of the call sheet. Everyone looked to her to see what she'd do. It didn't take long to find out.

'What's the set-up?' asked Todd.

'I thought … perhaps … we should … what do you think?'

Todd looked at her, hard. 'You're the director, Jassy. What do you want?'

'Let's start with … an establishing shot. Yes. We'll establish the location.'

Todd's eyes met Ludi's. The standbys exchanged a look. A nearby spark rolled his eyes. The grip said, quietly but distinctly, 'Jesus fucking Christ.'

'Okay,' called Todd, to the assembled company but simultaneously into his walkie-talkie. 'Setting up for a wide shot. No cast.'

The first chance he got Todd came straight to Sebastian and outlined the situation. 'You've got a nice girl who doesn't know shit from shiitake. It ain't going to work. I tell you this now because things can only get worse. By the end of the week you'll have lost the crew. Sorry mate, but you've got to fire her.'

'Don't you think that's a bit extreme?'

'No, mate. I think it's your only chance.'

They got Jassy's establisher, a shot absent from *Rough Diamonds* up to that point. Then she moved on to a dialogue scene, but every time they got to the end of a take Jassy had a new idea and needed to go again. By lunchtime they had fourteen takes of the master, each of them different, and eleven closer shots which didn't quite match any of them. Bernice said nothing but made copious notes on her clipboard. Helen Quigley was pulling her hair out, at first metaphorically, then literally. Katya had to keep patting it down. Sebastian strolled up to Jassy as casually as he could when they broke and asked her how she thought it was going.

'Fine, I think.'

'You've got a lot of versions of that master shot.'

'Yes, I like to be able to make choices later.'

'But you can't use any of them.'

'Why not?'

'Well, they won't match. The action's different.'

'So?'

'Well –' At that point his new Blackberry started to vibrate. Sebastian excused himself and studied the incoming email with exaggerated attention.

That night he discussed the problem with his co-producer.

'Daisy?'

'Mmm?'

'What are we going to do about Jassy?'

'Mm. Not now. Can you – ? That's it.'

A little later Daisy sat up and shook out her hair. 'We'll have to sack her.'

'Do you think so?'

'Definitely.'

'Do you think we should have …'

'Guessed earlier?'

'Yes.'

'Probably. Can't be helped. We know now.'

'Who shall we get to replace her?'
'Who's free?'

* * *

And so, a week later, the shoot resumed under the direction of
Bill Block.

24 It's a Wrap

For the next few weeks *Rough Diamonds* progressed just like any other production. It rained a lot, and the schedule suffered. Then it became excessively hot and sunny so nothing matched with the rainy footage. Then it was so windy that half the set blew away. Then it rained again, and a cherry picker sank into a muddy field and toppled over onto the make-up trailer, which fortunately was empty at the time. Katya took to drink, and Howard crashed his Saab. There was a crew revolt against red and green curry and they had to change caterers. Todd organised a go-kart race one lunch break and the camera car driver spun out and broke his wrist. Bill Block in his stained baseball cap and Ludi Schiaparelli in his black Armani battle-dress became close companions, and would go out together for gastronomic dinners whenever the unit was shooting within striking distance of a Michelin-starred restaurant. Gorgeous Gus arrived on set one morning covered in love-bites, giving rise to fervid speculation. Helen Quigley's wig went missing somewhere in Taplow. The page count mounted while the list of scenes remaining to be shot dwindled away almost to nothing.

Sebastian adjusted to his latest director. Bill grunted at him over his bacon roll in the morning, and Sebastian nodded back. Bill just … got on with it. Meanwhile Daisy and Sebastian were directing the second unit, picking up missing scenes and shots with which to patch up the holes in the episodes abandoned by Trevor William. Daisy began wearing a baseball cap, like Bill, only hers was from Dolce & Gabbana, not Millets. Sebastian didn't like the way she laid her arm on Jason Prynne's while she gave him notes.

'Notes! For God's sake, Daisy. All he has to do is walk across the road and go through the door. That's it. Cut. End of scene.'

'What's the matter with you? Not jealous, are you?'

Yes, Jason Prynne did cause some problems, now he'd finally joined the production. Sebastian couldn't avoid him forever, so once he was out on set Sebastian walked over and asked him right out how it was going with Jemma.

'Jemma? That was over ages ago.'

'Oh?'

'I'm seeing that runner, as it happens. Gus. Pretty fucking hot, actually. Why don't you come out for a drink with us tonight?'

* * *

Sebastian had been avoiding the cutting room for some time. The day had to come, though, and when he saw from the call sheet that Bill Block and the main unit were doing driving shots with Helen Quigley while Daisy and the second unit picked up a cutaway of Jason Prynne in his bath, he made an executive decision and went unannounced to Taki's Soho eyrie. Sebastian found him hunched glumly over the Lightworks.

'How's it looking?'

'Okay.'

'You don't seem too sure.'

'Take a look. Ringo, shove in the assemblies. I'll run three tapes. Then *you* tell *me*.'

Ringo clicked off the lights. There on the screen was Trevor William's DS Dan Beatty, a.k.a. Helen Quigley, her pale face swimming through the darkness.

'Okay. Hold that thought. Now look at this.'

The mood changed. Dan walking down a street. Dan in the underpass. Dan stops to look at a strange man.

'I shot that!'

Cut to interior disused crematorium. In reverse slow-motion a cloud of smoke implodes into a black casket. A hand, lacking an arm, twitches on the floor. The camera moves, finding Dan Beatty again, this time apparently dead. She sits bolt upright and opens her eyes, as the camera zooms very fast into the tunnel of her eye.

'What the hell's that? I don't remember any of it.'

'It's part of Phoebe's rewrite based on Trevor's leftovers and your second-unit stuff.'

'It's pretty weird, what you've done.'

'It's just a start. It's got something, though. Now look at this.'

Same lighting, same character. Dan Beatty walks into an office and meets a uniformed policeman coming out. They talk. Cut to Dan Beatty coming out onto the street. She gets into her car and drives off.

'Hang on, hang on. Why's this so …?'

'Stick with it.'

Car, doorway, another office, car, house. Two-hander with middle-aged woman. Door, car, travelling shot, police station. More dialogue.

'I don't understand.'

'Offices, cars, houses. We didn't have locations like that before. Ludi's matching the lighting as far as he can but you can't make an office full of fluorescent lights look Gothic.'

'It's a plod show,' added Ringo. 'Could be *Boys in Blue*.'

'Did Bill Block direct *Boys in Blue*?'

'I expect so. He's directed everything else.'

'Hang on, guys. What are you saying?'

'You've got three episodes of *Rough Diamonds* – well, two and a half, really – and three episodes of *DS Plod*.'

'Has Bill Block seen any of this?'

'He told me he never watches anything until he's finished shooting. Sometimes not even then.'

'But George's scripts – and Pat Quine's – they're not like that.'

'They are now.'

'Sebastian? Phone call for you.' Ringo passed over the handset.

'Hello? What? Okay, I'll be there as soon as I can.' Taki looked up. 'I've got to get back on set. We'll have to talk about this later.'

'Sure. I'll just keep on clicking the bits together.'

* * *

For some time trouble had been brewing between Bill Block and Helen Quigley. Foxed as she was by Jassy, Helen had been sorry to see her go. For her, Bill Block combined the worst of several worlds.

'What's the matter?'

'It's the nude scene.'

'Oh God.'

Pat Quine had written a scene where DS Dan gets emotionally involved with an attractive man who turns out to be the killer she's tracking. So far, so conventional. But in keeping with Pat's taste for envelope-pushing, further enhanced by George's polish of his script, Helen Quigley's character now found herself in the boiler room of a sinister hotel, naked, manacled, and blindfolded. Unsurprisingly, Helen hadn't been looking forward to this scene. There'd been discussions and Sebastian had promised all the usual consider-ations: closed set, no stills, no Polaroids, essential personnel only, dresser standing by with dressing gown, etc. And of course there was a nudity clause in her contract, which specified the production's right to carefully delineated portions of Helen's anatomy: full nudity (rear view), frontal nudity to include breasts (but not nipples), and an absolute ban on the lower frontal regions in general and pubic hair in particular. All fine. But when it came to the point Helen Quigley wouldn't do it. Bill Block was furious. He had his reputation as a man who shot the schedule to think of. So he'd sent for Sebastian to sort it out, summon agents, wave contracts in the air, threaten and cajole, whatever was necessary for Bill to get this scene in the can along with the rest of them.

Sebastian found Helen, upset but unrepentant, in her dressing room. They talked. No dice.

He spoke to Bill, who was getting a well-earned shot of nicotine outside. 'Give me my cast and I'll shoot it,' was all he said.

Sebastian had a ludicrous idea. He tried it out on Helen. She thought it was a joke at her expense, but then she smiled and agreed. Bill Block sighed, said 'If it's really necessary, what the hell.' The crew were harder to persuade, but when he got Daisy to tell them she was going along with it they muttered that they would if she would.

Fifteen minutes later Helen Quigley was naked except for half a pair of very sheer tights, a blindfold, two squares of gaffer tape over her nipples and quick-release handcuffs. Bill Block stood in his sagging Y-fronts and nothing else. He had an impressive beer-gut. Ludi Schiaparelli wore a black thong. Daisy was in her knickers, topless. Sebastian was wishing he hadn't chosen his Homer Simpson boxers that morning, but he had, and now everyone knew. The grip, strikingly, was elegant in Calvin Kleins. Gus the gorgeous runner apparently didn't go in for underwear at all and someone from wardrobe had to lend her a scarf to tie around her hips. Everyone in the room was similarly disrobed, and suddenly regained their individuality, lost for so long under identical jeans and anoraks and baseball caps.

'All right, let's get on with it,' said Todd, brilliant in a vermilion tanga. 'Stand by for a take. Final checks, please.' The make-up assistant darted out with her bag and pattered in bare feet to where Helen sat, to brush a shiny patch on her forehead.

'Ready? Quiet and still, please. Turn over.'

The camera motor began to whirr and the red lights came on. The clapper loader held the board at groin height.

'*Rough Diamonds*, slate seven hundred and sixty-two, take one.' He raised the clapper and brought it smartly down, retiring swiftly behind the camera.

'Thank you. And ... action!'

Once everyone was back in their clothes Sebastian sought out Daisy.

'I need a word with you in private.'

'The last thing I feel after that is frisky.'

'No, I really do need a word with you.'

They found a quiet corner at the far end of the corridor, and Sebastian told Daisy what he'd seen in the cutting room.

'Well, what did you expect? Trevor William was too arty for you, and now Bill Block isn't arty enough. Shit happens. We'll just have to do the best we can with it.'

'This isn't like you, Daisy.'

'Isn't it? I've just had the grip leering at my tits for the last hour. Thanks a bunch for that. Was it really necessary?'

'If you had a better plan, why didn't you say so?'

'I didn't.'

'Welcome to producing, Daisy. Whatever it takes to get it done.'

'This isn't like *you*, either. When did you become so cynical?'

'I'm not cynical.'

'No?'

'Desperate, perhaps. And pragmatic. This is a very pragmatic job. I thought you understood that better than anybody.'

Later, though, in the minibus back to base, Sebastian wondered about what Daisy had said. Perhaps in other circumstances he would have worried less about the budget and fought harder for quality, for what he wanted *Rough Diamonds* to be. In other circumstances, though, he wouldn't have been involved at all. Albie would have been producing it while Sebastian made gardening programmes on a Handycam.

Anyway, what did Sebastian want the series to be? The truth was, he hardly knew any more.

Yes, he did. Deep down he knew exactly what he wanted *Rough Diamonds* to be.

He wanted it to be over.

* * *

Giles Savernake continued to fence with Monopoli's hyper-expensive lawyers over the botched co-production. Daisy and Sebastian completed the second-unit stuff and Phoebe wrote and rewrote a new story around the pictures. Helen Quigley slipped into a catatonic state, giving her acting a sleepwalking quality that didn't help matters. Jason Prynne disgraced himself with the make-up assistant and started snorting coke in his trailer. Bill Block continued to shoot the schedule, but not much else. The air of gloom in the cutting room when Sebastian visited was almost palpable. He came to dread going there almost as much as a phone call from Mel.

Bill Block didn't respond well to suggestions. After looking at Taki's assembly of his cut scenes Sebastian had had a quiet word in the car park, while the director ate his jam roly-poly and custard off the roof of his Audi estate.

'All I mean is, it's a bit different from the early episodes we've already shot.'

'Oh aye.'

'It's a question of style.'

'Listen, son.' Bill jammed his big face close to Sebastian's, so close he nearly gagged on the director's sugar-laden breath. 'I don't shoot fancy bollocks, I don't wiggle the camera around for the sake of it, and I don't take notes from whippersnappers. I've been directing for twenty-six years and if you don't like the way I do it then you can fire me and I'll be off home now.'

'I just want it to match the rest of the series, that's all.'

'Maybe you should have come to me sooner. I'm matching nowt now.' Bill picked up his roly-poly and stalked off back towards the dining bus. Some of the crew were watching, interested, through the windows. Sebastian turned away and encountered a familiar face.

'Sophie? What are you doing here?'

'Hi, Sebastian. Making a programme about Helen Quigley. For the Soap Channel.'

'Have you talked to anyone about this?'

Sophie looked different. She'd lost the grungy media-studies look and had gone for 100% babe, titanium-coated. She didn't stop smiling and moved through the set like a bike courier carving through a traffic jam. A tiny DV camera never left her hand.

Sebastian called Molly, the publicist.

'Do you know anything about a programme on Helen Quigley for the Soap Channel?'

'No, darling. But it sounds a good idea.'

'What's the Soap Channel like?'

'Couldn't say, dear, I don't get it. But you never know what'll come out of these little snippets. It all adds up.'

Sebastian left Sophie waiting outside the make-up trailer and went to see if Ludi could help with Bill Block's shooting style. He had no joy with the DoP, either.

'But everything you shot with Trevor looks so different.'

Ludi spread his fingers expressively but said nothing.

'Can't you match what you did before?'

Ludi shrugged. 'I can photograph only what is there.'

'But can't you do it so it looks the same?'

Ludi regarded the producer pityingly. 'These directors. You have chosen perhaps not so wisely.'

'What do you mean?'

'They do not match. One is a chalk. The other a cheese.'

* * *

Less than a fortnight of shooting remained. Already people were smiling in anticipation, and portable objects were disappearing from the set and the production office.

Sebastian sat down with Munraj, now promoted to production accountant, and went through the cost report for the final week of shooting. They were slightly over in most areas, except for a few where they were massively over. Economies were called for. Sebastian cancelled the traditional free fleeces for the crew, opting for a job lot of novelty key rings with a plastic diamond on a chain, which Munraj's assistant had spotted on a stall in Brick Lane. He sent back half of Ludi's lights. He outlawed taxis and couriers. He did everything he could think of. But it was too little, too late.

* * *

The last day of the shoot dawned bright and clear, a brilliant sunny morning. The survivors were smiling and joking as they gathered around the tea urn before call time. Bill Block had a grin on his face as he squirted brown sauce into his sausage-and-bacon-and-egg-and-tomato roll.

By ten past six the sunshine had turned to a light drizzle, but not even the weather could dim the smiles as Todd waited with the rest of the crew for the focus puller to check the gate after the final shot.

'Clear.'

Todd turned and announced with a theatrical bow, 'That, ladies and gents, is a wrap on *Rough Diamonds*. Thank you all very much.'

A collective sigh of relief swept through the crew. Everyone turned to the person nearest to them and shook hands or kissed, except the sparks, who were working flat out for the first time in weeks, grabbing lamps and hurling gear into the back of the lighting truck. Sebastian held out his hand to Bill Block, who paused a second before taking it.

'See you in the cutting room, then.'

Bill grunted, and pulled his free novelty key ring out of his pocket.

'What's this when it's at home?'

'Something to remember us by.'

'Do you think I'd forget? What is it, anyway?'

'A diamond. In the rough.'

'Huh.' Bill Block shoved it into his pocket and padded off towards make-up for a snifter.

Half an hour later Sebastian was standing in the almost empty car park reading the notice on the back of the grime-covered grips truck. 'Ladies! If you think this van is dirty, you should spend a night with the driver.' He felt someone moving behind him and Daisy put her hand into his.

'We did it.'

'Sort of.'

'No, we did it.'

He turned to look at her. Her eyes were more blue than green in this light, and she was smiling.

'Thank you, Daisy. For everything.'

'Congratulations.'

Sebastian kissed her. They'd done it.

But what had they done?

25   Totally Fogged

The shoot might have finished but events elsewhere continued their relentless march.

BUNG BOUNCES BACK!
DRAMA CHIEF RETURNS

Brit TV's former drama supremo Steve Bung, who was replaced a month ago by Mel Gioconda, is back in the hot seat. Bung, 53, has been on gardening leave following allegations of improper conduct surrounding sales of shares in Brit TV hours ahead of the company's unexpected profit warning. Now Bung is back and says the whole affair is "history".

The move will come as an upset to Mel Gioconda, who left her job at The Channel to take over Bung's portfolio. Sources close to the board suggest that Gioconda will be given a new job title but report to Bung. In a separate move executive producer Richard Todge has left the company to pursue other interests. A spokesman said he will not be replaced.

Brit TV has come under pressure from shareholders to maximise profits in the wake of poor recent financial performance. Suggestions of swingeing economies and an imminent staff cull have been denied. In the past Brit TV has dominated the prime time audience but the latest figures have shown it giving ground to rivals, particularly in multichannel homes.

Steve Bung issued a typically forthright statement, challenging rival commissioners to "put their dicks on the table".

Mel Gioconda was unavailable for comment.

Sebastian had planned a lie-in. No early alarm, no trip round the M25, no call to the lab to check the rushes were okay.

In fact he woke earlier than usual. Sebastian remembered that he did in fact need to phone the lab. The unit might not be shooting today, or ever again, but they still had yesterday's rushes going through the baths. He phoned up the contact man.

'Sebastian? We've been trying to get hold of you. Your mobile's off.' It was six-thirty a.m.

'What about Daisy?'

There was a muffled groan from beneath the duvet. He remembered where Daisy had spent the night.

'Not to worry. What's the news?'

'Not good, I'm afraid. Are you sitting down?'

Not any more, he wasn't. 'What?'

'We've got a problem. Some fogging. Looks like a camera fault.' It usually did, when you were talking to the labs. Strangely enough, the same problem invariably looked like a lab cock-up when you talked to the cameraman.

'Bad?'

'Well, it's not good.'

'How many slates?'

'Quite a few. Most of them, actually. You'd better come and see for yourself.'

He put down the phone. 'Wake up, Daisy. We've got a reshoot.'

* * *

An hour later they were in the lab's screening room, somewhere in the industrial hinterland of Heathrow. Daisy and Sebastian watched as slate after slate rolled by, dimly perceptible through what looked like a heavy sea mist.

'And you think this is a –'

'Camera fault. Yes.'

* * *

They picked up coffee and some croissants on their way to the cutting room. While they queued behind the runners and early Soho risers Sebastian ran through the options.

'Chances are that the insurance won't cover it.'

'What's affected?'

'All of yesterday's unusable.'

'Can we tell the story without it?'

'That's what we're going to find out. Listen, about last night –'

'I don't want to talk about it. Let's move on.'

* * *

In the cutting room Taki ran the sequence again. The gaps made it mysterious, to say the least.

'In a way it's more like the early episodes.'

Sebastian saw what he meant. Trevor William had never bothered to join up the dots, nor bothered to shoot people getting in and out of cars, opening and closing doors, walking in and out of rooms. He did have something to say, however, and this was where he and Bill Block parted company.

'Hmm.'

'Think we can get away with it?'

If they were going to reshoot yesterday they had to set it up as soon as possible, before the actors and crew dispersed to the four corners of the earth.

'Let's check availabilities.'

That quickly settled it. Contracts notwithstanding, several key personnel – including Helen Quigley, Ludi Schiaparelli, and Bill Block himself – flatly refused to shoot another frame of *Rough Diamonds*, whatever the threats or promises.

'We'll cover it in off-screen dialogue if we have to,' said Bill, ever the voice of experience.

'Better to be a bit more daring with the storytelling,' Sebastian said. He was getting to like this idea of taking out some of Bill's more pedestrian sequences, and was expanding on this when his Blackberry started to vibrate. A familiar voice came across loud and clear.

'Sebastian Boyle?'

'Yes.'

'This is Steve Bung. You and I need to talk.'

His heart sank.

'Can you get over here right away? Bring me something to look at from your show – what's it called? *Rough* somethings.'

'Wouldn't you rather wait and see a fine cut?'

'No, I wouldn't, I just told you.'

'It's our first day in the cutting room.'

'So what? You've been shooting for months, you must have something to show for it. Bring over whatever you've got.'

'Will Mel be there?'

'Will she buggery. See you in half an hour.' And he hung up.

* * *

They waited on the leather sofas for the best part of forty minutes until Steve Bung was ready for them. Huge screens were playing Brit TV's forthcoming highlights. The more Sebastian saw, the more uncomfortable he felt. Neither version of *Rough Diamonds* was going to sit particularly comfortably with *Celebrity Lunchbox*, *Stars' Dirtiest Secrets*, and the rest of Brit's output. Daisy was still trying to do something about her appearance – combat trousers and yesterday's T-shirt wouldn't have been her choice for this meeting. Sebastian, as a man, had other things on his mind, and knew that Steve Bung, another man, would too.

'Jesus Christ, look at the state of you.'

'Hello, Steve. We wrapped last night. This morning we get a panic call from the labs –'

Sebastian was trying for a massively experienced, weary-but-wryly-amused tone. Steve waved his hand impatiently.

'Can't get involved in production problems, I leave all that up to you. Listen, what I want to know is: have you got my next monster hit in there?' He tapped the tape lying innocently on the table.

'Well, I –'

'Because if you have I want it on the air as fast as possible. There's a hole in the schedule and I've been asked to plug it. Between you and me and the gatepost some pretty fucking stupid decisions were taken while I wasn't around to straighten things out and now I've got to sort out the consequences.'

'Is Mel –'

'Don't mention that fucking woman's name in my office, no offence to you dear, what was your name?'

'Daisy.'

'Daisy. Right. So let's take a look at what you've got, shall we?'

Daisy slid the cassette into Steve's top-of-the-line player. The vast wall-hung plasma screen flickered into life. Sebastian slid back into the thick cowhide of the sofa and tried to make himself small. Daisy, braver, perched on the edge and sat very straight, with her chin out. Steve sprawled in his suede armchair, somewhere near the horizontal.

'Been offered a drink?'

For the distraction value Daisy and Sebastian both asked for a coffee, and Steve's assistant came in and took the order while the face of Helen Quigley shimmered into view.

'Who's that?'

'Helen Quigley.'

'She's looking rough. Who's the cameraman?'

Sebastian told him.

'Never heard of him. Where is she now? I can't even see her.'

In the end Sebastian had hedged his bets, and brought two tapes. Steve's reactions, he'd thought, might help them decide on the way forward.

'This is really something we're using for certain sequences – titles, that kind of thing.'

'Well, I don't like it. You can't see her eyes.'

'Have a look at this.'

Sebastian ejected *Rough Diamonds – The Movie* and inserted Bill Block's first episode.

Within three seconds they were bang into a big close-up of Helen Quigley's face – so close that, on Steve Bung's screen, they could see her contact lenses.

'Ah. There she is. The lovely Helen.'

Sebastian and Daisy watched, and waited. The coffees arrived and they sipped in silence as the magic unfolded on the screen. Master, two-shot, matching singles. Master, two-shot, matching singles. Master –

'Well, that looks all right.' Steve Bung killed the screen with his remote.

'Don't you want to see any more?' Sebastian asked, innocently. Daisy shot him a look.

'No need, Bill knows what he's doing. When'll it be ready?'

'The post schedule's ten weeks.'

'Ten weeks? Shit in a bucket! I can give you ...' – he looked at a calendar on the wall of his office – 'Five.'

'It's not enough!'

'It's got to be.'

'It'll cost more,' cut in Daisy.

'More? Why?'

'We'll have to have two teams working on it. And overtime.'

'Plus,' Sebastian added, 'our budget's based on working the most cost-efficient way, not the quickest.' He wasn't going to let Daisy make all the running.

Steve Bung sighed. 'Whatever. Just get it done. I want to poleaxe some new thing with Steve Quisling the other side are running in April. That doesn't go outside this room, of course. And for Christ's sake drop the weird stuff with the smoke and shit. Both of Helen's eyes, that's the rule.' He picked up a memo from his desk. The meeting was over.

'In a way it makes sense,' said Daisy, ten minutes later, over a slice of pizza. 'Bill Block's okay in short bursts. It's just hard to take over a whole episode.'

'What are we going to do about the first three?'

'I don't know.'

* * *

Back in the cutting room they briefed Taki.

'Total rethink. Mel and Trevor William are out, Steve Bung and Bill Block are in. So we can stop worrying about how to tart up the last three episodes and start wondering how we're going to crudify the first three.'

'But they're good. At least, the first two are good. The third one's good too, but it's still under-running.'

'Steve Bung saw ten seconds and hated it.'

'Mel Gioconda saw two hours and loved it.'

'And now she's out of a job. Could there be a connection?'

'Why are you taking sides? You produced them both of them.'

Good point. But Taki hadn't finished.

'Look, you're killing yourself trying to please these guys, and you're going to end up pleasing no one. Why not at least please yourself? Why not make it the way you want it? After all, isn't that why you started this project in the first place?'

Sebastian was just starting to explain to Taki that it wasn't that simple when he saw that perhaps, after all, it was. They'd survived the shoot, three very different directors and a trio of meddlesome executives. It was pretty clear that Sebastian couldn't give Steve Bung what he wanted, because he didn't have it. But, just possibly, they could make something that would persuade him to see it their way.

'Taki, you're right.'

'No he isn't. The only person who matters at the moment is Steve Bung.'

'Daisy! That's so … cynical.'

'No, Sebastian. Not cynical, pragmatic. If Steve Bung doesn't like it, he won't show it. Maybe he won't even pay for it.'

Sebastian felt himself going pale. 'That's never happened.'

'First time for everything. And he can just blame it on Mel Gioconda. Write the whole thing off.'

Daisy had surprised him again. Now she was thinking like an executive.

'So what do we do?'

Daisy shook her head. 'I don't know.'

'Come on. What would Steve Bung do?'

She looked at him coolly. 'I expect he'd fire the producer and editor and put his own people on.'

'Well, we can't do that, obviously.'

'Obviously.'

'And Bill Block will be in to edit his stuff next week.'

'So what do we do?'

However, it was what Bill Block did that mattered.

He died.

26 Not Really a Telly Person

Just as Dougal was coming home to recuperate at The Moorings, Bill Block had been admitted to hospital following a massive stroke. He never regained consciousness. The director's funeral a week later was an industry event, but Sebastian's new schedule couldn't accommodate the ceremony in Bridlington and Daisy sent a wreath.

Taki had been hunched for weeks over his editing controls. Now he trawled Trevor William's out-takes and discards for close-ups of Helen Quigley. Baltasar Musa was jettisoned in favour of old pro Nigel Bland, who knew how to help the story along with a sting here and there while promoting the idea, almost subliminally, that this was a classy and exciting show. They bolted on a theme tune from an upcoming girl band, a track called *Without You*, which seemed to tap into many of the series's themes.

Whatever they did, though, episode three wouldn't stretch to more than half an hour, and episode six ran a lot more happily at forty minutes than the contracted fifty. Then Steve Bung phoned.

'Sebastian? Listen, you're going to have to cut your running time.'

'Oh?' He tried not to sound too hopeful.

'Yeah, bummer, but there it is. We've all been there. They want to put *Worst Sex Crimes* in the first part of the slot so that only leaves you with three hours total.'

'You want me to chop my show in half?'

'Can't be helped, mate. We can do it, it's all there in the contract, take a look if you don't believe me.'

'But – what about the fee?'

'Oh, the same, makes no difference. Talk to Business Affairs if you want. Anyway, three hours it is, and we need it next Friday.'

'But that's only three weeks! You said five.'

'Yeah, well now it's only half as long you should be able to do it in half the time, which is two and a half, unless I'm mistaken.'

'It doesn't work like that!'

'It does here.' There was a click as he put down the phone. Sebastian could hardly believe his ears.

'Taki! New idea!'

'Tell me about it,' said Taki wearily, as he initialised yet another drive.

A month earlier Sebastian had had Taki and Ringo working in his home. Now he was living in their cutting room. The floor was knee-high in tapes and empty coffee cups, and the smell of pepperoni and burnt mozzarella never left their clothes.

There was one visit Sebastian had to make, and eventually he tore himself away and made the trek down to Alibert's Ait. The trees fringing the river were turning from green to gold, and fallen leaves floated past as Sebastian hauled himself across on the chain ferry. At The Moorings he pulled the handle and heard the ship's bell ring inside.

He waited on the doorstep. After a while there was a faint shuffling behind the door, and then it opened, and Dougal peered like a wary tortoise through the crack.

'Ah. Sebastian. Come in, dear boy.' He held open the door and Sebastian stepped inside.

Dougal was older and frailer still, the aged parent of the man Sebastian had jousted with over the *Rough Diamonds* budget. His eyes seemed set further back in his head, and there was a new, distant look in them.

'How's it going, dear boy?' he asked politely, but Sebastian could see his mind was elsewhere. Where to begin, with all that had happened since the climax of Trevor William's shoot?

'Fine. It's going fine. We're in the cutting room now.'

'Good, good,' Dougal muttered, vaguely.

Sebastian noticed the signed photos on the wall – Sean the Great, Sir Roger, Timothy, even the forgettable George. No Pierce, of course, too young, let alone the latest recruit. But all the senior Bonds had signified their appreciation of Dougal. Outside the floor to ceiling picture windows lay a small lawn with two geese settled comfortably beside a large rabbit hutch, and beyond that the thick grey ooze of the river. A small dinghy tacked across it, its single sail tugging in the wind.

'So how are you, Dougal?'

'Oh, you know.'

He patted his pockets absent-mindedly, found his pipe, paused a moment then replaced it. 'Not allowed. Keep forgetting. Can't quite give it up, though. I can hold it, even if I can't light the damned thing.'

'It won't be you without the pipe.'

He looked up. 'Exactly. I feel like I've left half of myself on the train. Keep hoping it'll turn up in lost property.'

They chatted for half an hour, an effort for both of them. Sebastian watched as the old man's fingers fluttered on his lap, as though working the keyboard of a phantom computer. As he pulled himself back to the mainland he wondered whether all productions were like this. Was it the effect of concentrating so much into such a short space of time? This was a time warp business, where months of development seemed to flit by with all too little to show for them, while a twelve-week shoot could last an age, and take years off your life, or end it altogether.

* * *

After the quiet desolation of Alibert's Ait the cutting room felt more hectic than ever. Steve Bung had waived the usual executive viewing before picture lock in the interests of speed, and also of his busy diary, which included some corporate entertaining that he had no intention of missing.

Helen Quigley's character had split into two – the tough-talking police detective favoured by Bill Block, and the haunted presence conjured by Trevor William. These became two aspects of the same person, the heart of the story her emotional and psychological disintegration as Dan's work took her deeper and deeper into an unsettling world of violence, darkness, and despair. That, at any rate, was what Sebastian wrote for the press pack, and it seemed to make sense at the time.

In spite of everything, spirits in the cutting room remained high. Partly this was the result of sheer adrenalin – having accepted a task that was, strictly speaking, impossible, they were all determined to achieve it. Perhaps their caffeine-laden and vitamin-free diet also had something to do with it, along with the clouds of smoke from Ringo's omnipresent joints, which filled the windowless cutting room. None of them had slept much over the past few weeks. All in all they were in no fit state to make rational decisions.

At last, though, the end was in sight. The negative was cut, the sound tracks prepared, and they stumbled into the dubbing theatre to put it all together while relays of runners fuelled them with tuna melts, chilliburgers, and bottled lager. The projected image of Helen Quigley loomed over Sebastian on the big screen as sound gushed through an array of huge speakers. In keeping with the new vision of *Rough Diamonds* they'd maxxed out on sound design, and the dialogue was embedded in a disconcerting aural undercurrent of nuclear explosions, industrial machinery, wheezy breathing, and the cries of wild animals. Much of Nigel Bland's score was dropped in favour of bells, distant chanting, and massed Latvian choirs. Baltasar Musa was back. As they replayed the final mix, everyone in the dubbing theatre seemed to fall under his spell.

* * *

Sebastian had spent an afternoon going through the various contractual obligations, which stated that person A was entitled to a credit of the same size and prominence as person B, while person C … It seemed impossible to resolve.

'Let's not credit anyone.'

'What – leave them all till the end roller?'

'Or leave that off too. If no one gets a credit, no one can complain.'

'But – won't that mean we won't get a credit, either?'

'Could be a very astute move.'

'What do you mean by that, Ringo?'

'Nothing. Just that – well, who knows how this is going to go down?'

'It's going to be massive.'

'If you say so. Then why don't we just fill the screen at the end with all the credits in one go – you know, a huge, continuous line? Just names, no job titles.' It was new, it was different, it was in your face, it had never been done before. It was very *Rough Diamonds*.

Friday, delivery day. They completed the titles, made up the creditless credits to the bewilderment of the online editor, and biked the transmission tapes over to Brit TV, together with the paperwork and an enormous invoice. *Rough Diamonds* was done and dusted.

Exhausted but happy, Sebastian arrived home with no other plan beyond going straight to bed and sleeping for several days. This, however, proved unexpectedly difficult.

'Mr Boyle?'

Sebastian blinked. The two men waiting on his doorstep looked like bailiffs or possibly loan sharks from some no-budget reality show, the kind who broke your fingers when you got behind with the repayments.

'Yes?'

'You do not have to say anything but it may harm your

defence if you do not mention when questioned something which you later rely on in court. Anything you do say may be given in evidence.'

It was Sebastian's worst nightmare. He'd become a supporting artist on *Boys in Blue*. Either that, or the skunk Ringo had been smoking for the last week had furred up the capillaries in his brain, and now he was undergoing some kind of delusional episode.

'Sorry, could you repeat that?'

Instead, one of the policeman steered him towards a silver Mondeo while the other opened the door and pushed him gently but firmly inside.

They completed the formalities at the police station, where Sebastian learned he was to be charged with fraud, obtaining money by deception, aggravated burglary, assault with a deadly weapon, and operating a television receiver without the appropriate license. He made his statutory phone call, leaving a message with Giles Savernake's assistant. Wishing he'd paid more attention to the many police procedurals he'd sat through, Sebastian lay on the bunk in his cell and awaited developments.

* * *

'Have you ever done anything to upset Bernie Gassman?'

'Not so far as I know. Except turn down his offer to take over the production, of course.'

'I mean something personal. Sure you didn't run over his mother in your car? Make his sister pregnant?'

'I think I'd have remembered. Why?'

Giles hitched up his tailored trousers and leant forward towards Sebastian.

'Because he's absolutely determined to see you get rogered.'

'But these charges are rubbish!'

'Are you sure?'

'All right, I may have forgotten to renew my telly license. What with one thing and another.'

'According to the long and detailed statement he's made, you tried to inveigle money out of Monopolimedia, misrepresenting the true state of your finances, and then sold him something which belonged not to you but to your bank.'

'Well, *technically*, I suppose, the bank does have *some* claim –'

'Removed private and confidential documents belonging to Monopolimedia …'

'Rubbish!'

'He described these as being copyright scripts … apparently you threatened his head of drama, someone called Jake Smith, with bodily harm.'

'That was just in the heat of the moment.'

'Then drove a scooter at him, causing him to suffer severe bruising requiring emergency medical attention.'

'Now that is totally untrue.'

'He claims to have several witnesses. The police are still working their way through the dossier he supplied them with.' Giles sighed. 'This isn't my line of country, Sebastian. You need a criminal lawyer, a good one. I'll find you someone.'

'What about getting me out of here? Don't I get bail?'

'It's unlikely, given the threats you've made against Bernie Gassman.'

'Threats?'

Giles got up.

'I'll see what we can do.'

Left alone once more, Sebastian summoned up what little he knew about Bernie. For some reason his conversation with Benjamin Prike and the squalid shoot for British Gas came to mind, causing the same uneasy stirring in his stomach as before.

At last Daisy paid him a visit. The look in her eyes, unambiguously blue in the fluorescent glare of the interview room, was cool, unreadable.

'I told you it was dangerous to cross Bernie.'

'No you didn't.'

'Well, it's obvious, isn't it? And I did say he had it in for you.'

'You could have come to see me earlier.'

'There's been a lot to do. Programmes don't produce themselves, you know.'

Sebastian felt his eyebrows rising and stopped them just in time. He must have picked it up from Dougal. He observed the small, hard line of Daisy's mouth, the tiny but unmistakable jut of her chin.

'So that's it, is it?'

'I'm sorry, Sebastian. But it looks like you could be here for some time, and I've got a career to get on with.'

Sebastian struggled to look on the bright side. After all, it was natural that Daisy should put herself first. Who didn't? At least she was honest about it. And being remanded in prison wasn't as bad as he'd expected. No one had taken a shine to him in the showers, so far, or shivved him, or made him hide their stash in his cell, or any of the other everyday events familiar to Sebastian from scores of prison movies. He struggled to think of this time as a sort of low-budget detox-and-chill session, and the prison as an entry-level Priory. Already he'd lost much of the weight put on by eating five square meals a day during the shoot and nothing but pizza since. His system was finally clear of Ringo's ferocious skunk, after weeks of secondary smoking, although the occasional flashback had him clinging to his bunk. The prison boasted a gym but Sebastian struggled to read the signals there, while grasping the essential point that whatever they meant he didn't fit in.

The library, though, was a different matter. Although lacking the elderly trusty and over-educated young convict found in so many prison dramas, the library did indeed contain books. Among them Sebastian found a cache of manuals relating to the performing arts, donated by some kindly drama type who'd once run a theatre workshop in the prison as a short cut to an Equity card. There were also some recent textbooks. Media studies seemed to be replacing psychology and sociology, inside prison just like outside, as the soft academic option of choice.

Sebastian was absorbed in a dog-eared copy of *Who's the Daddy? Blast your Way to the Top in TV* when he was informed that he had a visitor.

The elderly gent waiting for him in the interview suite looked like Dougal's louche elder brother, an unfrocked bishop gone to the bad. They recognised one another instantly.

'Sebastian.'

'Benjamin.'

'May I say at once how deeply sad I am to see you confined to this place?'

'Thank you.'

'If not entirely surprised.'

'What do you mean by that?'

'From our earliest collaboration, Sebastian, I felt that you were one who might all too easily find yourself caught in one of the many pitfalls dug to ensnare the unwary practitioner in our industry.'

'Really?'

'I fear so. And – forgive me for saying this – somehow you never seemed to me to be a telly person.'

'You may be right. Have you come just to gloat?'

'Not at all, Sebastian. I am here as an intermediary.'

'Between?'

'You and the party with whom you find yourself in conflict.'

'Bernie Gassman sent you?'

Benjamin Prike shot his cuffs, revealing elaborate gold cufflinks. Sebastian studied the seamed face below the long, swept-back white hair. The wicked old eyes twinkled.

'Have you made the connection yet?'

'It was Bernie, wasn't it? The runner on that shoot we did for British Gas.'

Benjamin Prike pursed his lips.

'But why –'

'I'd promised him a job. Then you came along and because I owed your brother a favour, I gave it to you instead. Two days' work as a runner was his consolation prize.'

'That's all it was? A job on a training video for British Gas?'

The old man nodded.

'Then Bernie should have it in for you, not me.'

Benjamin Prike sighed. 'Haven't you learned anything, Sebastian? Anything at all? The people we can't forgive are the ones who take what we believe rightfully belongs to us.'

'I had no idea he wanted my job.'

'Come on, Sebastian. In this business everyone beneath you wants your job.'

Sebastian thought about Daisy – her eyes blue, then green, now blue again.

'I'd forgotten all about it.'

'Of course. It's the injured party who never forgets.'

'So what does Bernie want from me now?'

'He wants you to remember. And understand. By the way, have you heard from that brother-in-law of yours recently?'

'He disappeared in Tajikistan some months ago.'

'I think he may have just returned home.'

'What are you talking about?'

'Mr Gassman has had people looking for him for quite some time. They found him last week not far from Dushanbe.'

'If he's back, then why haven't I heard from him?'

'I expect he's been rather busy with the sale of his company.'

'Albie's sold Brunt Productions?'

'Your erstwhile production vehicle is now part of the Monopoli empire.'

Benjamin uncrossed his legs and stood up.

'Well. I've delivered the message. I must be going.'

'What do *you* get out of this, Benjamin?'

'To continue my retirement in the Cotswolds in privacy and quiet, without my neighbours being sent photographs relating to an indiscreet liaison in Thailand several years ago.'

'So Bernie's got you where he wants you, too.'

'He's got us all where he wants us. Oh – there was one other thing Bernie wanted me to tell you, Sebastian.'

'And what's that?'

'You're fired.'

27   Closing Credits

Monopolimedia didn't like it and Steve Bung hadn't even watched it, but *Rough Diamonds* had a slot in Brit TV's star-studded transmission schedule. Phoebe Grolt was profiled in a style magazine called *Fist!* and talked at length about the woman-in-jeopardy as gay icon, with special reference to the *Buffy* phenomenon. Pat Quine was off in the US and couldn't contribute to the publicity, but somehow Pete Clapp got wind of their efforts and volunteered a think-piece for the *Guardian* on how television writers had become the unwilling and underpaid playthings of power-crazed executives and craven producers.

No one thought it appropriate to disturb the rehabilitation of the show's disgraced former producer.

Molly the publicist had selected as the *Rough Diamonds* launch venue the roof garden gracing the top of one of London's oldest department stores. Created in the 1930s, it now boasted full-grown trees and walks of pleached hornbeam as well as a fountain, Japanese temple, and small pagoda. There used to be flamingos, too, until executives of a broadcasting organisation enjoying a blue-sky event decided to liberate them, not realising that flamingos can't, or won't, fly.

Daisy addressed the audience.

'I want to welcome you all to the launch of what we believe will be a milestone in television drama.'

Two middle-aged women with big hair were reading the press pack with undisguised sneers. A third gazed out of the window at the rain. Near the front a young man with rimless glasses was giving Daisy his full attention. It wasn't exactly the full house Molly had confidently predicted. Even Daisy didn't want to be there, but Bernie had insisted. After all, Monopolimedia had invested heavily in the project.

She signalled to the back of the room and the lights went down.

'Don't worry about it, they don't like going to launches on Fridays, interferes with their weekend.' Molly sat with Daisy among the pristine tables with their untouched coffee cups.

'But you said Friday was a good day.'

'On this schedule we didn't have a lot of choice, did we?'

'At least that man at the front looked interested.'

'He's Swedish. Tries to sell things to the networks back there, takes a finder's fee.'

'Well, that could be useful.'

'He goes to everything.'

They sank back into silence. Daisy, elegant in her new black dress, decided to take a stroll on the roof terrace. Then she noticed some movement inside the dining room.

It wasn't journalists. It was a one-woman camera crew.

'Can I ask you a couple of questions?'

'I'm busy, Sophie.'

'Steve Bung had time to talk to me.'

Daisy spun round. The room was empty except for the waiter playing a game on his mobile phone and Molly van der Post, stirring her coffee with the end of a mini-croissant. Daisy hurried over to her.

'Was Steve Bung here?'

'Briefly, darling.'

'What did he say?'

'He looked at the guest book, then said he had to be somewhere else and left.'

The important thing was, according to Molly, the VHS tapes. 'It's the previewers and the reviewers who count, and they never come to launches. They just watch the tapes.'

'Have we got any covers? *Radio Times*, *TV Times*, *Sunday Times*?'

Molly looked at her. 'With their two-month lead times, and we're ten days from transmission? No, I'm afraid not. No covers.'

Daisy sank onto the nearest chair.

'Have a mini-croissant, dear.' She passed the laden plate. 'After all, you've paid for them.'

* * *

Sebastian was working in the prison garden when he learned the news. Following some high-level plea bargaining, Giles's colleagues on the criminal side had negotiated Sebastian's sentence down to a very modest eighteen months, half of it out on parole. With what he'd already served, another week would see him a free man again.

The warder stepped over the lettuces and showed Sebastian the article he'd ringed in that morning's paper. As a keen fan of Helen Quigley, now back in her minicab controller's booth in *Dalston Square*, he'd naturally homed in on the reference to his idol. Knowing one of the prisoners to be in some way related to the glamorous world of television the warder had hurried across to where a leaner, fitter Sebastian was hoeing the vegetable beds.

It had been some time since Sebastian had thought about Helen Quigley. He never strayed now into the TV room, preferring to spend his recreation time boning up on organic pest control. There was very little of his old life that he missed. He was curious about Daisy, and sad that Albie had never bothered to visit him. Jemma, who came every Tuesday, said it was probably better that way. So far as she was concerned, her brother should have remained in Tajikistan.

Apparently *Rough Diamonds* was up for an award. Unaware that the series had even been shown, Sebastian guessed that Brit TV had slipped it out late at night, probably in August when the regular reviewers were on holiday. Yet now, unaccountably, it had been judged a contender for Best Drama Series.

'They're showing the awards on the telly. You could watch it tonight.'

'Thanks. I'll see.'

Sebastian was hoping to find work as a gardener once he was released. A criminal record wouldn't count so heavily against him in that line of work, he reasoned, where people were entrusting him with nothing more valuable than their weeds and hedges. He and Jemma were thinking of moving up north. Giggleswick seemed a good idea. Instead of filming other people working on their gardens he'd be doing it himself. He was looking forward to it.

Sebastian picked up the hoe and returned to his weeding.

* * *

Steve Bung leaned across and raised his glass of champagne. 'Cheers. Here's to stuffing it up The Channel. This is my wife Samantha, by the way. Daisy, isn't it?' The slim young blonde, squeezed in beside Steve, smiled graciously. 'She produced that thing we did.'

'*Rough Diamonds,*' Rick Todge interjected helpfully.

'The one you didn't want to put out?'

'Strategic scheduling, or stuff the competition. That's the name of the game. And we did. That's why we're all here tonight.' Steve gestured expansively, and turned back to Daisy. 'You going to sit with us?'

Daisy shook her head. 'I'm with that lot.' She gestured across to another table where Pat Quine was sprawling beside Jeremy Cavendish.

'Monopolimedia? Yeah, I heard Jeremy's making you head of drama.' Daisy smiled. 'Shame his partner couldn't make it tonight.'

'Daisy!' It was Jason Prynne, resplendent in a double-breasted dinner jacket. He topped up her glass without asking from the magnum of champagne swinging by its neck at his side. 'So here we all are, then. Moment of truth. Do you know Jassy? Of course you do.' Jassy Cox came and stood at Jason's side in that way that can mean only one thing. She looked girlish, pretty, and very happy. 'We're working together again.'

'Oh?' News was that Jason was making a second series of *Bagels with Cream Cheese*, the sharp New York comedy that had rehabilitated his career. It was hard to see how Jassy fitted in.

'I'm designing the costumes,' she said. Daisy looked at her. 'Jason got me the job. I think it's so much more fulfilling, somehow, than directing.'

Jason smiled at her fondly. 'Let's sit down or I may have to ravish you right here on the floor.' Jassy giggled as Jason led her away.

Daisy returned to the Monopoli table. Jeremy and Pat had been joined by a knot of accomplices – Helen Quigley was there with her agent Lavinia, and a teenage actor from *Dalston Square*.

The lights went down a fraction and a TV comedian stepped up to the podium and began speaking. 'Tonight we're all here to celebrate the very best of British television.' Steve Bung turned round and cheerfully stuck two fingers up at one of his rivals across the room.

Uncertain how to place *Rough Diamonds* in their schedule, Brit TV had seized on Helen Quigley's widely publicised affair with the young actor as a launch pad for the show. Timely leaks about apocryphal three-in-a-bed frolics did no harm to the ratings, either. Certain critics, perversely, had warmed to the series, citing its moody lighting, enigmatic dialogue, and abrupt stylistic swings as evidence that there was still life in the British copshow. The fact that the transmission engineers loaded the tapes in the wrong order somehow only made it seem better.

The director's name was an asset, of course. By that time Trefor ap Gwyllm had become famous as his instant movie *Kaos* took film festivals by storm and landed him a job directing a Hollywood sequel. Sophie perfectly judged the moment to jump onto the bandwagon with her infotainment popumentary *Helen Quigley Naked*, which included interviews with all the main players as well as covert footage shot in the Brunt Productions office, on set, and in Helen's trailer. Phoebe Grolt wrote a stage play based on her experiences and was welcomed back upstairs at her favourite pub theatre.

Rick Todge stretched out his legs and poured himself another glass of Bollinger. If there was one thing he enjoyed almost as much as a new extension to his house, it was an awards ceremony.

'And the winner of Best Drama Series is ... *Rough Diamonds*.'

A stunned silence was followed by some sparse clapping, and an audible boo. Everyone knew that the six-parter about geriatric bank-robbers was supposed to win.

Steve Bung punched the air. Jason embraced Jassy. Helen Quigley was hugging Lavinia, the toy boy beside her temporarily forgotten. Daisy was shoved to her feet by Steve Bung and propelled towards the platform as Jason Prynne sprayed champagne in the air and yodelled.

Daisy shook the comedian's hand and grasped her prize. But there was a commotion in the room. A dinner-jacketed figure had appeared on the platform and was whispering urgently in the comedian's ear. The comedian shook his head violently. Oblivious, Daisy clutched her gleaming golden mask.

Now the comedian engaged in an undignified struggle with Daisy for the award. Steve Bung joined the melee as a group of harpies in shimmering gowns rose en masse from another table and stormed the platform. The comedian grabbed the microphone and shouted over the hubbub.

'Ladies and gentlemen, please! There's been a most unfortunate mistake. The award for of Best Drama Series has in fact been won by *Take the Money and Run*.' The chief harpy snatched the mask from Daisy and gripped it with scarlet talons. Daisy kicked her in the ankle with her Jimmy Choos, burst into tears, and ran from the room as Jason Prynne vaulted onto the platform and sprayed everyone with champagne.

Everyone agreed afterwards it had been the best do they'd had there in ages.

* * *

Sebastian opened the door to the TV room and looked inside. The only person there was the warder with a thing for Helen Quigley. Most of the prisoners in Sebastian's low-security wing were watching a re-run of *Desperate Housewives* in the cell of a disgraced governor of the Bank of England, who had cable.

'You've missed it,' he informed Sebastian. 'It's just writers and people like that, now.'

On the screen, a familiar figure in stonewashed denim with an unkempt beard stumped up the steps to collect a lifetime achievement award. It was the time-honoured way of telling Pete Clapp that enough was enough, the time had come to stop. Then the comedian-presenter, fully recovered from his earlier gaffe, leaned forward and frowned at the camera in an attempt to convey an air of gravitas.

'All of the awards made tonight have been voted for by our members, programme-makers and their peers. But there's one award made by the viewers themselves. Their choices aren't always predictable. They don't necessarily agree with those here tonight who make decisions in their name.'

Sebastian watched as though observing the rituals of a remote tribe. It was hard to believe he'd once stood shoulder to shoulder with Pete Clapp and spoken the same dialect as the tuxedoed presenter.

'This year the audience award goes to *Rough Diamonds*.'

Sebastian watched as Jason Prynne lunged for the award.

Unlike the others, this one was a sculpted block of crystal. The actor held it triumphantly aloft in one hand while he took in the audience and fixed it with a practised eye.

'*Rough Diamonds*,' he began. 'What can I say?'

Sebastian waited to find out. He saw Jason reach for his champagne, he saw the heavy chunk of crystal wobble, he saw the desperate fumble as Jason's brain struggled with decades of conditioning and urged his hands to forget the drink, for once in his life, and concentrate on the falling object. But it was too late. The audience award described a graceful arc and landed on the edge of the stage, where it exploded into flying shards, showering the black-tied guests nearest the podium.

The warder turned to Sebastian.

'They'll have a job picking that lot up.' He pointed the remote and zapped the television.

Sebastian watched as the picture shrank to a tiny white dot in the centre of the ancient screen and then disappeared. He smiled. Somehow none of this seemed very important. He wondered what the new prisoner on the next landing would make of it. People said he rarely came out of his cell, unless it was compulsory. Others claimed he was too busy with his work, planning a new cable channel targeted at corrective institutions. Everyone agreed, though, that he seemed quite at home, almost happy, working at his steel desk. The warders treated him with deference. After all, he was an important person. In the outside world he'd run a corporation. He still had influence, they said. You had to respect someone who tried to blackmail the Director of Public Prosecutions and very nearly got away with it.

And Bernie Gassman was going to be around for a very long time.

Printed in Great Britain
by Amazon